# Bliss

## Titan series, Volume 2

Renee Field

Published by Renee Field, 2015.

BLISS

**First edition. February 22, 2015.**

Copyright © 2015 Renee Field.

ISBN: 978-0991693290

Written by Renee Field.

# Prologue

Sesta's weary body vibrated through time. She couldn't believe it happened to her, again. *How dare he?* She fumed. The emotion was raw and powerful as she tried hard to shed the unwanted feeling from her celestial being. As the Sister of the Future she should have foreseen this.

"We were meant to be together."

Retan's voice was like a soothing drop of rain as it coursed through her consciousness soaking her with his love.

"You are my Sokhan. You are my only," he said, trying once again to wield his powerful magic into her soul.

Sesta shook her head. She fought the strange hum of desire spiraling like a hot red poker through her mind, twisting her thoughts from her original plan. "I can not," she squeaked.

A strange part of her ached for his dominance and his understanding, while a wild part of her yearned to give into his passion. It was a passion scorching all her souls. For in the intensity of that one emotion – passion - she recognized her old-self.

The self, before the Creator chose her to right the wrong. After all, that was what she had bargained for. If Retan, the Titan who loved her for centuries, learned the truth of what happened on that fateful day centuries ago then none of this would be. Of that she was certain. It had been her choice; her fate and she had embraced it lovingly at one time. Now, however, time was catching up with her. In fact, it was becoming her nemesis. She almost laughed at how absurd that sounded even to her consciousness.

However, it was now up to her. She had to right the wrong that happened centuries ago if her *mardom*, her people, the Sirens and

1

Titans of the undersea kingdom were going to have a chance. She owed them that. Even if it meant the end of her existence.

"Please forgive me." She whispered the words in reverence hoping Retan would forgive her sometime, even as she used all her power to spin beyond his control and into another time, and dimension.

His piercing scream soared through time and space as he fought to keep her with him. "No. I will never give you up. You are mine!"

It was a warning. All her long thought dead Siren senses awoke as they too clamored to the surface of her being, all but begging for his touch, his passion and his love. Mentally shaking herself free from the deep soul-ache she felt, she knew she couldn't stop. To do so condemned them all to Hades' wrath. *If only he would understood.* Sesta pressed on, her celestial body materializing for one nano-second in one time and dimension only to dissolve into the next. To stay in one spot for any length of time was certain death for all of the beings she loved. And, worse she would find herself once again caged by Retan's Titan demands.

Then she felt the brief touch of her siblings, her Sisters of the Past and Present. They were using their combined mind-link to sift through time. Sesta pushed herself well past her limit. She felt her sisters laugh vibrating through the time waves and that worried her. They probably thought of this as a game. Sesta knew it was anything but.

It was a deadly race against time. Time that was hers to wield. Time that for some unknown reason was only making things worse for her beloved creatures.

With a last push, she focused her thoughts and shimmered into reality. She felt the heat of another soul and sensed the purity of the being. She didn't hesitate as she gave up a fraction of her essence to the creature looking up at her with wide, dark brown baby eyes of wonder.

# Chapter One

Darius Fairbanks cursed in more languages than he could remember using in his long life. What had started out as a simple assignment had turned into a living, breathing nightmare. And it was only getting worse. While cursing alleviated some of his tension it did nothing to shed light on what had gone horribly wrong. One fleeting moment the ancient book had been in his hands and then whammo, an electrical bolt that packed more punch than Zeus' Triton had slammed hard into his left side, causing him to drop the sacred text.

He growled as Aphrodite's chief Titan slave trader chased him. *I'm not going down without a fight.*

He pushed himself up from the sea's floor. His muscular arms easily propelled him forward while his Titan form attempted to heal itself. Hot blinding pain filled his blurry vision when he finally righted himself. He shook his head to clear his troubled eyesight. His back itched with heat from the sea dragon's fiery brand he had received half a century ago. He ignored it all. Grasping the ancient book with one hand, he vowed to get it back where it belonged.

When it became known the book was missing it had been up to him as sea guardian for his kingdom, the North Seas, to track down the culprit. At first he had thought humans had somehow discovered it. Worse was finding out that the culprit was Zeus' own semi-god nephew, Rylan. The delinquent teenager was known throughout the realms for his pranks, and the kid did not disappoint. *He is a royal pain in the ass.* Darius was miffed that he'd been tricked into showing up at Aphrodite's harvest ball months ago with the promise Rylan would hand over the sacred relic – *as if!*

One look from Aphrodite and he sensed trouble. The goddess of love didn't take kindly to being turned down. But, Darius had heard enough over the centuries to know saying yes to her highness wouldn't have made a difference. He admitted she was a sight to behold. Hair spun of gold fell in waves to her feet. A sheer translucent gown edged with silver thread that let the viewer and everyone in the room see her perfectly sculptured body had been a shocking tease. While most of the guests were from the undersea kingdoms she had chosen her more traditional and alluring human form. After all, she was a goddess and she could do whatever she wanted.

When her pale blue eyes inspected him from head to tail he had felt his blood heat and his heart pound. That had been the moment when he realized that was exactly what Rylan had hoped for. If Aphrodite wanted him, she usually got what she wanted. After all you had to be nuts to say no to the goddess of love. But nuts he had been. There was no way he was going to be a pawn, played about like a chess piece. So, he did the unthinkable. He had turned away from those shimmering pale eyes and swum out the door vowing to get Rylan to hand over the relic at another time.

Now, after months of being hunted by Aphrodite's chief slave trader, Muroka, he had finally caught up to him. Another zap jostled Darius out of his daydream.

"Not so tough now, are we Darius," mocked the all too familiar voice of Muroka.

"Go to Hell!" Darius set his body into attack mode. The last thing he vowed was he would go down scarred, battled or even dead before ever giving into Muroka.

If it wasn't bad enough, having to continually dodge the infamous slave trader, he had taken the sacred Royal oath making him sea guardian and protector of all things sacred to the Titan way of life. That included the Text of Ashimori which had a detailed map of the ancient ruins of Atlantis – the so-called fable island that had made its way into human mythology. If Homer had been a good guy and a player Atlantis still would be a safe, sacred place for all of them. Now, however thanks to Homer's apt pupil, Ashimori, who had the audacity to draw a map outlining the Titan holy land, and where it was located in the Atlantic Ocean, their undersea kingdom was in jeopardy. If the ancient book fell into human hands it could be the end for his kingdom.

A second bolt of electricity caused him to gasp loudly as he drove his body hard into Muroka. The two clashed together like a mad cyclone, one trying to topple the other. Then a new sensation filled the water, causing Darius' nostrils to flare. *Please do not let that be who I think it is.* Instinctively, he sought the source of the irritation while trying to free himself from Muroka's death grip.

From the depths of the sea he heard a scratchy adolescent voice he dreaded. Before he could prepare himself and shout, "No!" he made out the faint voice of Zeus' nephew, saying, "I'll get you out of this mess in just a minute."

That was the last thing he heard before his body dissolved into a fine mist.

# Chapter Two

The fourth tequila burned down Kassandra Delong's throat, causing her eyes to tear. She forced the cough back down as her friends, Melissa and Sarah, pushed two more tequilas in front of her.

"Ahh, now that guy's a doll," drawled Melissa, her French accent getting heavier with every tequila she downed.

Kassandra fought the urge to look at the so-called "doll". She knew Melissa's type. A he-man clad in tight jeans equipped with not one speck of intellect.

"He is not. Gross!"

*Thank god Sarah agrees with me.* Kassandra squeezed the yellow tumbler which held her drink to oblivion and beyond and prayed it would soon work its magic. That's how her friends referred to tequila. Truthfully, oblivion and beyond, seemed to be taking one Hell of a long time. She gulped down her fifth tequila. This time there was nothing stopping the cough. As she sputtered and tried hard to regain her composure she heard the loud chuckles from her friends.

"Never could hold a drink down."

"She's not even tipsy. Bartender, two more drinks," shouted Melissa, over the loud crowd.

Not that Melissa needed to shout. Every movement brought her black, lacy, bra strap one notch lower, exposing her voluptuous cleavage. While Melissa looked like the typical blond, Kassandra knew she was anything but. Her naval reserve friend was brave, bright and fluent in three languages, including the most important one – how to get a man to buy you a drink. Since the moment the three of them had walked into O'Reilly's Bar, Melissa had worked her magic. She had flirted and flaunted it all – all for Kassandra's sake.

Her two friends were out to get her laid, as they not-so-politely told her. First their goal was to get her drunk as a skunk for her thirtieth birthday and then they planned on picking out her man of mystery for the night.

But getting drunk seemed to be hard to do. Her mind kept going back to what she had found closeted away in the back-storage room of the library. A very old book written in a strange language she couldn't decode. And that was a novelty for her.

Kassandra was the code cracker, as her parents and friends called her. Besides her love of all things ancient, she loved decoding things. She called it making sense out of the insensible. That was why she had joined the naval reserves in the first place. She had finally given into her father's argument that the navy was the best life. The reserve was her truce, her compromise, but truthfully from day one when she had joined at the age of seventeen she had loved it. Not that she'd ever tell her father. The last thing he needed was more ammunition to get her to quit her day job as Chief Librarian of Antiquity for the local university.

Truthfully, she loved the physical aspects of the reserves but what kept her in it over the years was one special section – intelligence. Two years into her part-time job her commander had taken her aside for a specialized series of tests. After that, well, she'd been granted access as a reservist, to something that only full-time naval intelligence had. Twenty hours a week she worked closeted away in the back room of HMCS Scotian. She was hooked up to Ottawa's naval intelligence via computer. Every day a series of suspicious letters thought to be from spies would arrive in her in-box. Her job was to decode any words that made reference to where Canadian naval ships or personnel were located.

"Kas, you paying attention to me?" Melissa gave her an elbow in the gut. "Pout your lips, toss your hair, come on, Kas, look sexy." Her friend whispered the words in her right ear as she wriggled her finger at the "doll" who was sauntering their way.

With long, chestnut hair and brown eyes, she knew from personal experience that she was plain Jane. No matter how many times her friends tried to dress her up they just couldn't make her look sexy. Case in point tonight. She attempted to paste a polite smile on her face as Melissa's beefy "doll" elbowed his way over to their station at the bar.

"Ohh, he's sooo handsome," drawled Melissa.

Kassandra gave her credit. She had it. And knew what to do with it to get what she wanted.

"Nice thighs," smirked Sarah, giving into another round of giggles.

As the man got closer, Kassandra felt Melissa give a tug on her sweater. Well, okay, not her sweater. The open neck purple cashmere sweater was Melissa's and she'd insisted Kassandra wear it, on two conditions—keep her hair down, and expose a bit of cleavage. Both concepts weren't the norm for her. But, heck, how many times does a woman turn thirty. She resisted the urge to push up the low-cut sweater, feeling very exposed.

"Ladies." The man nodded at them as he pushed his way into the center of their party.

Grabbing her last tequila, Kassandra prayed for the drink to take affect. She also prayed her friends didn't have their hearts set on her getting laid tonight. It wasn't like she was opposed to the idea. Heck, there had been a time the idea made her giddy. But that was a lesson well learned and one she had no plans on ever repeating.

Captain Tom Stronach, the man in her life for two solid years, had made her see the light. All men were sleazebags. What she really wanted, no desired was a prince in shining armor. One also equipped with a solid moral code of ethics. *Like that's ever going to happen.* Just once she wished her special talent for finding lost things worked her way. *Find me a prince,* she recited over and over again in her head, hiccupping against the round of giggles simmering below the surface.

"What do you think of my friend here?" Melissa flashed a blazing smile at Mr. Beef-cake while winking at her. Kassandra smirked. The guy was practically salivating all over Melissa while her friend tried yet again to get him to notice her.

Wrinkling her nose in disgust, Kassandra accepted without a word the tumbler Sarah was pushing toward her. Some of the liquid spilled onto the bar. Kassandra watched Sarah dip her fingers into the sticky liquid to lick the spill. *Wait until tomorrow.* She grinned with delight, when she would reveal that meticulous, germ freak Sarah actually licked tequila off the bar. Her friend wouldn't believe her, but heck, that's what drinking does to you. Tipping her head, Kassandra downed the burning booze.

She slammed the tumbler on the bar counter as she disentangled herself from her two friends. "I'm heading home." Straightening Sarah so she wouldn't topple off the bar stool Kassandra heard Melissa say, "Aw, come on, Kas, we'll find you one."

"You can borrow my Mike," said Sarah, her head leaning too far to the right.

Kassandra looked at her friend who was a cop. Tiny in appearance she could tackle anyone twice her weight thanks to years of karate training.

"Yeah, think I'll pass on that. As much as I like your Mike, I'm thinking he's not into the share department," she replied tartly, finally standing on her own. "Need I say more?"

Both friends turned to watch as Mike LeRue, Sarah's fiancée, elbowed his way to their corner. A good six feet in height, Mike was built like a tank. All muscles and bulges, but his heart was pure gold.

*Case in point tonight.* Kassandra watched Mike take in the scene with a practiced eye.

"Now, that's a pretty sight."

Kassandra wrinkled her nose at his sympathy wink. Pushing up the cashmere sweater she practically groaned with despair. "They made me wear it. I had no choice in the matter. Sarah threatened me with her cuffs." She wiped the sticky tequila from her hands and onto her jeans thinking she should have picked the cuffs over the sweater.

Mike laughed. "Honey, you can practice those cuffs on me," he said sweetly into Sarah's ears, while adjusting her more onto the bar stool.

Sarah playfully pushed him away. "Cut it out, Mike."

"You look pretty, Kas."

"Aw, Mike, Kas don't want to be pretty, she wants to get laid," slurred Sarah, just before Mike caught her from falling off the bar stool.

With her face in flames, Kassandra took a step back. "Thanks for sharing that info."

"She doesn't mean anything by it, Kas. Look, we just wanted to help." Melissa pushed Mr. Beefcake off her.

"Yeah, well thanks girls. I know. But, I'm calling it a night. Touch base with me tomorrow, okay? Take her home, Mike"

"That's the plan. Come on Sarah, it's time to go before you really regret it."

With a quick goodbye she fled the bar, happy for the long weekend ahead of her. The cool summer breeze caused her to pause. It signaled the end of one season and the beginning of the other. She could smell the salt from the harbor, a fact she rejoiced in daily. The small city of Halifax was home now. After years of wandering the continents with her military parents it had been the Atlantic coast that lured and snagged her. Her parents found it hard to fathom why anyone would want to live in one place for eternity. But that's exactly what she wanted.

A career, home, white picket fence, a husband, and let's not forget kids. Kids meant first getting laid. That thought sobered her, until she realized that with advances in medical science she could get artificially inseminated. "Yuck!" she said loudly, causing people to turn and stare at her.

O'Reilly's Bar was a good three blocks from her cozy apartment. Staggering slightly as the effects of the alcohol made its way into her system, she realized something that had been eluding her all night. Finally, the strange etchings on the ancient book made sense. A smile lit up her face. She had done it—decoded the symbols on the book she had found and taken the liberty of sneaking home with her for the long weekend.

"Damn, those tequilas were good for something after all." Muttering to herself she attempted to walk straighter and quicker back to her apartment.

"Now, let's see. I know it's in here somewhere." Mumbling to herself, Kassandra shrugged off the backpack. Task completed she delicately removed the precious cargo.

"Ahh, here it is." Setting down the ancient book she slowly unwrapped it from the heavy brown paper she had cased around it. Upon first glance it looked like it had colorful pictograms written on it. Now she knew what they were. Mirror images of the ancient Summarian symbols for the planets, the sun and the moon. In the middle of the book surrounded by a circle was one symbol, but it wasn't Summarian. It was the ancient Greek symbol for water and it was etched deeply into the cover. Tracing the etching with her finger she was surprised when a deep paper cut sliced into her causing her to bleed all over the book.

"Aww, shit." Scrambling to find a Kleenex, or anything to stop the flow of blood before it ruined the book, she ended up placing her finger in her mouth to suck on the cut. A warm sensation overtook her. Turning, she watched in amazement as the pages of the book opened on their own. Then a flash of bright yellow light filled her small apartment. When next she opened her eyes, she laughed.

"Finally, I've gone to oblivion and beyond." She chuckled to herself as she gawked at the naked Greek Warrior standing in her living room. Then with a powerful thump, she fell to the floor and started to snore.

# Chapter Three

*What by Zeus is going on?* Darius crouched his body for attack while taking stock of his surroundings. Blood dripped onto the floor from the slash across his belly. He watched as it left a bright red trail down his human looking body. One of his last thoughts was fighting Muroka who had been attempting to choke the life out of him. Straightening, he shuddered as another more terrifying thought popped into his head. It was the voice of Rylan. Horrified he remembered the kid muttering something and then his body had dissolved into mist. How he ended up here, wherever here was confounded him. The fact he had materialized into human form, not his true Titan body, equally confused him.

*And why is my body not healing itself?* The only good thing he noted was that the ancient book was here, directly in front of the strange woman, who had gawked, laughed and then collapsed at his feet.

"Humans," he muttered, grabbing the book. He ignored the searing pain from his wound and shook his head to clear his vision. It was still blurry. The sea dragon brand on his body burned his skin. Realizing he was still bleeding he snatched a nearby pillow to stem the flow of blood.

He paused. He couldn't leave without making sure the woman was okay. He knelt to examine her. She had a large bump on her forehead but otherwise she'd live. A small grin lit up his face when he realized she was snoring. The smell of alcohol and lavender perfume assaulted his sensitive nose. Even though his eyesight was no longer perfect he couldn't help but notice that the sweater she was wearing did nothing to hide her perfectly round breasts. Long, brown wavy hair spilled out around her. Deciding she would probably be better off in her own bed, he scooped her up off the cold floor. He tensed when her arms automatically circled his neck. And he cursed silently at himself when his heart accelerated with pleasure as she snuggled her face into his chest.

"Umm...you smell yummy...a bit salty...but yummy all the same." The woman slurred her words as she snuggled closer to his body.

*Get a grip, Darius!* He shook his head as he fought the urge to lean down and kiss the woman who was cuddling like a sea lion into his body. Looking down he noticed she had long dark eyelashes, and full sensual lips, but by far her best feature was her long, pale neck. A neck that begged to be kissed, bitten and licked. Groaning, he headed into the opposite room hoping it was her bedroom. Dumping her not so gracefully on the double bed he left the room hating his body for betraying him. He was rock hard for a woman he didn't know. A woman who was unconscious. A woman that Darius knew was drunk to the world.

Discarding the pillow, he grabbed a bathroom towel to hold against his bleeding stomach as he took another look at the woman sprawled on the bed. He was sorely tempted to leave her like that—uncovered. Instead, he did the honorable thing. Grabbing the yellow, knitted blanket at the foot of the bed he spread it over her. Remembering she had bumped her head, he grimaced, knowing full well he couldn't leave her like that either as the nasty bump swelled to egg proportions. Before he could stop himself, his lips were lightly brushing the swell on her forehead as he willed the bruise to heal.

*Great, my healing powers work on her but not on me. That just makes my day.* His hand absentmindedly moved a strand of her hair from her forehead. His eyes couldn't help but notice her bare skin, as the purple sweater slipped lower revealing lush, milky white breasts that caused his breath to hitch. Inhaling deeply, he breathed in her womanly flowery scent. Long legs clad in tight blue jeans bucked under the blanket, while his own throbbing arousal answered her call.

Cursing and groaning at once he dipped his head lower. His tongue licked at her neck while his hands inched out to feel her silky skin. A smile of satisfaction lit up his face when her nipples peaked immediately to attention. A small moan escaped her lips and he stilled. Shaking his head, he backed away from her inviting form.

*What by Zeus am I doing?* He ran a shaky hand through his hair, willing sanity to return to him immediately. Eyeing the bathroom door, he wondered if a cold shower would do the trick as he eyed his rock-hard state. Another moan of protest escaped the woman's lush lips as she turned onto her belly, giving him a remarkable view of her round ass. His hands burned to imprint themselves on her round cheeks. More than anything, he wanted to feel her cheeks rock back and forth as his erection entered her from behind.

*Wishful thinking.* Turning quickly from her, he grasped his own erection to force himself to leave the room. Definitely a cold shower. Realizing his naked state wouldn't go unnoticed as a human he searched her hall closet until he found a brown trench coat. Wrapping it around him, he belted the coat all the while grinding his teeth in frustration. He vowed to find out what had happened. Grabbing the book, he stepped out of the woman's apartment and proceeded to walk down the stairs.

Halfway down the stairs pain caused him to double over. Shaking his head, he straightened and looked about; trying to figure out what had caused him to almost fall to his knees. A prince of the Royal House, Darius wasn't any ordinary Titan. Belonging to the Spawn of Oceanus—the first Titan clan to rule the waters outside the Pillars of Hercules—his body had centuries of warrior training and was well equipped to deal with most things. Pain that came out of nowhere which caused him to almost fall to his knees was unsettling to say the least. And a pain that robbed him of breath was unheard of. Three more steps and he felt his breathing become even more ragged as he gasped for air like a fish out of water.

*What by Hades is going on here?* Cursing at his own limitations and weakness, it was then the hairs on his body tingled to stand on end. His nostrils flared when a familiar scent caused him to madly look around.

"I know you're here Rylan. Show yourself!" Forced to grab the banister to stop from tumbling down the rest of the stairs he growled in frustration.

"Now before you get mad, I mean really mad, just remember I was trying to help," came the scratchy, pubescent sound of Rylan's voice, as he materialized four steps in front of Darius.

"Just what by..." Darius paused, realizing it wouldn't be appropriate to use Zeus' name as a curse with that being the kid's uncle and all. "Spit it out. What have you done now?" He pulled his weary body up to stand to his full six and a half feet.

"Okay...just remember I was trying to help save you from that sea monster. I mean how was I to know this would happen. Really, someone should put those little itty-bitty clauses written in that tiny, miniscule writing much larger. I mean if I had read that first, I wouldn't have used that spell. Really when I look back on things I probably should have read it more thoroughly, but time seemed to be of the essence," babbled Rylan as he moved back and forth, and up and down the stairs.

More than anything, Darius wanted to grab the kid by the scruff of the neck and deck him. Anything to shut up his useless prattle. Forcing his anger down, he motioned the kid forward with his finger and forced him to sit. "What are you talking about?" He forced the kid to keep still. All that movement was making him dizzy.

"You're umm...bound to the book and the woman upstairs...and umm...I don't know how to fix it. I mean I'm sure I will. It's just a matter of time. But for now, I honestly don't know. To be truthful I didn't even think the spell would work. One minute that sea monster had you in a headlock that was sucking the very life out of you and in the next instant I watched ...really it was quite fascinating to watch as your body dissolved into a very fine mist right into the book. So, I grabbed the book and hid it. But then things got complicated."

"Complicated, like how?" groaned Darius, feeling like the weight of the world was on him.

"I lost it. I mean I lost you. I mean I lost the book and you and it wasn't until that woman upstairs...and I'm not even sure how she did it...I mean she must be really special...because there was this really hard riddle..."

"Stop! What are you saying?" Dread washed into ever cell of his body. Looking up at him with very blue human looking eyes, Darius couldn't help but tremble as the full force of the semi-god's words took meaning.

"I mean you can't leave her...that woman upstairs...or the book...which is good because you were looking for the book, right? Well, anyway, if you leave her or the book both of you will die."

An echo of silence filled the stairwell followed by Darius' animalistic bellow of outrage.

# Chapter Four

Darius wanted to slug the kid. Then beat the shit out of him. Those were the first thoughts resonating through his head and probably radiating out of the cold fury in his eyes because after that strained and very painful admission, Rylan had vanished. Alone and with his body cramping up in pain he cursed in the ancient tongues. He could have sworn he heard the Fates laughing in his head, which wasn't a good sign. But the idea of any weakness, and him being a Titan, a god worshipped by humans, caused another wave of anger to roll through him. As it was, he already harbored one secret. And, he'd be damned if he was going to let anyone know about that. He knew what that would entail – a pity party. Pity, a useless emotion. One he had no time for.

Groaning, he examined his options. Leave and die, which meant not returning the book. Go back upstairs to that woman's apartment and then what? *Explain who I am...like that's ever a possibility. Hell, she'd probably end up calling the police. And could I blame her. No, not really. What type of freak would she think I was?* A very naked one he realized, wishing humans weren't so bound to their clothes. Not that he didn't appreciate their clothing, but there were times, like right now, when having to wear clothing was a royal pain in the ass!

Decision one was made for him. Marching back up to the apartment he slammed the door and proceeded to find her phone. Looking down he noticed his bleeding had finally stopped, but he had a huge slice cut directly across his mid-section. The rational part of him realized that if his own Titan healing powers weren't working on him, he'd have to resort to the old fashion system. Needle and thread. Ugh.

Setting about to dial a number he knew by heart; it was at that precious moment he realized he had no idea how long he'd been trapped in that book. Was it just a few days, weeks, months, a decade? He searched for anything with a date on it. Finding none of the usual human paraphernalia, like TV, radio or a blasted newspaper, he ended up rifling through her writing desk. A simple postcard with a picture of a sandy beach from tropical Bermuda with a man wearing a snorkel and mask that said "Wishing you were here with me." Probably the woman's boyfriend, Darius thought. A quick glance at the top, where it was stamped and dated caused him to reel - October 14, 2006.

*I was locked up in that blasted book for a decade. Ten long years. What had transpired in that time?*

Ten years ago, he'd been on a crusade of sorts to find and keep safe all the writings pertaining to their undersea world. And a decade ago, he was sure he'd have found a clue in those writings on how to stop the deadly plague that was raging like a tsunami through his kingdom, killing his mardom, his family and friends. No, royal blood Titan and Siren born within the last four hundred years was safe from it. If you caught the disease as a freshling, you died. It was that simple. The unheard thing was happening to his race – they were on the verge of extinction.

The fact his twin, Seth, had found his Sokhan – his true soulmate – and married another royal blood Siren and now had a son, Reece, his first nephew, had made the race against time even more poignant. Now a decade had passed and a new sense of dread engulfed his senses. *What if? No! I'm not even going to think that.* Stubbornly, he refused to think the worse could have befallen his nephew.

Grabbing the phone, he punched in the number hoping against hope someone would answer it. By the tenth ring he hung up. No welcoming answering machine either. He cursed. The rational part of his brain reasoned the phone had still been working, which meant someone was taking care of his safe house.

After all he'd set-up his house for all types of emergencies. And this definitely counted as one. His instructions had been clear. If something happened to him another Titan, chosen by Seth was to take over watching the property. Who that Titan was, Darius couldn't even begin to speculate. He hoped it was someone with the good sense not to redecorate his house. Now, more than anything he wanted to rapture into Titan form and go home. Find out what had happened while he'd been cursed into that blasted book and then get on with his life. Then it would be pay back time for Rylan, he mused, cursing he had ever met Zeus's half-human nephew.

Sighing he realized getting home wasn't going to be easy. *By Zeus! How can I rapture when I'm bound to that woman, whose snoring sounds like a sea lion in heat.*

Then a soft, utterly, feminine moan stilled his thoughts, causing his ears to perk and his shaft to buck. The woman was dreaming. Stealthily walking back into her bedroom, he chuckled. She'd kicked off the blanket and managed to wriggle out of her tight jeans, providing him with a view of a bright red thong – a tiny piece of fabric – the best piece of clothing ever designed by humans. He licked his lips, watching as she rolled to her side, revealing two perfectly, velvety smooth cheeks that caused his knees to buckle. She had a small brown birthmark on her right cheek. His eyes were riveted to the spot. She looked entirely too erotic, to enticing and to innocent – a complete package that jarred his Titan senses. Taking stock of his hard and very aroused erection he growled.

A decade, stuck in that book. A decade of celibacy. *No wonder I've got a raging hard on.* Hell, his Titan body wasn't equipped to deal with that. The idea of no sex for ten long years was such a foreign concept to him he couldn't quite fathom it. He was Darius, prince of sex. He loved absolutely everything about it. And he'd had lots of experience doing it. Not just with Sirens, but with women as well.

Grinning, he recalled more than a decade ago when his father, King Sodak, had banished him to the land, stripping him of his Titan powers. He'd been depressed for days. Then he discovered as a human he could have long nights and days of hot, wild sex with women. It was a perk not many of his species had ever experienced and he had loved it.

Now, however, back in Titan form, he knew no human woman could survive his lust. Celibacy is going to be a bitch! Grimacing in sexual turmoil he watched as the woman rolled over onto her belly. Thankfully, he thought, she'd not managed to wrestle off her sweater. One sight of those breasts, and he knew he'd have come on the spot. What a weakling. Hating himself for watching her but powerless to move, he took a deep calming breath and tried to strop his heart from racing or his breathing to sound like he'd run a Titan marathon. Grabbing his erection in his hand he could feel the wet tip of it. More than anything he wanted to slide it up against her and rub his shaft shamelessly all over her body, but especially between those plump, ivory cheeks. Then he'd take his shaft in his hand and caress those lush breasts of hers, watching as the wet tip of it caused her nipples to peak and glisten.

Another mew from the woman and he stilled. What exactly is she dreaming? he wondered, as she turned yet again from belly to back.

*I've become a bleeping pepping Tom.* Darius froze on the spot. Even though part of him thought that, the other more powerful beastly part of him, the part that was bucking on its own in his hand, thought darker more sinister thoughts, as his eyes caught the black silky, curly strains of her maiden hairs peeking out of her sinfully red thong.

A small taste couldn't hurt, he mused, bending down over the bed. Trying hard to ignore the throbbing pulse from his own member, he leaned down, slid her legs open a fraction and moved his head lower, inhaling her utterly, unique womanly scent. And he stilled. She was untouched. Her scent was one of innocence and it wrapped around him, like an awakening wave to engulf and enflame all of his Titan senses.

Untouched. That was it. That was the difference between Sirens and human women. When he had been stripped of his Titan powers every woman he'd slept with he had been able to scent the others she'd slept with, even if it had been years. That had been one Titan sense that hadn't diminished when he had been banished from the sea. And from that he had learned each woman he'd slept with had her own unique scent – a scent that marked her as hot, wet and ready for sex. Whereas, Sirens had no unique scent. Born as sexual creatures their entire body radiated sex for all, while only a woman, and only once she let a man get intimate with her, did she let her scent radiate out to ensnare him. It was woman's gift to man. Her acceptance, her desire and by Zeus, he wanted more than to just sit on this woman's bed sniffing her like a freak'n freshling. He wanted to taste her. He wanted to lap her utterly salty, musky, scent into his body and suck on that small nub of pleasure so hard she cried out for more.

Placing one of his fingers between her legs he lightly felt the thong material. She was damp. Immediately, he knew she was dreaming of sex, as he watched for any sign of awakening on her sleeping face.

When her hand clamped over his forcing his hand to cup all that wetness, he couldn't help growl. His nostrils flared as her scent started to overtake his common sense.

*What by Tartarus!* Finally giving into the more powerful and sinister part of him that really wanted to just do it, he moved aside the material and delved a finger into her wet opening. She was tight. A blessed virgin! Never during his years of exile from the sea had he slept with a virgin. The idea of him being the first caused a shiver of delight to crash through his entire body which was thrumming with need so hot and hard he had to shake his head and force the beast within him down.

Another mew of delight came from the woman as she wriggled against his hand. He grinned, knowing what she wanted, but he wanted something more. With one yank from his teeth the sexy barrier was gone and her lower half was devilishly naked. There was no hesitation. He immediately placed his tongue at her opening and licked her for all she was worth. When her hand finally let go of his, he immediately pushed one finger into her and then another, all the while licking, sucking and grinding his face into her utterly unique feminine essence. He couldn't get enough of it. Like she read his mind her legs splayed themselves open even wider while her hand grasped his head tighter pushing his face into her. Her grip was almost death like, as if she feared he'd leave.

He could feel her pulsing around his tongue but he didn't want her to come just yet. He wanted her to beg for more. With two fingers sliding rhythmically into her opening he grazed her nub with his teeth. Her entire body jerked with pleasure and while a part of him was afraid she might awaken, at that precise moment, he didn't care. Grasping her cheeks tighter gave his tongue more leverage as it snaked into her opening. When she came, she grasped his hair tightly fisting it into her hands as waves of pleasure rode her body. All the while Darius kept his tongue deep inside her, letting her climax fill his mouth. He felt the sigh of contentment course through her body as she went languid against the bed. Giving one final lick he eased off of her.

His body burning with insatiable need. His erection begging for release. A quick drawn breath and he cursed. Instead of being satisfied with pleasuring her, he wanted more than anything to ram his rod deep into her. The beast within ached to turn her back onto her belly, raise that plump ass up, force her to her knees so he could rock her world. Running his hands through his hair, he backed completely away from the bed. From the woman. From temptation itself. There she was, her lower half bare to the world, her arms now sprawled blissfully above her head and by Zeus, she was snoring. Snoring! Again!

The gall of her. He wanted and almost wished she would wake up. Scream! Be terrified! Run. By Hades he felt that's exactly what he should be doing. Run as if Hades' pets, Tartahounds were after him and get out of the place. Out of her life. And never once look back. Because now he knew he would never be satisfied with what she could give him as a human woman. Now, as a Titan, he wanted the one thing he couldn't have. And what terrified him more was knowing he was bound to her and that blasted book until Rylan, or someone else, figured out how to release him.

Darius shook his head and tucked the blanket once again around her, knowing full well he was going to have to learn to deal with being rock hard, hungry for sex, wanting to pleasure the woman senseless and all the while knowing full well he couldn't. *They might as well have castrated me!*

# Chapter Five

Kassandra stretched. Her body felt good. Real good. So good in fact she stretched again. Curled her toes and extended her arms, cat-like above her head to flex her fingers. It was then she heard it. The soft, pounding sound of running water. Someone was taking a shower and she bloody well knew that someone wasn't her. But who? She was ninety-eight per cent sure when she'd left the bar she'd been alone. But that left two per cent of what if. She remembered getting home. Vaguely recalling she'd been looking at the antique book she'd smuggled out of the library. But something fuzzy and strange was starting to nudge at her conscious. Something eerily weird that didn't fit in with the night.

She sighed, realizing she must still be dreaming and tried to close her eyes again. Even with her eyes closed her other senses were awakening and screaming at her that all was not right. It caused her to clutch the blanket like a life-line all the way up to her chin. If she could have she'd have crawled under the blanket, but that was the cowardly way of dealing with the "what if". Taking a deep calming breath, she opened her eyes, and uncurled her fingers from the blanket to flex her legs over the side of the bed. It was then she noticed her lower half was naked.

Oh my god, what did I do? She fought with herself to not give into the scream raging around inside her head. Eyeing her jeans on the floor and ripped thong she groaned again. Wanting to beat herself up, she decided a calm approach was best as she shimmed into the jeans minus the underwear. The blasted things were tight. Not her style. But wasn't that the point of last night. She recalled giving into her friends who insisted she wear the tight-ass jeans, as they

29

called them, to show off her best feature. Best feature, my ass! She looked around for her favorite navy-blue sweats. But clothing was a good weapon, she thought, realizing the water had stopped and she was about to come face to face with the someone in her bathroom.

With her heart pounding in trepidation she forced herself to appear calm, and stood up. The last thing she wanted to be near was the bed. After all she wasn't sure what had happened in her bed. What she wanted was to be anywhere other than here – at the foot of her bed as the someone emerged from her bathroom.

"This has got to be the smallest towel I've ever seen," growled a rough, whiskey-soaked voice from the bathroom.

Kassandra tried to look up, but was afraid. From what she could see standing about four feet in front of her was the weird thing that had been nudging at the base of her conscious. It was the Greek Warrior come to life. A very naked warrior. Naked, all except for the wee towel she'd used yesterday. And from the gruff sound of him, he wasn't too pleased.

"You're awake. Finally," he said, advancing on her, causing her legs to automatically back up and bump into the bed. Her bed. The bed! The ohhhh, what did I do to deserve this?

Kassandra gulped away nervous tears and finally looked up. Way up. Bad, this is bad, she thought, taking in the full effect of him. He was drop-dead yummy. A man who radiated sex. A good six and a half feet of solid, bronzed muscle stood before her. Long black curly hair flowed well past his shoulders and every cliché in the book jumped into her head as she eyed his abdomen which looked like he did about two hundred sit-ups a day.

"I'm Darius. And you are?" he asked, giving his hair a good shake.

It was then she realized she'd been staring, actually gawking with her mouth wide open.

"Kassandra," she squeaked. "And you're dripping all over my floor. Did we...did we...what exactly did we do?" she forced the words out, not caring she sounded out of breath.

The man smiled a lazy feral smirk at her, while he arched his dark eyebrows in amusement. "Do? You don't remember." He advanced a foot closer to her.

Emerald green eyes flashed at her. His face was the stuff of dreams. Okay her dreams. A strong masculine nose, square jaw and dark black eyebrows framed mysterious eyes and he had the longest silkiest eyelashes she'd ever seen on a man. He was sinfully handsome. That wasn't good at all.

Then her eyes noticed his tattoo. She shook her head. His upper torso was covered with the intricate body art of a sea dragon. It was mesmerizing beautiful. That tattoo artist who did it must have been the best, she thought, eyeing as the body of the sea dragon draped itself over his right shoulder. She just knew it continued to his back. Silently, she wondered how low did it go. Immediate heat pooled to her face, flustering her thoughts. How on earth can I be thinking lustful thoughts with a guy I don't know. She was not pleased at herself.

Licking her lips, she broke the stunned silence. "No....I mean, I'm sure it was good....I mean...I don't really know what I mean," she confessed, bowing her heated face to collapse onto the edge of her bed. She bit at the inside of her cheek to come back to reality. This was not what she had expected. It wasn't every day one woke-up with a hunk of a man, who looked like a Greek warrior or who looked like he made a living modeling for GQ.

His fingers gently forced her head up to look at him.

"We didn't do anything, sweetlips. The day I do something like what you had in mind; trust me you'll remember it."

Kassandra knew a threat when she heard it and that thought caused her stomach to do flip-flops. She watched as he moved away from her. Bad move again, she thought, eyeing as he tried without success to keep the towel from concealing his very obvious arousal. Why that pleased her caused her to crease her brow. Maybe turning thirty made you instantly horny. But, still she eyed him. He was huge. Beautifully sleek, rigid and the racy part of her yearned to reach out and grasp him in her hand. While the other, the more rational part wanted to run screaming from the bedroom.

"We need to talk." He stated moving even further from her. Watching as he backed away calmed her breathing even though she knew she wasn't going to like what he had to say.

"This is going to sound weird. Because it is weird and I'm still getting used to it. But here's the jest of things. We're going to be together, kind of joined at the hip for awhile," he stated, crossing his arms over his chess, looking less and less pleased.

Kassandra shook her head. Like that is ever going to happened, she thought. "What are you talking about?"

"Okay lady, you asked for it. I was cursed into that book and you released me. Only catch is now we are bound together. And in case you are wondering what that means. I will lay it out real simple. It means I can not leave you and you can not leave me because we will both die. Got it!"

She giggled. Then chuckled. And then collapsed into hysterics on the bed. "Ooohhh that is sooo good. I'm going to get them. I mean you had me going for a minute. But I get it. I really get it. They are sooo going to wish they died," she laughed, groping around for the phone at the bedside table.

DARIUS WATCHED PARTLY amused as she punched in a number. Things weren't going exactly as he'd planned. The last thing he had expected was laughter. She thought he was a joke. Some prankster. She wished, he thought, moving into the living room.

Through clenched teeth, he muttered, "Rylan, get your ass here now!"

He could still here Kassandra laughing and chattering away in the bedroom and realized it was only a matter of minutes before she realized he wasn't a joke. And more than anything he wanted clothing. Anything to hide his friggin' erection. Seeing her in those tight jeans, again, did strange things to his body. Besides making him hard as stone, it made him mad.

"You called."

"What are you eating? No, don't tell me. Any luck on releasing me from the book?" he asked, eyeing as Rylan finally materialized in front of him, eating what looked like a powdered jelly donaught. He was making a mess all over himself, not that he seemed to care.

"Nope. But, don't look so glum. Things could be worse. She seems to be taking it okay," he said, shoveling another bite into his mouth.

"She thinks I'm a joke. And any minute she is going to come in here and probably call the police. Not that I don't blame her. But, before that happens. Get me clothes. Now!" he grabbed the kid by the scruff of his neck.

"Don't get sooo testy. Back in a flash with clothes."

With that Darius was left holding the donaught. Rylan's ability to pop anywhere at anytime was a nuisance usually, but for once he was thankful. Again, he wished he'd never met the hybrid half-human, half-god teenager. Now, however, the kid was his only help. Wanting to shake his head clear from that ironic thought, he calmly eavesdropped on Kassandra's telephone conversation. Even in human form his Titan hearing was a hundred times more acute. He could hear the nervous pitch in her voice as her laughter faded away.

"Aww, come on. Enough pulling my leg. Just admit it Melissa. I promise I won't be mad."

"For the umpteenth time. I did not send a GQ guy over to your pad. And I've got to go. Look call me later. And please do anything. Absolutely anything I would with him. He sounds delicious."

Darius liked the sounds of this Melissa chick. The click on the other end of the phone meant his minutes were up. Soon it would be confrontation time.

"Here. I had to guess your size. And I didn't have much time. I've been summoned by my uncle and I've got to go," said Rylan, his words a mad rush, as he dropped the heap of clothing at Darius' feet.

Darius knew he was wrinkling his nose. The clothes, if he could call them that weren't something he'd normally wear. More than anything he wanted to scream at Rylan and demand he go to Armani or Hugo Boss and grab something, anything from them. But with no other choice he shimmied into the faded jeans, amazed they fit. Then he grabbed the pink t-shirt and forced himself to not rip it to shreds. He could hear Kassandra talking to herself. Realizing she was mustering her courage to confront him, he grinned, as her words penetrated his brain. She was mumbling while brushing her teeth she'd be okay, cause he, the great hulking warrior was not going to be in her living room. She was finally going to confront turning thirty and not have it be a delusional birthday breakdown.

Darius wanted to laugh at that one. So that was why she had been drunk last night. She'd celebrated turning thirty and from what little he'd overhead, her friends had set about getting her laid. Only it didn't work. Why that thought made him happy gave him pause.

The last thing he needed was to think about her feelings, because the truth of the situation made things bad. Capital bad for her. If she found out he was a Titan he knew he'd have to kill her. That was the number one law of the sea. A harsh law that was a reality. If humans found out Titans and Sirens actually existed, their way of life would end. How he was going to explain things to a woman boggled his mind. Before he could think of some plausible explanation in walked Kassandra still muttering to herself.

"You're still here. Look mister, I'm not sure what game you're playing but I'm not in to it. I'm giving you five minutes to leave."

"I'm not leaving. Like I said...we're joined at the hip," he said, looking around for shoes and socks. When they didn't become apparent he rolled his eyes. Go figure, he thought, giving his body a good stretch in his new clothes.

...

Kassandra knew she was staring. Who wouldn't? Clad now in tight jeans that outlined the most gorgeous ass she ever saw or dreamt about; her eyes kept getting distracted by everything. His tight abs, his long dark hair that fell gracefully past his shoulders and those emerald eyes of his. They were sinful. Mysterious. And bad. Why she felt that she couldn't fathom. Some instinctual part of her knew she had to get away from him. She watched as he calmly stretched his body, long arms rose over his head and every muscle in his abdomen did a flex, causing her heart to accelerate. It was then she noticed his t-shirt. Bright pink it barely reached past his pecs. She watched as he turned and made his way into her kitchen. The words "Honk if You're Horny" outlined the back of his shirt in big black bold letters. Horny? The guy was a walking sex billboard. If she got any hornier she'd become a toad. She chocked on a giggle.

Then she realized he was walking away from her and into her kitchen. Like he was making himself at home. In her home? I don't think so. Her eyes narrowed to dagger points as she tried with all her willpower to get him to turn and walk out her apartment door. Exasperated when that didn't work, she asked the obvious, "What are you doing?"

"You humans always want coffee in the morning. So that is what I'm doing. Making you some. Where's your coffee pot?" he asked, his eyes skimming over her body in one fluid motion making her very conscious of her disheveled appearance.

"Okay, this is sooo not funny. For one, I don't have a coffee pot. I buy it. And for two, I didn't just wake up to you...a...ah...I don't know what you are...but I don't believe in genies popping out of books or things like that, that some romance writer might write about. Get it. The jokes over. I've got work to do. So, leave."

"Genie. You think I'm some freak'n blue bell...a tink. Do I look like a genie to you? Do you see me saying let me grant you three wishes, or better yet, let me give you what your heart desires," said Darius, closing the space between them in a heartbeat. "I'm not a genie. And if you're so smart. So, with the program, as you humans say. You leave. Be my guest. By the time you make it to the bottom level of those stairs out there ... you ... will ... be ... begging ... me ... back." The words came out forced and angry. Haunting sea green eyes bore into her, causing her to blush.

Mustering her courage, she snapped back "Fine. I'll leave. I'm going to go out get a coffee and come back. I expect you to be gone when I come back. Coppice!" she said with more flare than she felt.

She didn't wait for his reply. Instead, she grabbed the spare change in the change tray, and her keys and sauntered out of her apartment. Closing the door behind her she took a deep breath. Already she was feeling better.

This feels good, she told herself, marching down the stairs like she didn't have a care in the world.

When I get back he'll be gone. I'll get the book and get some real work done. Then I'm going to make Melissa and Sarah wish they had never played this practical joke on me.

When her feet hit the second-floor landing pain sliced through her body. White heat radiated instantly all over her, from her toes to the ends of her long hair. She couldn't catch her breath. She couldn't think straight as her body collapsed writhering in pain onto the landing. She felt as if she was being burned alive. She wanted to scream but couldn't. It felt as if someone was squeezing her lungs, making breathing impossible.

Her last conscious thought before another painful spasm wracked her was that death would be better than what she was going through.

# Chapter Six

Darius knew she was in pain, but still he lounged against the kitchen counter, counting the seconds. A second spasm of pain caused the hairs on his body to stand on end. He could feel his breathing becoming labored but still he waited. This was a lesson he only wanted her to experience once. A lesson learned once the hard way he mused was better than having her pretend he didn't exist.

The idea that she thought he was a genie was laughable. A tink. He wished he could share that thought with Seth, but like his healing powers his telepathic ability to speak with his twin were non-extent. The gash on his stomach started to bleed again, and he shook his head realizing he had forgotten to find a needle and thread. Taking a deep breath, he calmly walked out of the kitchen, out the door and down the steps. She had made it to the second landing. Crumpled in a heap, he watched as a painful spasm took hold of her body.

Cursing silently for waiting so long, he scooped up her limp body into his arms. Her lips were blue from the lack of oxygen. Without hesitating he kissed her. Luckily in human form he didn't have to worry about giving her the kiss of life. With his healing powers able to work on her, he willed his energy, his essence into her as it healed her body. Deepening the kiss, he felt the exact moment when she took a breath. His breath. He felt her arms snake around his head. He felt her mouth open wider, bolder, as she yearned for a second breath but he didn't want to break contact with her. The beast within him wanted her to breathe him...to scent him...to be his. Finally, breaking contact, he released her lips, and silently roared, as he bounded back up the stairs and into her apartment.

Like he owned the place, he marched into her bedroom and gently placed her down on her bed. Still cradled in his arms he leaned his body over hers. This time when he kissed her he did it the Titan way. With eyes wide open he watched as pleasure surpassed pain. He watched as her face flushed with desire. Plunging his tongue over and over into her mouth he devoured her. The fact that she answered his thrust with her own. That her arms clasped tightly over his head, caused his breathing to quicken and his blood to boil. Savagely, he pushed her back onto the bed, releasing his arms only to have them cup her breasts boldly as his hands pushed her sweater up. Still he kissed her not wanting to break the feel of her lush lips that molded his perfectly. He felt her hands in his hair and he growled deep in his throat. Reality would come back to him in a second, he thought, as he finally broke contact with her lips. Undoing her bra clasp, he pushed aside the flimsy material and wetted his lips in anticipation of devouring the peak dark rose buds that were tight with pulsing desire. It was then he realized her hands had stilled and her eyes were wide open. She stared up at him with innocence and wonder. And he hated her. Hated her for having this power over him. Hated her for not being able to accommodate his Titan nature. And more than anything he hated himself for taking advantage of her, again.

Growling he moved off her. Backed away from her lush body and forced his breathing to return to normal. "Like I said we are bound together. I hope you have learned your lesson," he said, marching out of the bedroom barely controlling the leash of his passion.

KASSANDRA FELT LIGHTHEADED. *What the hell happened?* The rational part of her brain said this can't be happening to her, while the irrational part said it was. But how? How on earth could she be bound to him? To that Greek warrior out there, who was prowling like an angry beast around her living room. One minute she'd been confident that once she got her coffee and waited a bit that he'd be gone and then whammo pain like she had never experienced before had consumed her. Then a feeling of bliss settled over her body as a warm, tingly feeling made its way from her toes to her head.

That was when she realized she was kissing him. Madly kissing him. Kissing him like her life deepened on it. And maybe it had. Because kissing him made her feel better. Much better. But the feel of his hands on her breasts had awakened something else within her. She wanted him. Wanted every inch of him. Instead when she looked up at him in wonder...wonder at this strange, unfamiliar feeling washing like crashing waves in the pit of her stomach, gone was the passionate lover and in its place was a stranger whose eyes were like nothing she had ever seen before. Something feral. Something wild. Something untamed and uncivilized loomed deep within him. And she wanted it. Wanted him. A man she didn't know. A man, she knew to the bone, was going to ruin her life.

Now, more than anything she wanted to run far away from him. But, the shocking reality was she couldn't. Somehow, and she had no idea how, she knew he told the truth about their being bound together by the book. But why? Why would she be bound to him. And who exactly was he? Because she sure as Hell knew he wasn't normal. Normal men didn't pop naked out of a book. Normal men didn't ooze sex like he did. And normal men didn't make her feel like this. Wanton and wild. She wetted her lips and took a steadying breath. Vaguely she recalled thinking last night she wanted prince charming to come and rescue her from her boring life. That was laughable.

Darius my prince charming. More likely the prince of darkness.

Angry at herself for somehow getting into this weird situation, she pushed down her shirt and marched into the living room. She could have sworn he had been talking to someone, but no one else was there.

"Okay, mister. For now, I'll play your game. We're bound by the book, somehow. So how do we get unbound," she said, walking right past him so she could plop herself down in her blush red lounge chair. Only then did she realize what he was doing. Stitching the gash on his stomach together with her one and only needle and thread. To be precise her red thread. Red because it matched her long, slinky red chiffon dress. "What are you doing? Okay, I know what you're doing, but I really think you'd be better off getting that done at a hospital."

He didn't answer her. Instead, he looked at her and it was only then she realized sweat was breaking out on his brow. The guy was in pain. And who wouldn't be? Before she could stop herself, she said, "Here let me help you."

She took the needle with the attached red thread from his hand, half expecting him to say no. Like she had done it a thousand times, Kassandra stitched away. "There all done."

He just stared at her. Hard. An intense stare that rocked her to her knees.

"Thanks," he said gruffly. "Pack your things we're going somewhere."

Kassandra knew an order when she heard it. Living with a military father did that to you. Fighting the urge to laugh in his face, she smartly asked. "Where?"

Instead of answering her, he walked back into her bedroom and started to throw things out of her drawers and stuff them into her knapsack. The nerve of the man?

"Ready?" he asked, an eyebrow rose like he was just wishing for an argument.

Fighting the urge to grab the knapsack and throw absolutely everything out of it, she stood and answered, "Sure, whatever. Just how do you propose we get to where ever we're going?" With her knapsack still in his clutches her hands were itchy. Itchy to touch him. Stilling the thought, she headed to the door and grabbed her apartment keys and wallet. No way was she going to follow him. That would be too much for her. Marching down the steps without incident she then opened the front door of the apartment building and breathed in the salty smell of the Atlantic Ocean. Instantly, she felt better.

She felt him still beside her, as if he too was breathing in the fresh smell of the sea. As if?

"Get in," he ordered.

So much for its calming effects, she thought. "Get in what?"

She watched him move towards a black sleek looking Ferrari. "That's yours? You've got to be kidding me."

It was then she heard the honks. Every car that drove past them honked its horn. Darius simply looked annoyed. Didn't the guy know what he was wearing? Or how he looked?

Ignoring the honking cars, he grinned looking like a Cheshire. "For now, this is my car, now get in."

Gallantly he held the door open for her in a very courtly old fashion gesture that caused her stomach to do flip-flops and her heart to race. How he looked polished wearing faded blue jeans, a pink t-shirt and barefoot bespoke just how damn good looking he was, she thought, as yet another car drove past this time to honk at least four times.

This isn't good. Don't get all goggle eyed at him, Kassandra told herself, as she slid her body into the warm black leather seat. Kassandra told herself once she sorted out the riddle of how to get unbound from him and the book, her life would go back to normal. The book? Where the hell was the book?

"Looking for something?" he asked casually.

"The book."

"Don't you worry about that. It's here. In the back," he said, smartly putting the car into gear. With a quick movement of his wrist they were moving. No racing. Winding their way through the small city streets. Heading east. She held on for dear life.

# Chapter Seven

Darius used the silence to think and plan. Again, he'd had to rely on Rylan's skills to acquire what he needed and that bothered him more than he cared to think about. The kid was the reason he was in this mess to begin with. Mentally, he said a silent thanks to the Gods the kid had taken to heart what he had said about cars. He had held his breathe as he made his way down the stairs hoping against hope Rylan would do what he'd ask. Seeing the black, sleek, Ferrari made him feel better.

He turned to glance at Kassandra. When he really thought about it she was handling things pretty well, considering how weird it all was. Truthfully, it had to be the strangest day he'd ever encountered in his entire existence. And at the age of two hundred and thirty in human years that left a lot unsaid. Stealing another glance at her he couldn't help notice how her long chestnut hair spilled gracefully down her back. Every once in a while she'd flick at her bangs to keep the curls away from her face. And those eyes of hers. Chocolate brown. Chocolate and thongs had to be his two favorite human inventions. In fact, he thought they'd be best served together. That idea immediately made him hard. Everything about her made him hard, and that unnerved him.

He had been amazed and actually tongue-tied when she'd taken the needle and thread out of his hand and set about to stitch him up. No one had ever done that before. Then again, he'd never had the need of stitching before. The fact she had undertaken the task without asking a ton of questions like why he didn't want to go to a hospital, gave him pause. She hadn't fainted at the sight of blood. Hadn't said she was squeamish at all. She had nerve. Gusty nerve, which he liked. And that wasn't good. He didn't want to like her. He wanted to get rid of her. Maybe once he reached his house he'd have more of a plan worked out. For now, he was going on instinct. And his instinct said to go home, slip into the sea and rapture. Hoping against hope that was possible, he slammed the gear shift into fifth speed.

He watched as her graceful fingers turned on the radio. Good, anything to break the silence. She fiddled with the knob until she came to a singer who was singing about something about a white flag going down on a ship. Her voice caused the hairs on his arm to stand on end.

"Is this okay?" she asked.

Giving a silent nod he answered.

"Good to know you like Dido, too?"

"What?"

"Dido, the name of the singer."

Go figure. Of course, he liked Dido. Who the hell could resist the charms of the fresh water Siren? She was a legend in her own rights. He vaguely heard Kassandra talking about her, how she was from Britain, played the recorder when she was younger and on and on and on it went. Part of him wanted to laugh at that. Dido playing the recorder. That he'd like to see. The last time he'd seen the perky fresh water Siren she'd been mopping around the Isle channels bemoaning over never finding her Sokhan, her true love.

She had sung for him then because it had been his awakening year, his 200 birthday as he recalled, and he'd been away from his people, his mardom. She'd taken pity on him and had sung a stupid human birthday song to him she had overheard. Her voice had been amazing and he had told her that. Come to think of it, didn't I tell her to stop mopping around. That her gift to the world was her voice. She wouldn't have, he thought, not liking the idea that she somehow might have given up her Siren nature to take human form.

"Are you going to tell me where we are going?" Kassandra asked, flicking the radio knob to the left.

"My house," he said, turning to give her a genuine smile.

An hour later they snaked their way onto a clam shelled road. He saw a man standing about two miles ahead of them, long before Kassandra did. His Titan eyes immediately recognized the towering hulk even in human form and a smile lit up his face. Ajoran. My cousin. A link to the sea. Finally! His cousin still had his back to him when he pulled up behind him.

"Who's that?" asked Kassandra.

"Stay here," he said, parking the car and jumping out, before Kassandra could ask more questions. He was eager to catch up on any news of his mardom.

"Not another step, Darius." The deep, shallow voice of Ajoran caused him to stop in mid-stride.

"What?" he asked, attempting to move forward, anxious to greet his cousin. "Using your powers again Ajoran even in human form...naughty," he said, wishing he could pull free from Ajoran's grip.

Darius watched as his fun-loving cousin turned towards him, slowly. His eyes missed nothing. He noted the way Ajoran shuffled back a step, almost like he was willing himself to stay and not run. And when his cousin fully faced him, Darius felt the anger rising in him. He didn't miss the audible gasp of fright that came from Kassandra in the car. Worse, he knew Ajoran heard it.

"What by Hades happened to you?" he asked, attempting to move forward. But, that was like trying to move a concrete wall with your pinky toe. He realized his young cousin had come into his full Titan warrior powers.

He noted that half of Ajoran's face was swollen, and that green ooze seeped from his right eye. The sight was truly grotesque. Worse yet was his body. Darius sensed by that one shuffle his cousin's body was quite literally falling apart. He could also sense the amount of pain Ajoran was bearing with typical Titan dignity. Clad in faded blue jeans, Ajoran wore no shirt. He knew the jeans were out of respect of the female his cousin must have sensed as they moved onto his property.

"Nice of you to return."

The sarcasm cut deep into him. Something was up. This wasn't like his playful cousin at all. Even after the many Titan battles they had waged together, Ajoran had always been the one to laugh at his scars.

"What happened to you?" Darius asked, wanting more than anything to lend his healing powers to his cousin to take away his pain.

"What happened to you? How could you leave us?" replied Ajoran.

Darius watched as a hacking cough tore through his cousin forcing him to spit out a gob of green mucous. "I didn't leave on purpose. It's a complicated story. Let's just say I was imprisoned for a while. So, what's happened to you?"

Darius barely heard Ajoran's whispered answer, "It's the plague."

The perplexed look on Darius' face said it all. "The plague?" Again, he tried to move forward. "Oh, for the love of Pasithea let me go. Now!"

In their undersea kingdom Ajoran had always followed the lines of respect that were Darius' by right and birth. The fact that Ajoran was a Titan whose father had been named a traitor during the battle with Zeus and banished to Hades' domain caused many in the undersea kingdom to view Ajoran as a second-class citizen. That had never set well with Darius.

Then Darius' eyesight cleared enough for him to catch the tattoo on his cousin's chest. The blue-green octopus shaped indicated Ajoran had finally reached his master Titan warrior level.

When Darius and Seth had discovered the young Titans natural ability with the Triton they both had set about to teach him how to tap into his warrior skills. The fact that now he had reached the master level made him an equal in Darius' eyes.

Darius felt the barrier holding him back dissipate and he inched forward.

"Please Darius you mustn't come any closer. We're not sure how it's spreading, but being in human form seems to slow it down.

"Seth is he..?"

"No, so far both Seth and Jamie are okay, but..."

Darius couldn't help move forward, "But what? Not Reece, please not Reece,"

Ajoran's look said it all.

Running a shaky hand over his weary face, Darius asked, "How bad is he?"

"I'm not sure, Darius. But that's not why I'm here. The Council of Cabiri has called you forward. They need the artifacts. Retan feels almost certain there's a clue in the five relics you've discovered. They need them. You have one day to make the summons. They will only be able to help until the full moon's high tide, after that they leave the realm." Another coughing fit took hold of Ajoran. "I looked through the house but I couldn't find the relics. Do you have them?"

The hope in his cousin's eyes seared him. Did he have them? By Hades, no. Well, some but not all. So now he had a day to get to the Council. Then what? In the meantime, what could he say to his cousin.

"Don't worry. I'll take care of it. You go back to the house and rest. I'll be there soon."

"No, you mustn't come into the house. I've been staying there for the past week ever sense this started. You could get contaminated. Go to Saad's house. Follow the cost further east, his house is about two hours from here. You can't miss it." Darius noted the sarcasm.

"Who by Hades is Saad?" he asked.

Darius watched as Ajoran hacked up another green glob of mucous before he spoke, "He's Retan's son."

"And Retan, remind me again, just who is he?"

"Retan is the only Titan sitting on the Court of Cabiri. He was invited by your father to come to the North Seas to help find a way to stop the plague. So far the plague is only affecting the North and South Seas. Saad's mardom is from the Red Sea. He's expecting you."

"Okay, fine. You go back to the house...I'll make my way to... where exactly are they meeting."

"They decided to meet on sacred ground. At Miradith." With that statement Darius watched as his once joyful cousin shuffled back up the clam shelled road to his house.

Of course, they'd meet at Miradith. Why not? Nothing was going right for him today or for that matter for the past decade. He fumed as he thought how by Hades was he going to get to Miradith in human form.

Miradith was located underneath an island about a hundred miles in the middle of the Atlantic Ocean. It was anything but easy to locate, because the island was constantly shifting. And, if the island didn't like you, since it was very much alive, it could decide to never let you enter the secret realm underneath the sea.

Lost in his thoughts, Darius was startled to see Kassandra attempt to get out of the car. Without a doubt he knew Ajoran was using his powers to keep the feisty woman from leaving the safety of the car.

"I've got to go Darius. Don't fail us. They're all counting on you." With that statement, Darius watched as Ajoran shuffled away back up to what had been the comfort of his house.

A sense of dread and doom settled on his shoulders. They're all counting on me; he wondered how many of his mardom were sick and dying all thanks to the plague killing his race. Worse, was the knowledge he had one day to get to the Court and petition for more time. At the moment he'd take a small miracle, like making the woman who was screaming her head off in his car, shut-up, so he could think.

# Chapter Eight

"Stop it. Now," shouted Darius, as he marched to the car, opened the door and slammed it.

"Why did you lock me in the car?" she screamed, wanting to punch him right in the face.

"I didn't. You must have hit a key that automatically locked it. Settle down, will you. I've got to think."

With that Kassandra watched as he dismissed her, turned the car around in one expert move on the clam shelled road to speed off down another small road. She was at least thankful it was paved.

She bit her tongue to stop screaming at her. Then it dawned on her. Big, brute he-man didn't like his women feisty who actually thought. "Go to hell," she said.

"Been there, sweetlips and trust me...it wasn't a picnic. Change of plans. We're going to visit ah... ah friend of mine on the east coast. He'll help us," he said, as he flicked on the radio.

Why don't I believe you? she thought, irked at herself for letting the guy get to her.

Flicking off the radio, she didn't miss the slanted, hard look from his eyes. "Care to explain all that," she asked.

"Not really."

"Try, it might make me feel better, because I feel like shit. My head is pounding," she said, gritting her teeth as he banked the car hard to take a sharp turn. Kassandra eyed the flimsy guard-rail and the cliff below. Even though he seemed to be well equipped to deal with the car, she wanted him to slow down.

Since she hadn't had her morning coffee she was so far gone beyond grouchy she was scaring herself. "What was with that guy?

He looked like he was falling apart and you just let him walk away. What's with that?"

Kassandra counted to ten before she let in on him again, because this time she was going to get some answers whether he liked it or not.

"So, here's the scoop. I'm going to keep talking...yup; I'm going to prattle on about whatever enters my mind until you, Mr., tell me what is going on. And in case, you're thinking I'll tire, not a chance. This is a game I used to play with my brother. If you could ask him he'd tell you it was pure torture and I always won. I'm betting on ten minutes tops for you and then your wall of silence will dissolve."

The car braked so hard she would have been thrown through the window if she didn't have her seatbelt on. As it was her shoulder felt like it was torn in two.

"Listen good, sweetlips. I'm stuck with you...all of you," he said, as his eyes gave her a slow once over that quite literally melted her bones all the way to her toes, "... and I've yet to figure out how to get unstuck without killing us, top that off with a family crisis in proportions you could never even begin to understand and a twenty-four hour deadline to get my ass to ...well to a place you're not going to like one bit. So, if you want to play your childish game go right ahead. For now, that's it. That's all you're going to get from me. When I decide, yes I decide, you can handle more, trust me you'll know it."

His face was inches from hers. She could feel his breathe on her skin and her heart had jumped straight to overdrive. She felt the irresistible urge to poke out her tongue at him. To taunt him to see how far he'd go.

Wetting her lips was the only invitation he needed. In the next instant, he had clasped her head between his large hands as his lips devoured hers. It wasn't a tender kiss, but she didn't care. This was a kiss to punish her. Her lips felt bruised and swollen as he deepened the kiss forcing her mouth to comply, as he forked his tongue deep inside her. Her lungs burned and she knew he was testing her limits. But she gave as good as he did. Opening her mouth wider, she relaxed into his hands, into his embrace. She stifled the groan that was on the tip of her mouth. Two can play at this game.

Then she felt his hand move from her face to grasp her crotch. She was so shocked by the contact she couldn't help the groan. Through her tight jeans she could feel his large fingers as he cupped her, forcing her thighs apart so he could stroke her intimately through her pants. Jamie knew she was in over her head, but she didn't care. God this feels so good, she thought, feeling her panties dampen and her body throb with a need she couldn't describe as she fought with her body not to arch more into his embrace.

Then as abruptly as it started it was over. His lips and hands left her body and she had to force her eye lids to open.

"It's going to be a long ride; I suggest you settle in."

That was it, she thought. The lecture was over. Her punishment, if she could call it that had ended and now they were back on the road. The road to hell, she thought, thinking of a way to escape one Greek warrior who knew just what buttons to push to make her pant and almost, but not quite, beg for more. Forcing her thighs together, she huffed at herself as she adjusted her body into the seat and looked out the window. Anything was better than looking at him, as she tried to quell her traitorous heart.

# Chapter Nine

Darius took one look at Saad's house and stifled a groan. *By Tethys, he's built a bloody palace in the middle of nowhere.* He fought the urge to swing the car around and drive like a bat out of hell somewhere else. If this is where I need to be while I find the artifacts, then so be it, he thought, parking the car.

"We're here." The gruff words woke Kassandra. He watched as she rubbed sleep from her eyes. When she finally focused on him, her doe-like chocolate eyes caused his blood to thicken.

"Agh," she moaned aloud, as she tried to rotate her neck.

"What's wrong?" Darius asked.

"Nothing," she replied smartly.

He watched as she tried again to sit up straighter and not grit her teeth as pain sliced through her body.

"Your neck is hurt," said Darius, moving slowly towards her. With his eyes watching hers he brought his hand to the back of her neck. Part of him wondered what he was doing. But the idea of her being in any pain unnerved him. He'd think later about his actions, he told himself, as he gently massaged two of his fingers in small rotating circles on her neck. The entire time he moved his fingers he willed away her pain. He felt her heart rate increase and worse he knew his own answered hers. The heat of their two bodies in the small confines of the car caused the windows to steam up.

"Okay. That's it. I feel better. Thanks," she said, curtly, moving away from him to put some space between them.

Darius realized that was probably a good thing, as his erection screamed in agony in the tight confines of his jeans.

"So where is here?" she asked, wiping the steam from the window to look at where they were.

With that question, Darius' Titan senses flared to life. "This is my friend's place."

"Some friend," she whistled.

He knew what she was thinking. A man who owned a place like this which was a sprawling mansion that could have made the cover of every fortune magazine didn't seem to fit in with the serene country lifestyle. The place was magnificent. It was like looking at a mini-castle, equipped with large marble columns.

"Yeah, some friend," grumbled Darius, as he stepped out of the car. "Stay here, will you and try not to lock yourself in," he said, sarcastically as he winked at her.

"Like hell, I'm staying here," she said immediately escaping the confines on the luxury car.

"Suit yourself," he replied making his way barefoot up to the massive oak door. For the first time in a long time, Darius felt under-dressed, to say the least.

The place gave Darius the creeps.

"I don't see any cars or people, your friend might not be home," replied Kassandra as she moved closer to him.

That Darius liked. He felt her nervousness and instinctively she moved towards him. Why that made him smile, he didn't know.

"Trust me he's home," he mumbled, slowing his steps up the long entrance.

In fact, all of Darius' seven Titan senses were reeling. He felt the intrusion in his mind as another Titan propped him. Instantly, he shielded his thought while letting the probe scan his intentions.

"He. Of course, your friends a he. Just my luck, he's another Greek warrior or maybe this one will be a genie. I've always been partial to genies. Yeah, that'd be good. I'd like a man who could grant me any wish right bout now. Cause number one up there would be a tall cafe latte with soya and whipped cream, then a ..."

"Trust me, he's not a genie," replied Darius, realizing Kassandra's prattle masked how nervous and uncomfortable she felt.

"No, I am not," replied a tall, dark skinned man who opened the door, dressed to kill.

With one look, Kassandra took in the tight black leather pants, white open-neck cotton shirt and looked around, expecting to see a black cape as she took in a Zorro wannabe alive and in the flesh.

"Ahh, Prince, it is a pleasure to have you."

"Prince?"

Darius ignored Kassandra's squeak, as she raised a questioning eyebrow at him. Bowing his head to acknowledge their presence, the man dismissed Kassandra as he turned his complete attention to Darius.

"Ahhh, you brought..." there was an audible pause that thickened the very air around them, "a human, how lovely," said the man.

Darius growled a low warning to Saad who gallantly took Kassandra's limp hand and raised it to his lips.

"Enough, Saad. I'm assuming you know why we're here."

"Of course, do come in. I am Saad, master of this small land dwelling. My house is your house. Please make yourself at home. Fiona here," he said, as he ushered the two of them inside, "Will take care of your needs, Darius."

*NEEDS, WHAT NEEDS?* Kassandra eyed the petite beauty sashaying towards Darius. She was exotically beautiful, so much so, she only made Kassandra feel more like a train wreck. Then again, sleeping in a car did that to you. Long, thick black hair fell gracefully down the woman's backside, dark blue eyes with long eyelashes eyed

Darius like he was a yummy chocolate dessert. To top it off she was a see-through sheer dress that left nothing to the imagination. Immediately, Kassandra hated her.

"I'm Kassandra," she heard herself saying, as she introduced herself to Saad, trying hard to overlook the hurt feeling that welled up in her, because Darius couldn't even bother. It was if she didn't matter to him. Not that he mattered to her, she told herself. After all, if she had her way she'd be at home, snug in bed and reading...no devouring the ancient book Darius had stashed under his arm as tight as a bug.

Without a doubt, Kassandra knew that book was her key to freedom. Her sole means of escaping the mad clutches of one so-called Greek warrior. But how? For the umpteenth time that day, she tried recalling what she had done to conjure up Darius from the book. The only thing she could think of was there must be some connection to the ancient Summarian symbols and the Greek symbol for water. Internally, she sighed, realizing that wasn't much help.

Realizing her host was speaking, Kassandra cleared her foggy brain and focused on his words. He had a slight accent, much like Darius, but Saad's was a bit more foreign. To say he wasn't a native was putting it mildly.

"Ah, again Kassandra Lilly Delong, it is my pleasure," said Saad, as he bowed to kiss her outstretched hand.

Kassandra couldn't help shiver. She felt Darius move closer, "Lily?" His breath was warm on her skin as she looked up at his questionable eyes.

"Saad," snapped Darius, attempting to move in front of her.

Really, though, Kassandra was back in la-la-land. Looking at Darius had that strange affect on her. And, boy did she hate him for that too. In fact, she was starting to think of writing up a long list of hates when it came to him. Controlling. Domineering. And, too damn masculine. Not that being to male was a bad thing, but when you combined that with oozing sex appeal, hauntingly good looks and a body to die for, it all added up to a pretty bad boy image that any male celebrity would die for. And, she most certainly didn't want that in any man. Let alone one who she was forced to stay in close proximity with until she found a way to escape.

When Saad's hand moved to her arm to propel her towards the large staircase, she stilled.

"Saad, she's with me," said Darius.

Kassandra watched as he freed himself from the little beauty that had been dangling at his side. If she wasn't so happy he had ditched the bitch she would have karate chopped him when his next words sank in.

"She's mine."

No one within the room could mistake that authoritative voice. Mine, like hell, she thought, even as she gave an apologetic smile at Saad and accepted Darius' outstretched hand.

Then he pulled her body in tight to his. His heat radiated like an arrow straight to her core. Yes, Kassandra thought, she was going to add humming to her list of hates, because boy did she hate how much he made her body hum for more... much more of him.

Leaning in even closer to her sensitive ear he whispered, "Don't fight me on this one, or you'll be sorry."

Before she could wonder what he meant he claimed her open mouth with a kiss that left nothing to the imagination as he pulled her body closer, cupping her ass with his large hands to mold her perfectly to his very aroused state.

Applause was the last thing she'd been expecting, but within the last few hours she'd given up expecting normalcy.

"As you say, Prince," said Saad.

Kassandra knew sarcasm when she heard it, after all it was her favorite way of speaking, but why Darius chose to ignore it, sent shivers up her. Or maybe that was him, still kissing her senseless, she thought, resisting the urge to scream "he's mine," to the exotic beauty who was sauntering away with Saad, not looking one bit pleased with the situation.

"We meet at half-tide," said Saad moving out of the room, "And in case you need more, Fiona is at your disposable."

The double-entrée did not go unnoticed by Darius, noted Kassandra, as she felt him chuckle and buck against her.

"You are such a brute. A big boorish he-man." She pushed at him madly, trying to force him to move even a fraction of an inch.

"I know," he said, winking at her with one of those very male 'I know you like it look'. She most definitely was going to add that look and wink to her hate list.

"What the hell was that for?" she asked.

Moving away from him she had to walk towards him again to hear what he said, "Just setting the rules."

"Rules! What rules? And where are you going?" she asked, curious to note knew exactly where to go in the spacious mansion.

"Have you been here before?"

"No. Never. But, I just so happen to know where our room is," he replied, striding up the long black marble stairs and taking a left on the top landing.

Hating she had to jog to keep up with him, she replied, sarcastically, "I just bet you do."

Holding a large door open for her he ushered her in, "Yes, sweetlips, our room. In you go."

The loud click told her all she needed to know but still she couldn't believe it. That bastard. That Greek warrior, he actually locked me in. Boy is he going to pay, she vowed, fuming like she'd never done before.

# Chapter Ten

It had taken a lot of telepathic talking to get Saad to agree to give him the top floor Even though he'd been suspicious as to the why, Darius had pushed the point that Kassandra liked heights. It was traditionally the Titan way to offer a guest the best accommodations, and being on the first floor made making a quick exist easier.

As he made his way to Saad's office on the first floor he couldn't help be annoyed. What right did Saad have reading Kassandra's mind. He fumed. He had been taught better manners. While in battle reading the opponents mind was okay, but never once in all his years had he invaded another beings consciousness without first their consent. The fact Saad had done it without asking and the fact he had seen inside Kassandra's mind, sharing something intimate with her, when he hadn't, caused his stride to increase.

He knew being angry wasn't going to help him. He took a calming breathe as he reached Saad's office. Plus, when he was really angry his eyesight got even worse and the searing brand of the sea dragon burned his skin. Not that he dared complain. The sea dragon had done more for him than he could have ever asked for. Not that he had, but without the sea dragon's special gift he'd be the first blind Titan in history. Now, that was one notoriety he'd rather be dead than have noted, he thought, reaching out a telepathic link to let Saad know he was coming in.

When the door opened he knew it was time to put on his game face.

"Done all ready with your human. I had heard they couldn't compete with one of ours, but she looked so pretty," said Saad, sitting regally in a large brown, leather chair behind a long marble table.

"Look, Saad, for one forget about her. Second, cut the Prince act, and third what's with you."

In a blink Saad was inches from Darius' face.

"You are what's with me, Prince. Where have you been for the last ten years while your mardom has suffered? Where have you been that now, only now, you show up? I promised my father I would help you, but I don't like it. By Hades, I don't like any of you. Because of you, because of that stupid plague out there destroying your people, not my people, I can't go home."

Ahh the crux of the thing, thought Darius, fighting to reign in his temper. "For your information, Saad, where I was isn't your concern," he said, slamming down the sacred book in one fluid motion that caused the table to shake. "I'm here and I'm going to do whatever I it takes to save my mardom. You got a problem with that." It wasn't a question, and Darius felt the taut leash of his temper fray.

"You found the ancient Text of Ashimori, Prince." Awe replaced anger as Saad reached out to touch the sacred book.

"Not so fast, Saad. The book has to stay with me. I'm here because I need to get to the Court of Cabiri," said Darius, securing the book back in his arms. There was something unsettling about Saad's reaction to the ancient text that left him feeling uneasy.

He watched as Saad sat back down. "You know the Court is at Miradith."

"Yes."

"Do you plan on taking the human with you?" Bright blue-eyes stared at him.

Not if I can help it, he thought, maintaining his shields so Saad couldn't read his mind. "Yes," he replied, running a hand through his hair.

"She will not make it."

"Oh yes she will," replied Darius.

"No, she will not. No humans are allowed on Miradith and well you know that. Why not leave her here with me while you meet with the Court. Or don't you trust me, Prince," asked Saad.

Trust? Hell, about as much as I'd trust Aphrodite to march in here and say she no longer wanted me for her Titan sex slave. Yeah, I'm big in the trust department, thought Darius, as his eyes narrowed in disgust.

"You leave the woman to me. I'm assuming I was sent here by your father so that you could help," said Darius.

"Fine. I can provide you with a boat and the coordinates to Miradith. But, Prince, as you know I can't guarantee she's still there," replied Saad, a little too sweetly for Darius' liking.

"When?" asked Darius, thinking he'd like nothing better than to leave right away.

"Tomorrow morning," replied Saad leaning back into the leather chair.

Darius did not want to stay under this Titan's roof for one night. Let alone a night with Kassandra, who would be madder than a crazed octopus about now. "Don't you have even one boat that we could use tonight?"

"The only boat I have is currently getting its motor fixed. I sense your disbelief. You have my permission to go to the wharf and check with my mechanic if that would make you feel better. Or Prince, you may read my mind," challenged Saad.

Standing at his full height Darius glared daggers at Saad. The insult did not go unnoticed by him. "Fine. In the morning," he said, turning to leave. "Oh, one more thing, Saad. Stop reading her mind. Now," he said knowing his telepathic brush past Saad's barriers would give his host one hell of a headache. That almost caused him to grin.

From now on Darius would have to keep Kassandra's thoughts shielded as well as his own. The thought of Saad reading her mind caused the beast within him to growl low and menacing. He didn't like that either.

Right now, there wasn't a thing he liked. Okay, maybe a little, he mused, looking forward to confronting the feisty woman upstairs.

"I'm back," he said unlocking the door.

Nothing. No pillows thrown in his face. No ugly words screamed at him. Only silence.

Just where was she? he wondered, coming fully into the spacious bedroom.

Then he heard it. Soft moans of pleasure that caused his blood to boil.

"Ahh, yes, that's right. God that feels sooo good," drawled Kassandra, her voice a low husky rumble cascading through all of his Titan senses making him feel as if he was swimming for the first time in a dark kelp forest.

Darius knew his mouth was hanging open and if he'd been a sea lion the beast within him would have been charging and barking its head off. The scene before him caused him to see red. He gasped as the brand on his skin burned bright and his eyesight turned. His vision cleared from being that of a Titan to that of a sea dragon. He blinked as his infrared eyesight caused him to see hues of colors streaming around him. The bedroom was blue but the heat coming off the two people in front of him was purple with streaking hues of orange.

Shaking his head, he fought to clear the angry haze. His head ached with the supreme effort but he managed to clam down enough to focus. The burning pain from the brand dissipated and his sight turned back to its fuzzy Titan focus. By the gods, how he hated that his Titan body hadn't healed properly from the poisonous black tar that had been absorbed by his cells when Princess Asta, a former lover of his, and co-ruler of the South Seas, had tried to overtake his kingdom. He knew he should be thankful to be alive, but a part of him resented the help he'd received from the infamous Ryuseikan. Why the mighty she dragon had sought him out to heal his body remained a mystery to him. When he had tried to question the sea dragon she had smiled, turned and slunk away before she could be detected in the healing waters. Part of Darius knew she had done it to thank him for healing her infertility crises. Using his healing powers, he had removed the blockage within her tubes allowing her to lay her eggs. Since a male Ryuseikan hadn't been spotted in over five hundred years he highly doubted she'd be able to find a mate to help her fertilize those eggs. In truth he'd always felt as if he had cheated her.

A moan from Kassandra caused his heart to race and his thoughts to focus.

In front of him lying naked with every glorious spec of her body on display was the woman who had been giving him a raging hard-on for the past twelve hours. She was on her back as a freshling, who had to be one of Saad's many step-brothers, administered a scented oil all over her body. An oil he was all too familiar with. The a'lamash was an ancient aphrodisiac made from the seaweed that grew deep within cold the Atlantic Ocean. It was an aphrodisiac that heightened the sexual drive. His nostrils flared as he caught the sweet scent of the oil and its effects on Kassandra. He could smell her warm, salty essence as it started to wet her opening, arousing all of her sensitive erogenous zones. Her arousal beckoned to him like a warm tide. A shiver ran through his body while his rock-hard erection throbbed even more.

*What by Hades is she doing?* When the *freshling* went to massage the oil all over her back, from the small dip of her backside, to her round plumb ass to the top of her neck, the Titan within him lashed out claiming what was his.

"Get out," he barked, moving so fast across the room the young Titan didn't stand a chance. In one fluid movement, he had the Titan dangling by his arm as he dragged him out the door. He knew by the crunch sound he'd broken the freshling's wrist but he was lucky he didn't smash Saad's younger brother into smithereens.

Shutting the door, he locked it again and then turned his attention to Kassandra.

"WHAT ARE YOU DOING?" she asked, disoriented as she attempted to grab the discarded sheet lying on the floor.

Kassandra's eyes widen as she watched him move like a wild beast towards her. A twinge of fear spiraled through her entire body. There was something wild, fierce and untamed about him as he advanced. She tried again to grab the sheet but before her fingers could make contact with it, it was yanked out of her grasp.

"You won't be needing that," he growled, pouring some of the sweet-scented oil from the vial into the palms of his hand.

She tensed her body ready to fight and flee. When his fingers gently took her foot in his hand she knew she was going to pay for taunting him.

Locked in the bedroom she had been furious. He treated her like a child and that made her even angrier. Barely speaking to her on the long drive he avoided answering her questions like the plague. Ignorance was not bliss. The last straw was being locked in a room. She had to fight to not give into a full-fledged tantrum and refrain from stomping her feet. She was an educated woman caught up in a weird situation, that was it, she told herself. So, when help came knocking at her door, she didn't hesitate to accept the gift. She simply lied. Claiming she'd accidentally locked herself in the bedroom she had been amazed the person had immediately opened it. And equally astonished to find another equally handsome man who looked a lot like Saad.

He had introduced himself as Saad's younger brother. His name had long ago left her memory. But, she remembered he had long, black hair that flowed down his back and while he wasn't nearly as tall as Darius he was imposing. Blue eyes framed an intense face. His offer of a massage for her neck cramp was her ticket. On a whim, she had vowed to get her revenge on Darius who had locked her in.

But, somewhere in the scheme of her plan something had gone wrong. For one, the scented oil seemed to dull her brain functions and two, she hadn't quite expected Darius to become this enraged, and three, all she could think about was how his body would feel deep within her. And that wasn't good. Not good at all, she thought, closing her eyes in pleasure as his hand moved up from her foot to her thigh.

The gentle caress on the inside of her leg caused her to instinctively move her legs apart. The soft chuckle from him caused her to grit her teeth.

"Now, now, sweetlips. A tad impatient aren't we," he said, just before his tongue gave a long, leisurely lick on the inside of her calf. It was so erotic, the rough feel of his tongue on her sensitive skin, she bit the inside of her mouth so as not to give into the moan struggling to escape. The tangy, bitter taste of her own blood brought a semblance of rational thought back to her.

"Stop that. I need to get up," she snapped, attempting to push him away. Since that accomplished nothing, except to cause him to chuckle more, she got even madder.

"I said stop that," she said, attempting to kick him with her dangling foot.

Before she could react he flipped her body over onto her back, so that her legs were left dangling down the sides of the massage table. Her front and everything else was dangerously exposed. Sunlight streamed in through the large wall to wall windows and she knew her face was flaming red with embarrassment.

Not once with Tom had the lights been on when they had made out. It wasn't like she was ashamed of her body; it had just seemed safer to be in the dark with him. Now, even in the day she knew she wasn't safe from Darius.

She felt raw, vulnerable and wanton. Most of all, she was afraid of what she'd unleashed by pushing Darius. In the last twelve hours while she didn't gleam very much information from him, one thing had stood out – he was a man you didn't mess with. And mess with she had.

"Nice and wet. That's how I like you," he said.

His words caused her heart to accelerate, as the feel of his large body moved to stand between her legs. She tried clamping her legs shut but his hand cupped her womanhood so hard she knew that was futile.

"Now, now. None of that. I'm going to let you play with a man for a change since you seem so interested," he said, backing away to shuck off his t-shirt.

Kassandra ached to close her eyes. But then she heard him unzip his pants, and she gulped.

"Open your eyes, Kassandra. Take a good long look, sweetlips. I dare you?"

"Look Darius it's not like you think...that guy was just..."

"I know what that guy was just thinking, and trust me, he won't ever think it again about you," he said, slipping his jeans down low so they rested on his hips. Dark, curly hair peeked out of the top as she wetted her lips in anticipation.

"That's right, sweetlips. You want to see it," he said, a husky whisper of its former self.

Feeling braver than she felt, she relied to his challenge. "You know I've seen lots of guys before you."

"I just bet you have," he replied, giving her another smoldering look as if he knew she was lying and that she wanted so very much to see all of him.

Kassandra willed herself to not look at the sheet lying on the floor which she wished was covering her up. Instead, she tried hard not to gape, as the man, the oh my god man, stepped out of his jeans. That was it. No underwear, no socks, nothing else to look at except all of him. She had seen him before when he'd come out of the shower, but nothing like this. He was fully aroused and massive. A long, hard thick penis jutted at full attention just for her and her eyes couldn't take in enough of him.

"I'm going to make you beg, again and again, because..." he said, leaning in closer, so that the hot, tantalizing feel of his rock hard erection now rested between her legs as she tried to shuffle further back up the table, "I know you want it," he said, shamelessly taking his cock in his hand to rub it against her wet opening.

He was magnificently beautiful. Long, dark hair flowed past his shoulders. His face was flawless, and his emerald green eyes seemed to be read her every wish and traitorous body. His skin was the color of bronze everywhere and his erection was something she'd never seen in her life. Sleek, huge and thick, and she wanted more than anything to clamp her legs around him and let him continue to rub her sensitized nub over and over again, cause it felt so damned good, she thought.

Then she shook her head. This was something she'd dreamt about in the dark as her own fingers tried hard to fulfill her sexual fantasy. Now, however, it seemed that fantasy was about to be fulfilled and she knew her fingers were nothing compared to the massive action-packed rocket that was fueling her own imagination.

"That's it, sweetlips. Give into your womanly passion. Let me make you come. Let me make you scream," he breathed the words into her as he pulled her body closer to his, almost but not quite claiming her lips.

"Darius I..."

"Shh let it happen." Again, his breath was hot and heavy just inches from her lips.

*Why isn't he kissing me?* She tried to sit up so that her head was closer to his, willing his lips to connect with hers.

"Ahh, darling if I kiss you, I'll take all of you and I can't. So, I'm giving you a bit of heaven instead," he said, his voice confident, as he once again brought the wet tip of his cock to her opening. She felt him gently push the tip of his hard, throbbing length inside of her. She was so wet he simply slid in. Her body opened to him greedily. She couldn't help moan. Then as quickly as it happened he stopped. He pulled out. Gone was his large, throbbing presence within her and in its place was his rough tongue that delved deep inside of her taking all of her.

She tried to control her body but it did no good. She felt as if her senses were on fire. Never had Tom done anything like this to her. Even though she had known oral sex could be pleasurable, something all of her girlfriends had told her over and over again, the idea of it has simply been that – an idea. Now, it was reality. And it was pulsing hot. So much so she throbbed. Her body humming in sweet anticipation of something just beyond her grasp.

"That's it sweetlips, let it happen," he said, gently nipping at her sensitized nub.

The pain and pleasure of it caused her to groan and moan at once. Then he slid his tongue deep within her opening and made full circular sweep with it so deep inside of her, she all but screamed.

"Open your eyes, Kassandra. Watch what I am doing to you. Watch as I make you come," he demanded.

The sight that she took in caused her body to squirm. It was the most erotic thing that had ever happened to her. In broad daylight, she was naked and her Greek warrior had his head between her legs working her with his tongue.

"You like?" he asked, glancing her a sly, 'I know you like' look, that she wished at that moment to hate, but for the life of her she couldn't. Then, with another one of his infamous winks, he slid not one but two of his fingers into her drenched opening as his mouth moved to suck on her nub. She arched her back on her own accord and actually felt her legs open wider.

"That's it. Spread your legs wide for me Kassandra. I want to look at all of you."

His words almost sent her over the edge. He was sinfully sexy and knew which buttons to push.

She complied, hating herself for the sheer pleasure of what he was doing to her body. She felt like she was hanging on to a cliff and about to have the best free fall in the world.

Then she felt him still, stiffen and run from her like there was no tomorrow.

What did I do?

She laid there like a used limp dish cloth back onto the massage table. Her breathing was ragged, her heart still accelerating and her body was thrumming for the almighty one that was a fraction of an inch beyond her reach. God how she hated him.

Kassandra wanted nothing more at that moment than to kill Darius. Then she'd beat her own traitorous body up herself. No amount of bruises she could self inflict would make her feel better. That only made her feel worse. Deep down she hated admitting she had really liked what he'd been doing to her and only wanted more. And, like a lesson learned the hard way she knew her heart couldn't stand to want Darius. Men, as she knew from experience, only thought about themselves. Next time she'd make sure things were different. There would be no more what her body craved for. No more silly frivolous dreams. No, the only thing she had to concern herself about was how on earth she was going to escape Darius' clutches without losing her heart or her innocence.

# Chapter Eleven

Darius only had a minute before the words flashed bright inside his head.

"Help me, Uncle."

The haunting sound floored him into action. No matter how long he'd been away there was no mistaking his nephew's voice. Or his need of him.

He only spared a moment to look at Kassandra. While the beast within him was urging him to give into his Titan nature and claim her, he knew he couldn't. Seeing pleasure ripple over her face had been rewarding itself he tried to tell himself, but leaving her like that, aching and teetering on the blink of climaxing was cruel, but it couldn't be helped. There was no way he could ignore the summons.

"Darius, another Titan comes near," said Saad, already on the beach and getting ready to walk into the welcoming surf.

"Stay here Saad, I'll handle this."

Saad's hand on his arm stilled him. "You can not. There are sharks in the harbor."

"I'm not afraid of sharks. I suggest you get your hand off my arm before I permanently remove it," he barked, attempting to move forward. Saad's grip only increased.

"These aren't ordinary sharks, Prince. They have been enhanced."

The last word was said so softly that at first Darius thought he might have misheard him. But the look in Saad's eyes told him that was not the case. "You and I are going to have a long chat when I get back. For now, I'm going in after him," he said, briskly moving away from Saad.

Saad moved as fast as any Titan would to block Darius' path, but with years of Titan warrior training inherent in his genes, Darius side-stepped him easily.

"You won't last five seconds. Can he shift?"

"No...I don't know. Now get out of my way," he said, giving Saad a good push, watching with relish as his host fell back into the welcoming cold surf.

Just as Darius' feet touched the water pain sliced through him. By Zeus, I can't go to him. I'm still bound to Kassandra and that blasted book. What by Tethys am I going to do?

Panic causing him to bellow in rage. He had never felt so useless in his entire life. He knew, Reece, his nephew needed him, but he was incapable of helping. He wanted more than anything to kill Rylan for getting him into this situation.

Before he could ponder his next course of action, his eyes caught the slight change in the water's surface. In the next instant Reece burst forth. Dazed, completely exhausted he looked like he'd been to Hell and back. Worse his skin now in human form looked like it was molting.

Reece took a stumbling step forward on unfamiliar legs and fell into the swell of the surf which propelled him forward. He crocked out only one word and it was enough to force Darius to move ignoring the burning pain as he stepped out of the boundary that bound him to the woman and the book.

"Uncle."

"I'm here, Reece. Everything will be okay. I promise you.' He reached the young Titan just before he collapsed face first into the sea.

Cradling his nephew in his arms, Darius made his way back to Saad's house. He knew Saad was mumbling a bunch of nonsense over and over again and all that Darius wanted was for him to stop so he could finally enjoy the true pleasure of seeing one of his mardom in the flesh.

"Darius, how could he have survived those sharks? They're designed to attack anything within two hundred feet of my beach. Hell, they've even tried to attack me, and I'm the one that re-arranged their instinct protocols. I'm not sure how he made it, but by Zeus he did. Too bad you're going to have to return him to the sea."

That stopped Darius cold. "What are you talking about, Saad? This is my nephew. He needs my help and that's just what I'm going to do," he said, once again moving with determined steps while he cradled the unconscious child in his arms.

Darius marveled at how much Reece had grown. Long, dangly legs gave way to a thin frame. He was blessed with the long black curly hair from his mother, Jamie. Everything else was pure Seth, right down to the shade of his eyes.

"You can not bring that freshling into my house. He has the plague," stated Saad, once again moving to intercept Darius.

Darius eyes had noted the pallor of Reece's skin and how some of it seemed to be flaking, but the thought of returning his nephew to the sea was to painful to comprehend.

"What's going on?" yelled Kassandra, as she ran down the beach towards them.

Why that made Darius feel glad he couldn't tell.

"Oh my god what happened to this child?" she asked.

Darius noted that she had put her clothing back on, and that she walked with her hips swaying from one side to the other as her bare feet attempted to find their balance over the beach pebbles that lined Saad's beach. She was an intoxicating sight. A breath of fresh sea water and his heart speed up.

"Darius.."

"Don't you say another word, Saad. I mean it," said Darius, telepathically as he pushed past Saad's defenses. He was angrier than a crazed Tartahound. Just how the hell was he going to explain a naked, unconscious child to Kassandra?

"What are you two waiting for? Bring him inside, now!" commanded Kassandra, ushering them into movement.

Bless the woman, he thought. That was twice now she had surprised him and that wasn't easy. First with stitching him up without questioning his desire to not go to a hospital and now this, ushering them forward which gave him the chance to completely ignore Saad.

But, deep down Saad's thoughts unsettled him. As if he heard Darius' private inner conversation, Saad pushed past Darius' own natural shield to have the final word. "If he has the plague you will not be able to save your mardom. And you will have condemned both of us to a living hell, Prince."

He wanted to tell Saad to shut-up, instead he ignored him.

Kassandra on the other hand seemed to be in her element. "Here bring him in here," she gestured to the room they had shared.

He gently laid his nephew on the large bed, silently wishing it was shaped in the traditional scallop shape he knew Reece would be accustomed too. Then he stood back and watched the woman who was more of an ignominy take control. His heart beat fast with pride as he watched her command Saad's servants to do her biding. She was polite but firm with a smile of thank you always on those luscious lips of hers.

"His pulse is strong and steady. I think he's just exhausted," she said, removing her hand from Reece's wrist. Tenderly, she tucked the blankets in tighter around his nephew. Why that touched a cord deep within him that swelled to the point of almost bursting he couldn't say, but for a moment he wished that was him lying there helpless in the bed so Kassandra's fingers could comfort him.

His eyes missed nothing. High-tide was ebbing, dusk was setting quickly and the black of the night would soon be upon them. He watched as Kassandra ran a tired, shaky hand through her long hair. He knew without a doubt this had to be the strangest day in her life. How many women wake-up to a living legend, only to find out they are bound to an ancient book, then ushered into a car only to confront what must have looked like a walking zombie and now this.

"He needs to rest. I think it would be best if one of us stays with him in case he wakes-up, but by his breathing I'd say he'll be out for a while. Long enough for the two of you to explain what happened and how you happened to come across a naked child on the beach." Kassandra's eyes were intense. Her arms were crossed and she stood at full attention, demanding a reply.

"I will leave that for you, Prince," said the mocking voice of Saad, as he bowed to Kassandra and backed out of the room.

Coward, thought Darius, eyeing Saad's retreating form.

"Prince? That's the second time he's called you that," she stated, maintaining her pose, her foot tapping away impatiently, looking more and more pissed off.

Darius reached out and wiped a stray lock off Reece's forehead. His voice was filled with need. "It's nothing. Just a nickname. As much as I'd like to tell you all about him, I can't."

"Can't or won't?" asked Kassandra.

Ever the perceptive one, he realized. Darius took Reece's hand in his own. "Can't." The word was torn from him. "I can handle this Kassandra. Why don't you go...?"

"Go where exactly, Darius? The last time you left me pain consumed me. I felt like I was on fire. If you think for one minute," she said, moving closer to the bed, "that I want to stay with you....you are sorely mistaken. If I could I'd have walked away a long time ago."

Grabbing her before she could take a second breathe, Darius growled the words out low and throaty, his body shaking with unleashed desire. "You will leave only when I tell you to. Do you understand?" The scent of her was driving him insane, he thought, trying to leash the beast that ached to claim all of her.

Kassandra's eyes burned into his soul. He watched as she wet her lips. He had one moment of satisfaction noting she was not as immune to him as her sweet, feminine scent flowed through every pore of his body. Instantly he harden not caring that his rock-hard erection jumped to attention only to settle poking into her belly. He felt her in drawn breath, her heart beat speed up and growled low in his throat. Pushing her away he forced his attention back to his nephew. Out of the corner of his eye he caught her rubbing her arms. It was then he noticed the burns.

Once again he moved in a blink of time, pushing her sleeves up. "What happened?"

Pushing her sleeves down she tried to step away. "You happened," she snapped, turning her head, so he wouldn't catch the telltale trace of tears that were thickening in the corners of her eyes.

Without hesitating he focused his thoughts, his hands tight as he held both of her wrists in compliance. His eyes closed in satisfaction as he healed her, attempting to right the wrong. Because he knew without a doubt the only reason she'd come to the beach looking for him was because the pain of being separated from him had been too much for her. As it was the burn marks were an indication she'd held out as long as she could. Guilt washed over him in long, shallow waves. It wasn't an emotion he was comfortable with, and he wanted more than anything to try to ignore it. Instead, he did the honorable thing and used his healing powers to heal her.

"Just what are you?" she breathed the words out, fright causing her heart to beat irregularly.

Darius watched as she rubbed her arms, marveling that they were now healed. "Can you heal him?"

The words resonated deep within his soul. *Why didn't I think of that?* Without a word he turned his full attention back to Reece. He placed one hand on his nephew's forehead and the other over his heart. He didn't care that Kassandra was in the room to witness what he was about to do. All he cared about was healing Reece.

His palms itched and then burned as he fought past Reece's natural shields which were surprisingly strong for a freshling. He felt the sea dragon brand sear his skin and fought hard to keep the infrared vision from taking over. He heard Kassandra's gasp as a blue haze outlined the child's weary body. Sweet trickled down his forehead but still he pushed past his limit, seeking the source of his nephew's infection, attempting to make Reece whole again. He knew his form was shimmering but still he pushed on trying to find the source of his illness. His breathing was becoming ragged and he knew he had nothing left to give. And for the first time he doubted his Titan abilities. The soft touch of Kassandra's hand on his shoulder broke the spell. He felt a cool washcloth on his forehead as she wiped away the sweet without comment.

Then the child-like voice of his nephew cut straight to his heart, just as the full force of his words penetrated his exhausted brain.

"Uncle, I don't have the plague. Mother sent me to find you. I turn a decade tomorrow at full-tide."

Darius knew what he'd see if he looked into Reece's eyes – fear.

# Chapter Twelve

K assandra eyes looked at the child and then at Darius. *Uncle?* Her brain screamed the word over and over, again. She noted the same thick, black hair, the same emerald-green eyes and square chin. Sure, there was a resemblance, she must have been blind not to see it, but hell, and it wasn't like she expected the child to be related to her Greek Warrior. *My Greek Warrior?* Why that thought caused her cheeks to blush she didn't want to think about. Things only got weirder and stranger with each passing moment. She'd like to think the kid was delusional but knew from the tender look in Darius' eyes that was not the case.

She watched as Darius' gently swiped a stray lock off the child's forehead. She heard his voice drop low, as he spoke in calm, reassuring tone to the frightened child whose eyes were now as big as saucers as he took in his surroundings. She knew exactly how he felt.

There were so many questions scrambling around in her brain that she felt fried. Who? No. What exactly was Darius? Was he a Prince? What was wrong with the child? Where did he come from? And worse, was she ever going to get free, unbound from him and that ancient book. The book she was now wishing she'd never found and never opened.

That old proverb, "Curiosity killed the cat," haunted her thoughts.

Momentarily drawn back to their strange conversation, she blinked. "What's wrong with him?" she asked, watching as the child started to convulse.

Ushering her to the door, Darius said, "It's nothing. You need to leave," as he darted anxious glances to his nephew.

83

Great we're back to the one syllable answers. "Fine, I'll leave. I'll be on the other side of this door. I'll just sit, propped up here like a puppet. Oh my god, foam is coming out of his mouth. Darius we need to take that kid, your nephew, for god sake to a doctor. Now,"

"No, we don't. And, we aren't. This is a family matter. Look, I'm sure you'll be safe on the first floor. Take a look around. I need to stay with him for awhile."

That was it. The door closed quietly this time and as much as it killed her to not intervene something within her told her it would be no use. So engrossed in her own thoughts, she practically jumped out of her skin when Saad's fingers brushed her arm.

Why his formal speech grated on her nerves, she didn't know. "I did not mean to frighten you, my lady, but there is nothing you can do for them. Why don't you and I take a walk? I believe dinner, as you say, is being served. Come, please be my guest," he said, ushering her forward down the long hall to the dining room, like she didn't have a choice.

Kassandra wanted to say no; partially she was afraid that moving to far from Darius would start that burning pain again, but also, because she felt uneasy around Saad. He was polite and all, but there was something within him that warned her instincts to flee. Pasting a polite smile on her face she turned and took his offered arm.

They made their way down the long corridor to the formal dining room. Formal, because it happened to have one of the largest dining tables she'd ever seen. It easily could seat a hundred people around it. Made of red cherry wood, it gleamed as it caught the light from the old-fashion iron wrought chandelier.

He clapped his hands twice and a dozen servants walked in with dish after dish of food. It was a feast fit for a king. He gallantly pulled out the mahogany high-backed chair for her. She sat and eyed the banquet. There was fresh poached salmon with dill sauce, fried kippers, lobster on the half shell, lobster bisque, snow crab legs glazed in a garlic cream sauce, mussels, and urchins. That was it. The guy must have a hankered for seafood, she thought, noting no vegetables lined the table.

She watched as Saad picked up a crab leg and sucked the meat out of it. "So, my dear, how is our young patient?"

"Fine," she answered, deciding to tackle the lobster bisque first.

"Fine. I am most sure he is not. But enough of that, do tell me, how do you know Darius,"

It wasn't a question. It was a command and her back immediately went up. Before she could respond though the exotic beauty who had attempted to latch herself onto Darius when they arrived sashayed in. This time she wore a concoction that reminded her of the show I Dream of Genie.

"Sorry I am late, master. I could not find the diamond anklets you gave me and I sooo wanted to wear them," she moaned out the last words and it was all Kassandra could do to not gag on her soup.

"Third dresser drawer to the right," she blurted out before she could help herself. She tried smuggling another bite hoping her words would have fallen on deaf ears. Instead, when she looked up four piercing blue eyes were staring at her.

Saad placed the crab leg down and leaned over the long table, "What did you say?"

Taking a large spoonful of soup, she gulped, "Nothing."

"No, my dear, you specifically said third dresser drawer to the right. Fiona please excuse yourself and take another look, exactly where our guest told you to."

The look Fiona darted her way before gracefully exiting the table was pure hatred. The silence in the dining hall was suffocating and Kassandra almost wished Fiona would hurry up and return so she could get the meal over with and then get back to Darius.

"She was correct, but I never put it there," pouted Fiona, flouncing back into the dining room to resume her seat.

"Ahh, my dear, does Darius know?" Saad eyes gleamed with triumph and the smile that lit up his face only heightened Kassandra's unease.

"Know what?" she asked, long giving up on trying to stuff her mouth with more food.

"My dear, you are a Seeker. This is truly delectable."

Seeker. That sounds ominous. "Do I want to know what that is?" she asked, slanting her eyes.

The smirk that arouse on Saad's face caused her to flush. Why she felt he was reading her mind scared the shit out of her. Great now I'm paranoid which tops being delusional.

She watched as he reached out and grabbed the lobster. "Does he know?"

How he managed to eat the lobster without sending shards of it clear across the room amazed her. It was a talent she'd love to learn. "Know what?" she asked, reaching for the snow crab, watching as the melted butter dripped onto the polished table. Great no stains until I come along, she thought, holding her breathe as she waited for the reprimand that always followed. Her father believed in spotless, neatness and manners that would have made the Queen happy.

"You can find lost things."

He said it so matter of factly she actually stopped chewing and breathed. He said it like it was normal. Like it was okay. And that really scared her. Part of her ached to deny that but one look at Saad and she knew it would be futile.

"I will keep your secret but heed my advice, tell him soon. He is not a being that takes kindly to secrets, especially from a woman." The word woman was said with such contempt he actually grimaced. Scorned and burned, I'd say, thought Kassandra.

"Saad, shall I dance for you," asked Fiona, sweetly as she gracefully rose from her chair.

She had been so quiet while Kassandra ate she had forgotten she was still in the room with them. Eyeing as the exotic beauty stood, Kassandra inwardly groaned. Great, just what I want to watch genie-girl flounce around the room, jiggling it all for Saad. Kassandra quickly lost her appetite.

The shrill scream that rent through the air immediately broke the mood and actually caused the chandelier to vibrate.

Without preamble all three rushed to the source – her bedroom, where the child and Darius were. Kassandra didn't hesitate opening the door as another piercing scream curdled her blood.

"Get out!" The command was so strong she turned back towards the door, but then she caught herself. What else could he do to her, she thought, a slight shiver of the unknown, the fear of disobeying him running like cold water over her skin.

"I told you he had the plague," said Saad, ushering Fiona from the room with one look.

Kassandra noticed Saad didn't stray to far from the door or step into the room.

Darius stood awkwardly by the bed his hands clenching and unclenching. He looked like a caged beast that had run a marathon inside his cage only to find out there was no way out. His tone of voice was even and steady and Kassandra knew how much of a struggle that was for him. "It is not the plague. He turns ten at high-tide."

"Great the kids writhering in agony on his birthday...just what every kid wants as a gift," said Kassandra, her voice laced with sarcasm.

"Tie him to the bed then," said Saad, as he turned his head and walked away with Fiona on his arm.

"Tie him to the bed. You're sick, twisted and so wrong...that I seriously hope you're kidding, right?" she asked, as he shut the door behind him. Turning her head, she eyed Darius. "He's sick....really sick," she repeated, not understanding why Darius' eyes looked so pained.

"It would be better for him." He said the words so low that at first she didn't believe what she had heard.

She took two steps towards him. "Darius the kid needs a doctor. Not tonight...not tomorrow...now!"

She watched as he ran his hands through his hair like the weight of the world rested on his shoulders.

"Darius your nephew needs help. We really need a doctor."

"You do not understand. It is our way. Our tradition. I cannot interfere. He must go through this on his own." The words were a heartfelt admission. It was the most she had heard him say about who he was, and his family. Her heart clenched with fear as he turned to give her a penetrating look.

That's it, thought Kassandra, throwing up her hands in the air. Her body bounced with angry energy and she wanted to hit someone – okay him. That's the weirdest thing I've ever heard. But, what did I expect from a Greek Warrior who pops out of a book? How about the truth, she wanted to scream that thought at him.

"Okay, your tradition really sucks. You know from what I've learned over the years from reading countless historical books, is that tradition is a lame excuse for not taking a chance, not changing, not growing. Tradition can be what you or anyone else wants it to be...but don't let it be this. Don't let it give you an excuse to do nothing. That's your nephew. He needs you. If you're not man enough to get him help, then I will."

Kassandra turned and marched towards the door. She burned and seethed. Fear pounded straight to her heart because she knew without a doubt, he wouldn't let what she said go. As if on cue, he grabbed her, bringing her body roughly to his. She could feel his heart beat as her head made contact with his chest.

"No, you are not." The words were a mere whisper, as he proceeded to pick her up like she weighed a feather when the truth was far from that. Carrying her over his shoulder, she struggled and squirmed but his hold was tight. She was hot and embarrassed beyond words with what he'd done to her. The hot part was because his large hand was now firmly over her bottom holding her in place and it felt sinful and wicked. His fingers were splayed wide and she could swear the feel of his fingers was being seared into her flesh. He proceeded to carry her across the hall to dump her on a small bed.

Thinking she was finally free of him she was startled as the full force of his weight came crushing down on her. She couldn't breath. Slowly inch by inch his hard muscle-toned body came off hers. Then as if it was an after thought he grabbed her face to frame it in his large hands and kissed her. Demanding a response. Demanding she comply. Demanding she melt against him.

She fought it, or attempted to fight it, but he pushed past her defenses like her thoughts meant nothing. She felt his thumb pull her chin down forcing her mouth to open wider, allowing his tongue full range as he marked his territory. Plunging again and again deep inside her. Then he teasingly withdrew only to lightly skim his tongue across the tops of her teeth. She shivered as desire gained head way. She felt hot and wet. Wanting him. All of him. And she was angry at herself. But, at that moment she didn't care. Part of her wondered what he would do if she bit him. Somehow she sensed that would only turn things up to full volume with this guy and her body instantly responded. Her nipples peaked as if on cue and she felt drenched with need for him. She continued to fight her own inner battle and had to force her hands from reaching up to grab his silky hair as it brushed across her face. Her lips felt bruised, battered and swollen and ached for more.

A whimper of protest escaped her lips when he pulled back. His face a breath from hers. His hands moved from her face to cup her breasts. His fingers played with her nipples and she thought she'd go crazy with desire. More than anything she wanted his mouth to suckle her swollen nipples. To nip and bite and more. Then she looked at him. Heated desire blazed from his emerald eyes. And the look of pure possession caused her breathe to hitch. She felt raw and vulnerable beneath him. She watched as a flicker of a smile lifted the corners of his mouth. She wetted her lips in anticipation as his eyes leisurely moved over her body. His words hummed through her being, causing desire to run like a crashing wave through her entire system.

"This," he said, his finger pebbling her nipple into a tight point, "and this," he said, his hand moving between the v of her jeans as his thumb pressed on her damp invitation, "are mine. I intend to claim them very soon, but for now, you will obey my wishes and not interfere. I will mark you like you've never been before. I plan to worship your body like there is no tomorrow. And I promise you will enjoy every long moment, and beg for more," he said, as his hand at the junction of her legs began to rhymatically move up and down causing her to squirm and reach for more. Pleasure streamed through her. His words were a hot, erotic promise. It did more too full her desire than she thought possible.

"Darius, I..."

His mouth clamped over hers once again forcing thoughts to scatter. She felt her back arch all on its own as he then left her mouth and claimed her peaked nipple, his mouth suckling hard through her thin cotton shirt. His tongue deftly flicking her nipple and then the small nip she ached for. All the while his hand continued to shamelessly rub her, causing her nub of pleasure to harden, and her panties to become slick with need.

"Stay here. I will come back."

The order rocketed through her crazed desire-stricken brain and she once again wanted to scream. She watched as he walked away from her, gave her one last penetrating, heated look and then locked the door. Forcing her compliance. Her body couldn't do anything. Looking down she noticed the wet stain on her shirt from Darius' mouth, and then his words came back to haunt her. Without a doubt she was in well over her head, because when he came back she knew she'd get what she desired, wanted and ached for, and that scared her more than being once again locked in a room.

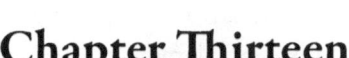

# Chapter Thirteen

His body was taut with unleashed desire and his breathing sounded irregular to his own highly trained Titan ears. It took every ounce of control to not stake his claim. Not give into his sexual Titan nature and brand the woman his. The beast within him growled for gratification and more. It was the more that scared him.

The whimper from his nephew turned his blood cold. This was his awakening year. The first decade of passing, the first molting of his skin, the first Titan memories he would accumulate, passed down from one generation to the next. By rights, his awakening time, should take place deep within the safety of the healing waters, but that was impossible, now. Darius pinched the bridge of his nose, deep in thought. He'd never known a Titan to go through the transformation in human form and that worried him. He could still recall his own first awakening.

He'd been terrified. Deep within the healing water's undersea caves his father had bound his body and arms together, saying it was for his own good. Wave after wave of searing pain had crashed through his body but the worst part was the burning sensation. He'd actually thought at one point that his skin was on fire only to writher in agony as he began to transform and watch as his skin flaked off of him. Bound he'd been unable to scratch. But, bound he'd felt vulnerable like never before.

Then Kassandra's words came back to haunt him. Some family I've got, he thought, realizing he hadn't been alone during that first painful time. His twin brother, Seth, bound in a similar fashion in a nearby cave had sought him out. Gifted telepathically they also shared a unique twin bond. He remembered the first wisps of his brother's thoughts – it had been calming, reassuring him all would be well, even though, he had known his brother was going through the exact painful process. Shaking his head, he realized what he needed to do. To hell with tradition. Opening the bedroom door, he finally give into what his heart demanded.

KASSANDRA HAD NO IDEA how long she'd been in the room but she'd obviously slept through the night. How that could be she couldn't fathom. The click of the lock opening woke her, as a servant walked casually in to set down a breakfast try for her. Her first thought was thank god there was coffee; her second one was where the hell were Darius and the child. Downing two gulps, she ran her hands through her messed up hair, straighten her disheveled clothing and marched out of the room.

At the adjacent bedroom she hesitated. Putting her ear to the door she could hear nothing. Drawing in a breath for courage she turned the doorknob and stepped inside.

She blinked, thinking at first she must have made a mistake with the rooms. Then her eyes caught sight of Darius, his body slouched over the figure in the bed. The pink t-shirt with the words "Honk if You're Horny" still blazed across his back.

"He will be okay."

The husky, timbre of the voice caused her to stare. Gone was the child in its place was a man whose chiseled chest, long thick black hair, resembled Darius so much that a lump formed in her throat.

"What the...who are you?" she said, backing towards the door.

In the next instant, Kassandra watched as in one fluid motion Darius awoke. He moved lithely away from where he had been his body tense and ready for action. She watched as he looked at her and took a second look at the man now lying in the bed, only to shake his head.

"What the...?"

Good to know I'm not the only one with questions, thought Kassandra, watching as Darius took in the scene.

"It's okay, Uncle. It's me, Reece," said the man, as he attempted to slide his long, muscular legs over the side of the bed.

In a movement so quick, it almost didn't register, Darius moved to intercept him. "Reece, what happened?"

"I'm not sure. I felt you lending me your strength throughout the night as the pain took hold of my body, but as for the rest I'm not sure. All my life I've heard stories of the awakening year. How the first time it tears through your body and the memories get burned into you, but Darius, I have all the memories. All of them. And my body. Somehow, I don't think this..."

Kassandra watched as he took a good long look at himself.

"... is what mother had in mine for me when she said I would have a growth spurt. Is this my final form, well okay, final human form, that is?" he asked, as a smile lit up his face, his eyes wide still with that innocent child-like stare.

"Your mother is going to kill me. Okay, let me rephrase that. My brother is first going to kill me and then knowing your mother, she's going to do it all over again," Darius said, as he stretched his body.

Kassandra was reminded of a large, wild, untamed tiger as he lazily stretched his arms above his head and flexed on the balls of his bare feet.

"Hello guys, I hate to interrupt but dare I ask what went on here last night?" asked Kassandra, finally finding the courage to move away from the door.

"Who let you out of that room?" demanded Darius, advancing towards her, his eyes blazing at her.

"Good morning to you too, Darius," smirked Kassandra, vowing to not move an inch.

"Uncle, this is..."asked Reece, swinging his legs over the side of the bed.

That stopped Darius cold. Kassandra watched as he ran his hands through his long hair and part of her envied those long fingers of his. With a chagrin expression on his face, Darius finally introduced her.

"Reece, this is Kassandra. Kassandra, my nephew, Reece."

Kassandra watched as Reece cocked his head to the side like he was listening to someone. Again, she felt as if there was a private conversation taking place between Darius and Reece, but that was impossible.

She watched as Darius grabbed the blankets to keep Reece covered. "Do you think this could be a reaction to the sickness?" Darius asked the question but in reality Kassandra knew he was thinking out loud.

"This might be the reason mother sent me to find you. She and um...your mother.. were unusually worried about my awakening year. Now I know why. I must say I'm happy to have that done with. At least I won't get to repeat that anymore," he said, his voice breaking out with a laugh that did more to rejuvenate Darius than anything.

Kassandra watched as Darius grasped the man arm to arm, kissing first one cheek then the other and finally a kiss on the forehead. The scene was incredibly touching and it brought a tear to her eye.

"Well, I'm glad to see you two are fine. As for me. I think I'll just leave you in peace because I know my questions will get no answers, so with that, adieu," said Kassandra.

Darius turned towards her, "Kassandra."

The way he said her name caused goose bumps to break out over her entire body.

"Um, Uncle you wouldn't happen to have some spare clothing I could wear," said Reece, taking a good long look at his naked self.

Kassandra giggled as Darius noticed what she did. Reece was one fine specimen of a man, well endowed in all the right places. She laughed harder when Darius placed his body in front of Reece's to block her view and grabbed the blanket to cover him up, again.

"I'll get Saad to bring you some clothing and food. And after breakfast you and I are going to have a long talk about things....every thing," he said, turning his attention once again to her.

As if on cue in walked Saad with an entourage of servants, some barring clothing and others with breakfast. Kassandra watched as Darius made swift introductions. She also watched Reece exchange what must be the formal greeting with Saad and then back up, like he was thinking something. Tension filled the air and it was Darius that broke the silence this time.

"Kassandra, have breakfast with me," he said.

Part of her wanted to inform him she didn't care to be ordered around, but the other more traitorous part of her yearned to be near him. He looked happy for a change and it filled her heart with something she wasn't keen to discern.

"Sure, why not," she said, saying a final goodbye to Reece who was eyeing the pretty girl that was serving the breakfast.

"You might want to have a talk with him about the birds and the bees," she stated not missing the look of sexual interest Reece seemed to have for the young serving girl.

"Birds and the bees. What are you talking about?" asked Darius, moving towards a patio off the dining room.

Kassandra stopped walking. "You know..." she eyed him, looking for recognition of what she was talking about.

"No, I don't, just spit it out," he said, forcing her to move again.

She gulped, and wetted her lips. "Sex."

"What about it?" he asked casually, his eyes gleaming with the mere mention of the word.

"I don't get you. Last night there was a kid withering in that bed and now, this morning he's a full-grown man, eyeing that pretty little serving girl. I'm thinking he might need a bit of guidance, now, that's it. You might want to have a sex talk with him," she stated, feeling the blush move from her face to her chest.

Laughter was the last thing she expected from him. It softened his features, made him look more approachable and that wasn't good. "Reece will be fine. You don't need to be concerned. Let's enjoy our breakfast and get to know each other for a little bit, before the next crisis falls in our lap," he said.

Sarcasm and laughter. Two traits she would have sworn he didn't possess yesterday.

"After you, my lady," he said, gallantly holding open the patio door for her to step through. She almost felt like she was stepping into another world. Clad in his tight-fitting jeans that hugged his hips, with his bright pink t-shirt on he appeared like an old-fashion gentleman as he ushered her onto the patio.

Servants followed in with trays of fruit and salted cod, and kippers. The smell of hickory coffee wafted on the light breeze causing her to give a slight shiver.

"Are you cold?" genuine concern filled his voice.

Hugging her arms for warmth and safety, she replied "No," not wanting anything to interrupt the mood.

He eyed her like he wanted to say something but then smiled charmingly, like he had a secret. More goose bumps formed over her skin. She watched as he pulled the chair out for her and motioned for her to sit. Then he picked a lush strawberry from the pile and brought it to her lips.

She had to tilt her head back and the affect was more than she bargained for. His towering body stood over her, his hand holding the berry just inches from her mouth and his emerald-green eyes blazed with hot desire. She couldn't help wet her lips as he brought the red, ripe berry to her mouth. She bit into it, causing juice to spill down her chin. Immediately, his fingers were there, wiping away the excess from the berry. In a world of her own she watched as he brought the juice from his own fingers to his lips and suckled. The erotic image of that caused her nipples ache. Hot desire flooded her body.

Oh, how she hated him, she reminded herself. Shaking her head slightly she cleared her thoughts. Today, was going to be the day she figured out how to escape without getting herself killed.

She turned her head towards the smell of the hot coffee. Anything to distract her from her own passion and desire that wanted nothing more than to rip all of Darius' clothing off of him and bring him to his knees.

As if he could read her mind, she watched as he grinned and took a seat, gulping down half a dozen kippers and half a honeydew melon before he raised his all-knowing eyes to hers.

"So, what do you think of our little adventure, so far?" he asked, eyeing the hot steaming brew that sat next to him.

"Well, let me see. First I get you...and I'm not really sure what you are...and then I'm forced, did I mention I hate to be forced to do anything, into a car for a wild adventure ride only to run into a Michael Jackson look alike zombie. Then we end up here, with our host Saad, and his exotic female pets, and to top it off you come back from what I can only assume was a leisurely call to walk the beach and you find your naked nephew ...oh I know, skinny dipping without his parents...I'm thinking I wish I was on some medication of some sort, because there is no way anyone...okay maybe Melissa and just maybe Sarah would believe me, but hell, I'm not even sure I believe myself," she said, her heart beating wickedly as he stared at her like there was no tomorrow. And for all she knew, with him, that could very well be true.

"You seem to be handling things pretty well," he said it casually, while his large, muscular leg moved between hers. She felt his toes gently scrap the inside of her calf and she gulped. She was no longer cold from the breeze as passion rippled through her, flames lit up from her calf to travel to the pit of her stomach, leaving her all but breathless.

"Whatever," she replied, trying once again to assume her sarcastic tone as she reminded herself he didn't matter.

"Kassandra, I know this has been strange. Heck, it's been somewhat strange for me too, but I like your courage, your spunk and your...uhm, ability to adapt. I've got to go somewhere today and you're going to have to come along with me because of that damn book, but trust me, once I've figured out how to get unbound from it, I'll let you go back to your normal life. As for today, I hate to say it, but it's not going to be a picnic. Saad, has arranged for us to use his yacht and after breakfast we're going out to sea."

"That sea?" she asked, noticing how the swell had picked up.

"That sea," he said, taking a small sip of coffee, his face immediately grimacing.

"I take it you don't drink coffee," she said, almost laughing.

Leaning back in the patio chair she watched as he stuffed two large strawberries in his mouth, before answering her. "That stuff is disgusting, how you humans drink it I have no idea."

Why does he say that? You humans, she thought, once again wondering just who and what he was.

"The yacht is ready at your disposal," said Saad, entering the patio, with his favorite female pet hanging off his arm.

Immediately Kassandra's back was up, as she eyed the beauty, who was all but salivating as she eyed Darius.

"Would you like me to come with you, Darius?" asked Fiona, dropping Saad's arm to sashay towards their table.

Kassandra fought the urge to throw a piece of fruit at her.

"That won't be necessary. Thanks Saad," said Darius, as he got up and moved her chair back for her.

She fought the urge to flash Fiona a wicked smile. That would be way to childish for her, she mused.

"Darius before you leave, a moment of your time," said Saad, as he held the patio door open for them.

"That won't be necessary Saad, I will see you later tonight." His tone broke no argument and once again Kassandra watched as Saad bowed his head in acknowledgment.

"The sharks..."

Darius turned to face Saad, his voice gruff as he said, "I am not worried and nor should you be. We will be fine."

"Take this, just in case," said Saad, handing Darius a large blue crystal.

Kassandra watched as he cradled the crystal in his large hand. "Where did you...."

"Your mother," said Saad, as he brushed past them.

She watched as Darius eyed their host, conflicting emotions played themselves out on his face.

"Darius where are we going?" she asked, finally finding her voice, wishing he wasn't standing so close to her.

"To hell and back...I hope," he replied, taking her by the arm, as he marched them out of the house.

Gone was the compassionate Darius and once again the imposing Greek warrior that chilled her heart and soul stood shoulder to shoulder with her. And once again, Kassandra shivered with mixed emotions.

# Chapter Fourteen

The yacht was speedy and in no time Darius found himself exactly where he wanted to be. Now comes the hard part, he thought, trying to figure out a way to rapture into his Titan form without killing Kassandra. Piloting the yacht, he'd been surprised to see joy light up her face. He had watched amused-like as she sauntered about the deck with sea legs that would make an accomplished sailor proud. As it was it made him hot and hard for her, as his eyes kept getting diverted by her cute, little behind as she romped playfully around in the tight space. Knowing she was wearing a lacy, white thong that his Titan eyes could discern didn't help matters. And, just where had she gotten those short-shorts, or that blasted tank top that barely concealed her bountiful breasts, he wondered, wishing he'd tied his long hair back with something to keep it from flying into his eyes.

There had been a time he'd kept it cut short and neat. No longer. What was the point? Once he raptured into his Titan form his hair grew back to its shoulder length so keeping it constantly trimmed was had become a nuisance.

Kassandra's laugher broke through his thoughts. He watched amused like as she stood at the stern of the yacht, her arms outstretched, her face titled back in joy as the sun's rays steamed over her slim body.

He had thought she'd be nervous on the water. Learning she practically grew up on boats of all sorts explained her ease on the water and for once he was thankful.

"What's that?" she asked, moving from the stern to stand next to him as she reached for the binoculars.

Darius didn't binoculars. He could hear the hum of life coming from the island, even though it was dark and fuzzy to his Titan eyes. He knew to the human eye; it would look like a small island. To him, it was Meredith, the place the high court of Cabiri had currently chosen for its location and his summoning. The fact Meredith was one temperamental very much alive island bothered him Why Sangarius, a mighty river god and first-born son to Oceanus, had created the island still remained a mystery to all. Currently, it was more of a headache than anything else, thought Darius, stopping the yacht.

"Is this it?" Kassandra asked, putting the binoculars back in their case.

Darius moved to the side of the boat. A slight cool breeze ruffled his hair as he breathed deeply the scent of the salt water filling his Titan senses. His heart filled with longing for the sea. As if it could read his thoughts, two dolphins surfaced, spraying him with water.

"Dolphins, Darius. Look at them, aren't they beautiful," said Kassandra, her eyes sparkled in the high sun.

"Yes, beautiful," said Darius, turning to look at her. He watched her turn her face to his, a pink blush spreading across her cheeks. Grabbing the rail, he fought the urge to take her in his arms and kiss those lush lips of hers. Knowing his voice was gruffer than he intended, he asked "Do you know how to snorkel?"

The light disappeared from her eyes as she replied, "Yes."

"Good, put this on and we're going in," he said, handing her a snorkel mask and flippers.

He watched as she slipped the flippers onto her small feet.

"Darius where exactly are we going?" she asked.

It was on the tip of his tongue to say 'to hell and back' but instead he said, "To that island," as he undid the top button on his jeans.

"You're not..."

"Not what, Kassandra, stripping...no nothing like that," he said, grinning, as he shrugged his body out of the tight confines of his jeans, hoping for once his bloody erection wouldn't command any attention. He heard her hitch her breath and the Titan part of him almost purred in satisfaction knowing she wasn't missing anything as he stood before her in all his splendor.

"Darius, seriously, you're planning to skinny dip in the Atlantic?"

Was that a touch of fear in her voice? The Titan in him said so what, while the compassionate part of him tried to reason her fear. Swimming in the middle of the ocean wasn't that unusual, but the chill of the water would nip into her skin after about ten minutes. By Zeus, why didn't I think to bring along a human wet suit for her. Mentally annoyed at himself, he realized he didn't have time to care for her feelings. And that irked him more.

"Um, those jeans of yours are going to have to come off," he said, fighting the urge to grin. He watched as she looked down and realized she'd put on the flippers without taking off her pants. He especially liked how her eyes grew wide with shock as the full meaning of what he said penetrated her brain.

"What...oh...I hadn't thought of that," she said, her cheeks now flaming red.

Crossing her arms, in a stance he was becoming all too familiar with, he wasn't surprised by her request. Humans and their modesty, he thought, yearning to simply rip off her clothes.

"You look the other way. And Darius, no peeking."

Knowing they'd never get in the sea unless he complied he forced his body to turn in the opposite direction. He could hear her unzip her jeans and tried to think of some mundane thing before his erection took on a life on its own.

"Ready," she replied, giving him the grace to turn around.

Darius knew he was staring. Who wouldn't? He eyed her graceful form. She wore a white thong, its lace barely covering her dark curls and worse she'd taken off her shirt. His heart did a double take. That was the last thing he had expected. He'd tasted her. Knew she was an innocent, yet there she stood before him holding herself proud, her chin tilted up in defiance, while her breasts beckoned to him. The beast within him roared to life. His eyes couldn't be pried away from her dark rosy buds as they peaked from the gentle breeze.

"Darius..."

He couldn't stop himself. He advanced toward her, knowing his erection was huge and pulsing. He heard her indrawn breath and knew her heartbeat was accelerating. There was more than a whisper of fear in her voice, as she tried to back away from him, but she was tight up against the yacht's rail with no where to turn, except to him.

His arms circled her small waist, grabbing her ass, bringing her in tight and close to his arousal. Her head barely reached below his chin.

"Darius, we should..."

She tried to bring her arms up between them in a pathetic attempt to put some distance between them, but he growled, a low, throaty warning that vibrated through him.

"These are mine." There was no hesitation. No pause, as he breathed the words into her lips and then moved his head down to claim her peaked nipple with one long suckle. He felt her body bend to meet his need and it took every ounce of willpower to not hoist her ass up high onto the railing, fling her legs around his waist and rip that thong to shreds with his teeth and delve his painful erection into her tight sheath. He inhaled deeply revealing in her scent. He suckled harder bringing as much of her breast into his mouth as he could. He cupped her ass cheeks, his fingers pressing into the round globes in earnest as he stepped between her legs. His erection throbbed against her belly as he managed to bring her in closer, so he could deepen his suckle. He heard her moan of delight and moved a hand down from her ass to feel what his senses could smell. Her lacy thong was damp with sex. He felt her move her trembling legs a bit further apart and he didn't hesitate. Sliding his hand inside her thong from behind, he dove one finger in deep. She was hot, tight and slick with need. She arched her neck back in pleasure and he took a small step back to admire the view.

Her head was thrown back as pleasure crested in her brown eyes, turning them a dark shade of chocolate. Her chestnut hair fell down past her shoulders, swaying in the breeze. She reminded him of the graceful Royal blood Hu'lan sirens, who lived in the Red Sea. The Sirens there lived in harems where they were trained in the art of sexual pleasure, a finer art, he couldn't imagine.

His eyes burned as the pain of the rapture, the pain of wanting to claim her, tried to take over. He watched as she slowly opened her eyes. In an instant her dark brown eyes took him in. He could just imagine what he looked like to her. His body was straining to keep the rapture at bay. He knew his arm muscles were bulging and that his erection was huge and pulsing with a need that made him grit his teeth. The pain of the rapture, the desire to claim her was running like a cyclone through his veins.

He saw her small hands reach out to grasp him and heard his own indrawn breath as both of her hands claimed his member.

"You are so huge, beautiful and so sleek," she mouthed the words as her eyes took in all of him. "And there is no way we could ever..."

He knew what she was thinking as she eyed his arousal, warily. There is no way we can make love. For once he damned his Titan lust that was raging like a rutting sea lion in heat. Why she wasn't running from him remained a mystery to him. He knew he looked like a caged beast, but the Titan in him, wanted more.

"You ain't seen nothing yet, sweetlips," he snarled, grabbing her hands from his engorged member as he turned her around, locking her arms behind her back. He bent her over so that her round ass was his. The slip of white lace resting between her cheeks did more to arouse him than he thought possible. He wanted to rip it to shreds, but knew better. Instead, he grabbed his throbbing erection in his hand and slid it between her cheeks. He could feel her dampness seep onto him as her smell took over his senses. He stifled a groan in satisfaction as she leaned back to match his rhythm. The tip of him was wet and the sea dragon's brand on his skin was blistering with intense heat. He was so close to rapturing it hurt to breathe. It took every ounce of willpower to not give into his Titan sexual drive. As it was he knew he was dangerously close to going over the edge.

A splash of cold water from one of the dolphins brought sanity rushing back to him.

In one fluid movement he lifted her hips. "In we go," he said, hoisting her above the yacht's railing to drop her into the cold Atlantic Ocean. He heard her gasp of surprise, as he prepared to dive in. Flexing his feet on the railing, he dove straight up from the boat's rail into the sea, hoping against hope rapturing wouldn't kill her or him.

In a millisecond the sea's powers claimed him as he continued to dive deeper into the cold water. He couldn't hesitate another second. Finally, he gave into the pulsating need and raptured into his Titan form. Strength and power flowed through his veins as his body reveled being back in its original form. The sea dragon's brand burned hot into his Titan skin, but this time it was a welcome relief. As always the brand gave him more strength when he was in his true form. He sensed all the sea beings' thoughts and more importantly he was able to telepathically seek out his mardom. A splash from above brought his attention back to Kassandra. To the woman who was turning his world quickly upside down.

With a long sweep from his tail he swam upwards.

# BLISS

YOU KNOW I ALWAYS WANTED to swim with dolphins. I just sort of pictured doing this...oh I don't know...how about in Florida, with trained dolphins, thought Kassandra, looking around for the umpteenth time for Darius. You are so going to pay for that. Just you wait.

However, waiting was beginning to become a problem for her. She had watched spellbound as Darius, in all his naked splendor, dove head first into the sea. Honestly, how long can a human hold their breath? She forced the strange sweep of panic from taking hold. The rational part of her that had been drilled with years of survival training all thanks to her military father and her naval reserve training told her she had lots of options. Like swimming back to the boat and getting out of the freak'n cold water, and hightailing it out of here with the motor at full tilt. While the other irrational part of her screamed where the hell was he and are those sharks in the distance? Getting tired of treading water, she eyed the boat again, thinking he might have crawled back into it. I wouldn't put it past the weasel, she thought, her body starting to take on a chill.

Then she sensed movement in the water. Something was moving towards her, fast. *Okay, Mister, that's it. Time's up and I'm out of here. So, what if we are bound together, obviously he doesn't care.* Kicking her feet into high gear she moved, only to feel something warm and satiny brush past her legs. Her entire body shivered from the warmth of the contact. That stilled her. Immobile, she forced herself to take a calming breathe.

Then he shot up out of the water, looking for all the world like what she imagined the sea god, Poseidon, would look like. His hair was wet, slicked back from his forehead, falling down past his shoulders. Shoulders she could have sworn were larger, more muscular, as if that was possible, as she blinked all of him in. His chest magnificent before, was something else, entirely. He looked bronzed and chiseled all at the same time, and worse he was grinning like the weight of the world had been lifted off his shoulders.

It was the grin that did her in. She watched as he playfully splashed water in her face and that did more to make him loveable, make him more trusting, than she liked. Cold, tired of treading water and reminding herself that she was mad at having to wait for him to come back from who knows where, she fought to remain pissed off at him. That idea though simply vanished from her mind with one look at his sexy, charming smile.

"Are you okay?" he asked, gliding next to her.

How he could tread water without using his arms remained a mystery to her. "Sure, I'm fine. Who doesn't like to swim in the cold, Atlantic Ocean every day? Give me a break, Darius," she said, slanting her eyes, hoping she looked mad.

"Glad to hear you're okay. I've got to go to that island. I'll try not to be long. Stay here."

Oh, he must be insane. I know he takes me for an idiot, okay a drooling sex-starved idiot, but help me god he can't be serious. Before she could say anything he was gone. A swish of movement from below was the only warning she got before his upper body, head and all, once again disappeared bellow the surface. Again, her legs felt the brush of a strange, warm, satiny something...a really long something. That must be seaweed; she tried to reason with herself, vowing to kill Darius for playing that trick on her. She was angry he assumed she'd stay, as she treaded water in the middle of nowhere. However, her scattered thoughts got diverted as four dolphins leapt directly over top of her.

So much for Florida? Smiling with her ring side seat, she watched what had to be the best sea water show she'd ever seen, and she forgot all about being cold and mad.

Twenty minutes later it all returned to her. She ran her hands up and down her arms attempting to add warmth but truthfully she knew her body couldn't stand another second of being submerged in the water. Her shivering had taken on convulsing proportions, and she knew her lips had to be blue. Hell, even my nipples hurt, she mused, trying for the third time to rub some sensation back into them with her own hands.

Just as she was about to latch onto the boat's side, the side with the dangling rope that thankfully Darius has thrown overboard, she felt a hand grab her ankle. That scream most certainly did not come from my mouth, she thought, kicking her feet from whatever it was grabbing her back into the sea.

"Darius, you dimwit, stop that!"

"Darius...I don't think so," said the man, surfacing inches from her. "Why pray tell is a silly, little human female doing swimming in the cold Atlantic Ocean?"

Kassandra's entire body clenched in fear. More than ever she wanted to get on the boat, out of the water, away from the danger she sensed from the man, who eyed her like she was a morsel ripe for the picking. The man had a chest that rivaled Darius' but his skin was as dark as Saad's. A bald head gave way to two piercing blue eyes and from his left ear dangled what looked like a fish-hook. He was handsome and worse, she sensed he knew it. White teeth gleamed at her as he smiled, but it wasn't a genuine smile. It was the type of smile you see on a cat just before it pounces on its prey.

"I heard that Darius had a female, and I just had to see," his eyes raked over her and it was then that she remembered she was practically naked. "..for myself." He actually licked his lips. She felt his hand back on her ankle and this time she didn't hesitate. She kicked him for all she was worth. However, it was obviously not much. He simply grabbed her, chuckling at her feeble attempt.

"Look, I don't know who you are, but get away from me." Even to her own ears that sounded pathetic.

"Feisty little human aren't you. I like that," he said. "I can see why Darius is attracted to you, but it won't last."

"What won't last?" Like that was smart. Blathering idiot that I am. Kassandra hated herself for talking to the man who was scaring the pants off her, that is, if she had been wearing any. Inwardly, she was screaming for Darius to get his butt back here this instant.

"You won't last. Darius likes variety. You're a treat, but trust me little lady, he'll use you and then abuse you. I on the other hand only want a sample," he said, grinning as he attempted to pull her in closer to his body.

# Chapter Fifteen

Sweat poured off Darius' body and for the fifth time he yanked on the metal chain. Chain! He practically screamed in fury, as he shook his head which caused the heavy, rusting chain to rattle and clink. Around his neck was a black, iron collar clenched as tight as possible. Tiny iron spikes from the collar where embedded into his neck, preventing him from rapturing into any type of sea creature at will. He yanked again in frustration, knowing he had to get out of the dank underground cell he'd been put in before time ran out. His heart thundered when he thought about Kassandra. What must she be thinking?

Things had been going well as he swam like a mad Titan to reach Miradeth's entrance. That had been the easy part. After much pleading and even bowing in reverence to the living entity she had granted him entrance to her Great Hall. Thinking the mission was almost accomplished he'd momentarily let his guard down. Now, here I am back to where I was at the beginning of this mess. He gritted his teeth in agony as the taste of the metal spilled into his body.

"Enjoying your nice, new surroundings," said Muroka, as he ambled forward.

Ten years had done a lot of damage to him, thought Darius, glad his former opponent didn't look as impressive as he had a decade ago. Nasty, jagged scars ran down his face and his chest, and there was a gaping whole where his right eye used to be. The fact Muroka's Titan powers hadn't healed him remained a mystery to Darius. The only other scared Titan he knew was his twin, Seth, but that had been a deliberate punishment inflicted by their father's Triton. From what he knew that was the only thing capable of scarring a Titan. He highly doubted, though that his father had anything to do with disfiguring the infamous Titan slave master.

"You look charming as ever, Muroka. Why don't you go take a bath, or better yet, brush your teeth," he taunted, eyeing as the large Titan moved closer.

In a flash, Muroka punched him in the chest, causing him to double over in pain. The chain, embedded deep into the sea yanked him back as he almost toppled over. He felt Muroka grab his hair tearing the roots out, causing his eyes to sting. Inches from his face the slave master sneered at him and he fought the urge to gag. Besides his outward appearance the slave master smelled like rotting fish on the inside.

"I saw you looking at me, freshling. I consider myself lucky. For ten years I've searched these waters for you, and now," he chuckled, the sound like someone rinsing out their mouth, "she's going to do things to you that even in your wildest dreams you wouldn't imagine."

So that's how he got the scars. Aphrodite can be a bitch, but I didn't think she was that bad, thought Darius, trying to figure a way to get the chain off his neck. Maybe the direct approach will work.

"Look, Muroka, it wasn't my fault for what happened ten years ago. When have you ever known me to shy away from a good Titan fight," he grinned, hoping to catch Muroka's attention. After all, he knew the Titan slave master loved a good fight. Pushing his luck, he ventured forth with an idea that had been simmering in his head.

"Look, let's just you and me pick-up where we left off a decade ago. A good clean, Titan fight."

"No," answered Muroka, giving another hard yank on the chain. "I promised Hera I would bring you to her for your...um," he chuckled again, causing Darius to get a good whiff of his rotten sea breathe, "your punishment."

"Hera? What does Zeus's wife have to do with me? I thought Aphrodite was mad at me. Have all the gods gone mad? I haven't even seen Hera in over a century," he said, frowning, trying to figure out how he could have insulted Zeus' touchy wife.

A rough yank on the chain by Muroka unhooked it from the sea floor. Then his body was dragged unceremoniously down the long corridor. The so called, Great Hall Meredith had let him enter. No wonder. Traitorous entity.

"You sneered at Aphrodite," answered Muroka.

It took Darius a moment to realize that Muroka had answered him.

"What! What are you talking about? I didn't sneer at Aphrodite," he replied, attempting to haul his upper torso off the crusty seabed cutting into his skin. Did I? he thought. "I simply had something more...something more important to do" ...like run in the opposite direction, he thought, "but I most certainly did not sneer." Do I sneer? "And, what by Zeus...okay, bad choice there, what does that have to do with Hera?" he growled.

"She took offense to you. And you might as well stop your sniveling, freshling. She will enjoy filling you in just as much as I'm sure she will enjoy inflicting pain on you," said Muroka, dragging Darius' body down the long corridor.

She took offense to me. By all that's reverend. Somehow I've managed to piss off Hera when she's obviously on a woman rampage. The last time she went on one of her famous rampages the Trojan War broke out. And just who is he calling a freshling. I don't think so, fumed Darius, his Titan anger rising like never before.

"You there. Just where do you think you are going?" said a booming voice from the end of the corridor.

While his Titan eyesight was blurring causing him not to see the figure clearly, he immediately recognized the voice. The oh, I can't believe it voice, he thought, knowing he was going to regret what was going to happen next before it actually did. Madly, he looked around for an alternate escape route.

"Drop him. You are not to come any nearer with your foul Titan body. I will take the prisoner from here."

"But, Hera said I..." began Muroka, only to be cut off as the figure loomed closer.

"Are you disobeying my direct orders, slave. Need I remind you of the consequences?"

Darius watched mildly amused as Muroka's body actually shook in fear. He felt the heavy chain drop, allowing him the dignity to move his Titan tail underneath him to propel his upper body up off the floor.

"Enjoy yourself, freshling," taunted Muroka, making his way back down the long corridor.

Darius watched until Muroka was completely gone before he made a grab for the figure. "What are you doing here, Rylan?" he demanded, grabbing the kid by the scruff of the neck.

"Rescuing you...you're um, choking me, Darius," said Rylan. Back was the pubescent, scratchy voice that Darius recognized.

Releasing his choke-hold on the kid, he backed up, allowing Rylan to remove his disguise.

"I was visiting with my Uncle and really it was a good thing too, because he's got this whole new plan...you should see it...I mean it's really good, not like the last time, when you know he accidentally started that little war," blathered Rylan, as he finished taking off the cumbersome Titan disguise.

Darius felt his eyes roll back in his head. Why the kid didn't spell the disguise away annoyed him. Thinking about that made him realize it was probably safer for him if Rylan didn't use his powers. Every time he used a spell something went wrong. Seriously wrong. Case in point his current predicament.

There had been one moment when he'd felt actual joy at seeing the kid, and being freed, but that feeling evaporated the minute Rylan mentioned Zeus' name. The kid is a babbling idiot, he thought, attempting to sort out from Rylan's spiel what was important.

"Enough, cut to the chase, Rylan, but before you do that get this blasted collar off my neck," he yelled, causing the kid to jump in fright.

In a blink, the collar and chain were gone. Ahh, the joys of being a semi-god, thought Darius, eyeing the kid, warily.

As if there was no interruption in his monologue, Rylan continued to blather away, "So, anyway, in walks Hera, and well...we all know to leave the palace the minute she's anywhere in sight, but I hid behind this large pillar and overheard her talking about you. Well, I couldn't believe my luck, so here I am. What's our mission?"

Darius crossed his arms over his chest and counted to ten. Then he closed his eyes and started to name all of the sea creatures he'd transformed into over the centuries. Finally, he opened his eyes and looked at Rylan's hopeful gaze. What do I do with you? he thought. The kid was a freak of nature but he realized at that precise moment his options for help were limited.

With his hands crossed over his torso, Darius said slowly, hoping Rylan would get the jest of what he had to say the first time. "The only mission you have Rylan, is to find a way to break that spell. Remember." His eyes starred directly at Rylan's shifty eyes.

He watched as the kid shifted his gaze to observe the seabed. "I haven't forgotten....in fact...I think I've almost found a way to break the spell, of course there was that little bit about having your body dissolve for all times, but that's not really a big thing," rambled the kid, unaware of the building fury in Darius.

Darius wanted to take the kid by the shoulders and give him a good shake or deck him one. Decking him was starting to sound really good to him, as he absorbed what Rylan was saying.

"...so anyway, Hera said she was going to castrate you and..."

"What!" bellowed Darius, his eyes wide in disbelief? "The goddess actually said that to Zeus. She said she was going to..."Darius couldn't bring himself to say the word. It was an abomination. His whole body was now in a rigid state of shock.

"You know that was the tame part of what she was saying to my Uncle, who I have to tell you was laughing so hard he almost fell over," answered Rylan, crossing his arms over his chest to mimic Darius.

Zeus falling over that I'd love to see. Darius swam nervously back in forth in one spot. He needed to get to the High Court of Cabiri, get back to Kassandra, and then he'd find a way to torture Rylan for doing this to him, he vowed. First thing first, getting to the court.

"So, what's with that woman you were with?"

That stopped Darius cold. "What do you mean?"

"Why did you leave her swimming in the Atlantic? On my way here I saw her latching onto Rajheb," said Rylan walking ahead of Darius down the long corridor.

No longer in Titan form, Rylan looked like a typical human teenager. Clad in ripped jeans, he wore a simple white shirt and sneakers and a gold necklace. Once again Darius was reminded this wasn't just any kid he'd got saddled with. It was Zeus' half-nephew, and half of him was a bloody god! The kid could move at will through all the realms, including his undersea kingdom. That knowledge infuriated him.

Taking stock of what Rylan said, Darius' did a double-take. What! screamed his brain. His heart clenched in fear. There was no way in Hades' Kassandra would latch herself onto Rajheb. More likely the Titan rake was trying to latch onto her, wanting to sample a human female for a change. Every cell in his body went into overdrive. He had to force himself not to turn and swim for all he was worth back to her location. As much as it killed him he did have a mission to fulfill. Get to the court, talk to them and try to find a way to stop the plague from killing his mardom. But, he vowed silently to himself, if Rajheb touched one hair on Kassandra's head, he'd kill the Titan with his bare hands.

# Chapter Sixteen

Ten minutes later task one was accomplished. He'd meet with the thirteen Cabiri members and now he knew what he had to do. Only find all seven ancient relics from each of the seven seas. That's just great. Nothing else could be easier. Just seven relics, one from each of the blasted seas, and guess what Darius you've got all the time you need. Two days! That's it. Two blasted days! Or that little plague that's killing all your mardom in the North Seas will in all likelihood start to consume all the seas. That had been it. No advice. No good luck. Simple instructions that could have been delivered by one of their pitiable servants.

Darius saw red. It's impossible, he thought, like they'd listened to him. There had been no argument. No debate. Just simple instructions and then all thirteen divine beings had vanished back to wherever they came from.

"So, what did they say?" asked Rylan for the umpteenth time.

Darius couldn't speak. He growled a low warning to Rylan hoping the kid would get the hint, shut-up. He swam to the entrance – the Main entrance this time – avoiding Meredith's Great Hall – as the entity shifted in another one of her attempts to block his exit. As the opening loomed in his sight, he gasped. Blinding pain sliced through every cell in his body. His chest constricted as his body started to rapture back into human form.

"No!" he shouted, fighting the rapture that was taking over his Titan body. There was no way by Hades' he'd survive in human form this far down under the sea. The pressure would kill him, let alone the water, which he'd drown in as a human. That's irony for you, he thought.

121

...

"Get your paws off me," said Kassandra, gritting her teeth, as she tried to calm her breathing.

"Why? What are you going to do about it?" asked the man, pulling her in tighter to his chest.

"This," answered Kassandra, head-butting him for all she was worth. He was so stunned and surprised by her move he let her go, giving her the time she needed to grab the rope to pull her body up out of the water and onto the boat. Her head hurt more than she thought possible and her ears rang. Great, if that creep gives me hearing loss he's going to pay big time. She moved to start the boat, only to realize the key wasn't in the ignition.

"Going somewhere are we?" taunted the man, hanging onto the rope that in her stupidity she forgot to haul back into the boat. "I don't think so," he said, rattling the boat keys like they were a toy while his lower body remained submerged in the water.

Not good. This is not a good situation. Quickly Kassandra took in her options. None. No, that's not right. Her father said there were always options; it was a matter of how far one would go to get them.

Sighing in frustration, she asked, "What do you want?"

"You," came the man's husky reply as he made his way up onto the boat's rail.

"Oh, I don't think so, Rajheb," said Darius, giving the rope a good yank causing the man to drop back into the water.

Kassandra stilled herself from doing the happy dance. Where did he come from? Who cares, she thought, thrilled to have her Greek warrior back. Then she frowned. I'm still pissed at you and I can't believe you left me in that water, alone, for so long, she told herself, as she hugged herself to keep from jumping into his arms.

As if he could read her mind, he whispered, "I'm sorry," as he leaned further over the boat to speak to the man.

It had been a long time since Kassandra had heard Greek spoken, and even longer since she heard ancient Greek spoken. It was obviously his native tongue, she realized, loving the cantor and roll of his accent that reminded her very much of her father's. She almost laughed. What language did she expect a Greek warrior to speak, she thought, biting her lip to stop from gawking at him.

Naked, he was one fine specimen of a man, as her friend Melissa would joke, while her other friend, Sarah, would chime in with some retort about, "size has nothing to do with it." Deep down, Kassandra was starting to doubt that. Size seemed to have a lot to do with Darius. The guy was unusually tall, broad in the shoulders, with a six-packed chest that lead to the most marvelous butt she'd ever seen, and his...she couldn't even say the word, as the picture of his erect state still burned brightly in her mind. Quickly, Kassandra looked the other way, her face heating from her own wicked thoughts.

Even though she had turned in the opposite direction she could make out every word Darius was saying. After all, it wasn't like he was trying to be quiet. He was shouting and growling all at once to the man in the water. And, while it might have been a long time since she heard ancient Greek, her heart speed up when she realized what he was saying.

"...you take one more look at my woman, and you won't live to see another high tide. Do I make myself, clear?" It wasn't said as a question. It was a clear statement. A command.

Kassandra couldn't hear what the man said, but she didn't care. Her heart was fluttering in excitement. His woman. *Did he say what I thought he said? And, why does that make me happy? I don't even know this guy. He just popped into my life and ever since then my normal life has evaporated.* Why that sounded hollow even to herself gave her pause.

Then she heard one loud splash.

*Hopefully, creep-o is gone. Gone for good.*

She felt Darius' arms gather her to him. She realized she should have fought him, but his body felt so damn good. His body heat was like a furnace in overdrive. "Kassandra, I'm sorry. I had no idea it would take me that long. The good news is that we are done and we can be on our merry way. And trust, me that guy won't bother you ever again," he said, tilting her head up to look at him.

Kassandra stilled. I am not a weak woman and I certainly don't need a He-man to look after me. Then why do I feel so good? Why am I so pleased he got rid of that creep? "Where did he go?"

"Don't worry about him. Kassandra...I," Darius angled her head, providing her with an out if she wanted it.

Instead she closed her eyes, eager for the feel of his lips on hers. Part of her knew she should shove him away. After all, she was still mad at him. Instead, she gulped as tears from who knew where threatened to spill from her eyes. Damn, damn, damn. I am not about to cry because my prince in shining armor just rescued me. She gulped, hoping he'd take command of things. Thankfully he did.

The rough, crushing feel of his lips on hers awoke the simmering passion within her. He cupped her bottom closer to his, wedging her body tight into his muscular thighs. One of his hands grabbed her hair, bunching it tight as he applied more pressure to the kiss, forcing her mouth to open wider. His tongue dueled with hers as she fought to regain the upper hand. It wasn't going to happen, she realized that the moment he released her hair and grasped both of her butt cheeks to haul her up to his waist. The rock-hard feel of his throbbing erection tantalized her. Since he was as naked as a jay bird, and with her only wearing a thong and the diving flippers on her feet, without a doubt she knew she looked ridiculous even as she moved her legs to circle his waist.

When he finally did release her lips, he whispered into her ear, "Ahh, sweetlips that will never happen again. I would never let anyone harm a hair on your head. It's okay."

Okay, she thought. It most certainly was not! Realizing as the cool ocean breeze buffeted her skin what was going on, she immediately chastised herself. "Darius, I.."

That was all she could say, before his lips gently claimed hers, again. If it had of been another rough, forced kiss, she would have fought back. Instead, he gently tilted her head, and ever so lightly his lips grazed hers. Then his tongue licked her lips in what had to be the most erotic sensation she'd ever experienced. She knew in his own way he was asking permission. And she complied. Opening her mouth, she suckled his tongue bringing him in. His arms were still holding her body tight to his. But this time, her nipples were standing at attention, begging for him to move his lips lower for a taste. She felt every ridge of his planed muscles, including his impressive member that throbbed against the vee of her secret garden. A garden that was hoping to get weeded any day now. His hands roamed in small circles over her bottom. For once she wished she was as nude as him, even though she only wore her thong.

"Hey, where did Rajheb go?" asked a scratchy voice, in ancient Greek, to her left.

Thankful that Darius had turned her so that her back was to the strange voice, she had to tilt her head up over his shoulder to find the source of it. Who is that? And where did he come from? wondered Kassandra, eyeing the strange looking teenager.

"Wow!" said the voice, as he stood on the tips of his feet to get a better look at her.

"Turn around, Rylan. Now!" commanded Darius.

"Okay, okay. Look, it's not like I haven't seen a woman before, geesh," replied the voice, in one of the sulkiest tones she'd ever heard before.

"I'm only going to tell you once. Look at my woman again, and I'll tear out your eyes," said Darius, again speaking in ancient Greek.

*This is too much, really.* "That's enough," she whispered the words in ancient Greek into Darius' back.

She felt his entire body go rigid. The look of pure disbelief on his face made her smile.

"You speak ancient Greek?" asked Darius, giving her a penetrating stare.

"Yup."

"Since when?" A frown creased his forehead.

Eyeing the teenager over his broad shoulder, she replied tartly, "Ever."

"Not many hu...not many people know how to speak ancient Greek anymore. Who taught you?"

"My father." *Boy, these one-word answers are a real treat.* Kassandra enjoyed finally being able to give back to him his one-syllable answers. She knew she was toying with him and relished the moment.

"I'm Rylan by the way, your one and only Greek..."

"Teenager," cut in Darius, turning his head he gave a glaring look to the gawking teenager.

"Nice to meet you, Rylan. So where did you come from? Oh, let me guess you just popped here, didn't you?" Sarcasm laced her question but the kid seemed not to get it.

"It's complicated," replied Darius. "We need to get back to Saad's and then be on our way. Rylan go below while Kassandra gets dressed," commanded Darius, in a tone that broke no argument.

"Below, I think I'll just..."

"No, you will not. You will go below and do as I say," growled Darius.

Kassandra knew he wanted to advance and usher the gawking teenager down below deck but that would mean releasing her and for once in her life she was grateful his large body was covering hers. The minute the kid was below she broke free from his grip. She knew letting him hold her almost naked body would be too much for her frustrating hormones. As it was they were screaming at her in complete disbelief.

"So why do you speak ancient Greek?" she asked, taking another step away from him.

"Why do you?" he asked, glowering at her.

"Because I can," she replied, tartly, wondering how long this tête-à-tête was going to last.

"Same here," he replied, as he walked away, picked up the keys creepo had dropped onto the deck to start the yacht's engine. Talk about a nice view, she thought, wishing her hormones would shut-up for once.

"Come here," he said, crooking a finger at her while at the helm.

Oh no, thought Kassandra, shaking her head. She knew if she did that, they'd be back where they had been, not once but twice...with her getting all hot and bothered for nothing. Mustering as much courage as she could, she grabbed her tank top, yanked it over her head and shimmed into her shorts. Covered, she tried hard to ignore him as she turned to the stern of the boat, hoping the cool ocean spray would cool her irrational behavior.

# Chapter Seventeen

Saad leaned back in the large indoor salt pool he had specially built into his bedroom. In Titan form he enjoyed the cool feel of sea water running over his body. He wanted more than anything to feel the full power of the sea fill his essence. But, that would have to wait. He'd promised his father, Retan, he would find the sacred text and hand it over to him. The only problem was Darius either had the book in his hands at all times or he'd hidden it using some type of Titan spell making it invisible to his eyes.

Lazily, he watched as Fiona sauntered in dressed au naturelle. In human form she was beautiful. In Siren form she was breathtaking. "Shall I?" she asked, dipping one foot into the pool. Even though it had been a full day without partaking of her pleasure, Saad was not in the mood.

That probably had everything to do with Dr. Lancaster who had dropped in unannounced today. It had been Trevor Lancaster's famous idea to reprogram the sharks into more controllable, lethal weapons that could be controlled by humans. As if, Saad thought, for the hundredth time. However, the proposition had spiked an interest in him to see if it was possible. Could one actually manipulate genetic behavioral coding? That answer had been a resounding yes. Were they then able to control the sharks that had been released into the ocean? At first it had appeared that they had, but within a few months the experiment had gone horrible wrong. Worse, the sharks had somehow been able to trigger the aggressive gene in all the other sharks they had encountered. Short of killing every shark that roamed his ocean frontage, Saad was momentarily at a loss to explain what had happened. Strangely enough, Trevor hadn't seemed one bit worried about it. In fact, he had seemed euphoric about the possibility of their specialized genetically engineered sharks triggering the aggressive gene in sharks naturally. As he had rambled on about the possibility of what this could mean for the Canadian Navy's specialized marine service core, Saad had tuned him out. Now, he wished he'd paid more attention to what he'd said.

Even when Fiona dipped her other foot in the water to entice Saad, he didn't bat an eye.

"Leave, Fiona," said the commanding voice of Retan as he materialized in human form to stand by the pool to look down at his son.

"Father," said Saad, quickly, rapturing into human form to slip out of the pool.

"Aja Master," said Fiona, meekly, bowing low as she left the room.

"I see you brought some of the Um'elle's with you," his father said, sarcasm lacing his words.

Saad was not in the mood to discuss the Um'elles. He knew from previous frustrating conversations with his father that he disapproved of his choice of Sirens. Why that bothered him he didn't understand.

"Where is the book?" his father asked bluntly, turning his back to his son.

Saad took a moment to admire his father's physique trying yet again to guess his age. He seemed timeless and immortal all at once. His father like him did not bother with human clothing. They were equally comfortable in their own skin.

"Saad, where is the book?" asked his father, this time turning to give him a penetrating stare.

Saad knew it would be useless to stop his father from reading his mind, so he didn't even bother to shield his thoughts. "I don't have it."

"What!" bellowed Retan, his eyes turning a dangerous shade of dark blue that Saad knew only to well.

Saad choose to ignore his father's rage. Instead, he sat down on the rouge velour settee and grabbed a nearby oyster to eat. "I'll get it. Don't worry."

He watched as his father leashed his temper away. "You had better. I need that book."

"What's so important about that book anyway? It's not like there's a cure in there to stop the plague from killing our mardom," he said, watching as his father's face took on a guarded look. "Is that it? That's why you need the book. There's a cure in there for this blasted plague spreading through the seas. By Zeus, just tell Darius, I'm sure he'd hand over the book. In fact, I know he would. This plague has killed more of his mardom in the North Seas than anywhere else," said Saad. Then it clicked. His father wanted the first spawn of Oceanus, the rulers of the North Seas to die. That was it. He wanted the book not to cure them but to ensure they all died.

He watched as his father grinned. It wasn't a pretty sight.

"Your thoughts are correct. Darius has been sent on a wild goose chase by the Court of Cabiri, when in reality all I need is to get my hands on that book," said his father.

Reaching for another shucked oyster, Saad asked, "Does mother know?"

"Your mother is in denial. Her plans are why I've been forced to interfere. She is blind to her own plight. Once I get that book, she will come to me," replied his father, smartly.

Saad had never met his mother. All he'd heard growing up were stories of her from his father. At one time the stories had been of a loving, tender Siren, but then as the years passed and the centuries accumulated, his father's tales grew darker and more sinister. Gone was the loving mother he'd fantasized about and in her place was a creature so mysterious, so unreal, he knew he never wanted to meet her. As it was, he had to grow up with the shame of being a zeta – a son without a history, a son whose mother had deserted him at the moment of his unique birth.

Growing up with his father had been anything but gentle. Even though his father had taken three other Siren mates producing two half-brothers, and one half-sister, he'd always felt like the outsider in the family. And, he'd always felt as if his father was testing him. Looking for any type of weakness in him, anything to disown him. After all, he knew that every time his father looked at him, he was a reminder of the one and only time in Retan's life when fate had interfered and he'd lost the thing that had mattered the most to him – his own Sokhan.

Over the years, he'd come to realize why his father's tales had turned sinister. His father suffered from a broken heart. Getting his father, the famous Titan that the all-mighty Creator had taken into confidence, the only Titan to ever serve on the Court of Cabiri, to admit that would be a major coup.

"You need to get that book to me. Do I make myself clear?" demanded his father.

Saad nodded his head in acknowledgement only to find himself once again alone as his father vanished from the room. How he was able to do that remained a mystery to him, but then again, most things about his father were mysterious. It was why so many Titans and rulers feared him.

"Your father sent me back to you. Are you in need of service?" asked Fiona, as she walked in the room wearing only a pale blue bathrobe.

"Yes," he replied, "take it off."

He watched as the material slid to the floor. Ushering her forward to the pool he spoke to her telepathically. Still sitting on the settee, he watched as she raptured into her natural Siren form. His breath hitched as the power of the sea claimed her. Not one to waste the moment he walked into the pool and raptured into his Titan form, looking forward to a very physical evening.

# Chapter Eighteen

Darius was no longer in the mood to talk. More than he cared to think about it unnerved him that Kassandra could speak ancient Greek. From following the course of human history over the last few centuries he knew only a handful of people today actually spoke the original language. Many of those were Titans who had given up the sea to live on land. Could it be? No! There is no way she's a Siren, even as he eyed her graceful form. She stood tall and regally proud at the tail of the yacht, her long hair streaming behind her from the force of the wind, looking so much like a current washed Siren that for a moment he wondered if the Fates were playing him for a fool. He wouldn't put it past them. His eyes narrowed in disgust at the current predicament he found himself in.

Shaking his head, he turned his thought to other more pressing matters. Getting seven blasted ancient relics from seven seas. That's just great. And task completed in two days. What could be easier? He laughed loudly when he'd telepathically told his twin what the Court demanded of him.

"You've always been up to a challenge," Seth had replied, and Darius could almost picture his boyish grin. There hadn't been much Darius could say. He knew his brother was in no condition to help. As it was, it had taken every ounce of his own willpower to force both Seth and his wife, Jamie, from venturing to Saad's to see their son with their own eyes.

It hadn't been easy but he allowed them both into his mind to witness what had happened to Reece. He had heard every painful cry from both Seth and Jamie as they witnessed his memories first-hand to see what had happened to their son. Knowing that the plague had somehow been responsible for forcing Reece to mature into a full-blown Titan scared them. But, it had been Jamie who had quietly informed him that Seth was affected by the plague, also. Not wanting to risk anyone else getting infected, Seth was forced to rely on his younger brother for a change, and Darius could just imagine how much faith he had in him. I won't let you down, brother. I will get those relics no matter what I have to do. I will succeed, he vowed.

Cutting the engine quickly, Darius docked the yacht. He expected to see Saad not Rajheb standing on the dock. His eyes narrowed in disbelief. Is that freshling looking to get killed today, he thought, not forgetting for one minute how scared Kassandra had been. Not that she'd let on for one minute.

He felt Kassandra move to his side. "Is that who I think it is?" she asked, squinting her eyes to make out the shape.

"Yup," he replied, throwing the rope onto the wharf to fasten the yacht.

"Nice to see you again, Darius. I don't believe we've been formally introduced. I am Rajheb, Saad's brother, and you are..." said Rajheb, holding out his hand to help Kassandra up to the dock.

"None of your concern, Rajheb," replied Darius curtly, as he hoisted Kassandra up to the dock by circling his hands possessively around her waist. In one leap, he landed on the dock, enjoying the look of disbelief on Kassandra's face.

He watched as she composed herself pulling down her tank top to reply, "It's Kassandra. So, you actually have a name. Tell me Rajheb do you make it a habit to harass women on the high seas, because I have news for you... pirating isn't a turn on."

Rajheb bowed gallantly. "You have caught me, Kassandra. Fiest and fire, I like that Darius."

"You can like all you want, Rajheb, but that head-butt you received is nothing short of what I will do if you ever lay a hand on me again," said Kassandra, as she stared down her opponent.

Laughter from both Darius and Rajheb quickly filled the silence and broke the tension.

"You actually head butted him?" asked Darius.

"It completely caught me off guard. Like I said, she has spunk," chuckled Rajheb.

"Why do you continue to talk about me in the third person. I'm standing right beside the two of you. And, as much as I'd like to be somewhere else, I can't."

Darius knew Kassandra wanted to push both of them off the dock and she was mad as hell, but he wanted to make it plain as day to Rajheb that she was his woman. Since actions speak louder than words he pulled her in close to his chest and proceeded to thoroughly kiss her. The last thing he expected was for her to bite his lower lip.

He knew the yelp of surprise wasn't a very Titan sound, but no woman, or Siren had ever bitten him before, except when he'd wanted them too, of course, relishing those wicked times.

Without another word he watched as she walked away from him and Rajheb.

"Like I said, Darius, fiest and fire and I'm thinking she's more than you can handle," replied Rajheb.

Darius grabbed Rajheb and dangled his body over the wharf not caring that the Titan's elegant suit was being rumpled. "In case you didn't understand my earlier message, stay away from her or else." Using his telepathic abilities, he easily pushed past the Titan's barriers to inflict what he knew would be a serious migraine on Rajheb. He watched as the young Titan's face contorted with pain, but still he didn't release him.

"I haven't heard a reply to my statement. And until I get that, well let's just say what you are experiencing is just a tad of what I can make you feel."

"Okay, Darius, stop being such a beast. She's yours. Hands off. I get it. Now, let me go," replied Rajheb.

"With pleasure," replied Darius, as he eyed the murky water below.

"Darius, can I come up now?" asked the pubescent voice from bellow, just as he dropped Rajheb into the water.

"What the..."said Rajheb before his body went under the water.

Ryaln's body materialized next to Darius' "Is that who I think it is?"

Darius eyed the kid. While Rylan had been below deck he'd taken the liberty of talking telepathically to him trying to get the half-god teenager to understand why he had to act like a normal teenager and not simply pop here and there. It wasn't like he wasn't grateful to the kid for saving him again from Muroka and from rapturing underwater into human form, it was simple, whenever the kid was around things seemed to get complicated. Like now. It was bad enough having to make up another lie to explain Rylan to Kassandra, but the last thing he wanted was for Saad and Rajheb to know what really happened to him.

"I told you know popping around," said Darius.

"She was gone. No harm. That is Rajheb. Why is he in the water in his Armani suit?"

Darius watched as Rylan's eyes looked at him. "Ooh, I see. You threw him in. Hey, Rajheb, do you want some help?" yelled Rylan to Rajheb who was fumbling none too gracefully to the shore in his very wet, expensive suit.

"Darius if that is who I think it is, you are in big trouble. Get that kid out of here," growled Rajheb, slinking out of the water looking like a drowned rat.

"Aw, come on Rajheb, not happy to see me," smirked Rylan, actually punching Darius in the arm, like they were boozen-buddies.

Darius heard Rajheb's telepathic message loud and clear and for once he actually agreed with the annoying Titan. "I mean it Darius, make him go. He's trouble."

Trouble, Rylan? That was an understatement, he thought. "Rylan, what did you do to him. No, I take that back, I don't want to know. You said you were close to finding a spell to get me unbound to the book and Kassandra, I need you to get that pronto. Can you do that for me?" asked Darius, forcing his tone to be gentle while persuasive.

"Can't I stay with you? You've got this great quest and I never get to go on any adventures. That's why I was taking all those relics in the first place. It was an adventure. Now, thanks to my Uncle, and yes I know you're listening," shouted Rylan to the wind, "I've been grounded."

"Grounded?" asked Darius, wrinkling his nose as he forced his mind to pay attention to the kid. Just how does one ground a god...okay, semi-god?

"Uncle said I had two choices. Stay with him at the Palace or be with you. So, I picked you, okay? Because really after two days of being in the Palace the place is so boring, unless you happen to catch Apollo or one of his winged horses to play with. But, come to think of it, the last time I did that Apollo locked me up in the stall with Thagesaurs, and that wasn't fun, at all...."

"Shut-up!" bellowed Darius.

Darius knew his eyes were blazing with fury as he advanced on the kid. "No, it most certainly is not okay with me." This was the last thing he needed. How by the gods can I get all seven relics in two days if I have to baby-sit Mr. Catastrophe?

Forcing a calm, he didn't feel, Darius continued, "You promised you'd find a way to get me unbound from your last misadventure, need I remind you," he growled, standing at his full height as he towered over the kid.

"Okay...don't get so riled. I was only trying to help, need I remind you...I did just save your life, twice. Not that it seems to count for anything these days," muttered Rylan.

Darius rubbed his face with both hands weary of the situation. He felt as if he was sinking into a deep underground sink hole and quickly going nowhere. Or worse, heading straight to Hades' lair. Bowing his head in defeat, he knew Titan honor bound him to repay Rylan for saving him and that grated him. "Okay, you can stay," he muttered, turning towards Saad's house.

Darius closed his eyes momentarily, as Rylan proceeded to jump up and down in excitement. "Did you hear that Uncle...I can stay. He said I could stay. I'm going to help him. You'll see," shouted Rylan, as Darius left the dock, wanting more than anything to avoid everyone so he could get on with his quest. He could have sworn he heard Zeus laughing in his head which really worried him.

Forty-eight hours that's all I have, he thought, knowing he'd need to look at Saad's undersea maps of the seven seas. Before he could do that though he needed to have a talk with Kassandra to set some things sort of straight.

# Chapter Nineteen

Kassandra strode into the bedroom with the grace of an angry barracuda. That had been her father's nickname for her as a kid whenever she'd had one of her major tantrums. She avoided answering Saad's pointed questions about the trip or meeting his brother. She was sick and tired of them all. How the hell in only twenty-four hours did her life go from the truly mundane to frightening, to the ridiculously bizarre.

Thankful for the change of clothes laid out on her bed, she stomped into the bathroom and proceeded to take a long, hot shower. Once cleaned and clothed she felt more human. Attempting to braid her long, wet hair into a ponytail to keep it off her head, she felt Darius' hands on hers before she heard him.

"Why do you always do that?" she asked, tartly, trying to brush off his hands. His reply was to push her hands away so he could finish braiding her hair.

"I like your hair down," he said, as his fingers twisted the ends into a tight braid.

"There we go again. You never answer any of my questions, Darius. You know I can keep a secret," she replied, watching his reflection through the mirror.

"Can you, Kassandra?" he asked, turning her body around so they were face to face.

"Yes. I can. I'm not your average woman who blathers away about things. In my line of work, keeping secrets is what I'm good at."

"Your line of work?" he asked, his eyebrows rising in speculation.

"I told you I work at the library but I'm also a Captain in the reserves. Naval reserves. I...uhm...break codes," she coughed.

She watched as he backed away. A huge grin lit up his face and his eyes actually sparkled. "Go figure. That's why you were able to open this blasted book. Just what else are you keeping from me, sweetlips?"

Kassandra gulped. She wasn't ready to share everything with him. And as much as it killed her to lie, and ignore Saad's earlier warning that she disclose to Darius she was able to find lost things, she hesitated. Heck, it's not like he trusts me either. "Nothing. That's it. You know the rest. I can speak ancient Greek, and four other languages as well."

"Do tell, what are they?" he asked, a smug smile lighting up his face as he moved to perch on the edge of the bed.

"Well, it's not really a language anymore, more a list of symbols," she paused as his eyes bore into her, "Okay, I can speak, French, Hebrew, Assyrian and uhm, decode Summarian symbols."

"What the? You're serious. Who taught you?" he asked, disbelief written all over his face.

For once that made her feel good. She'd been thrown surprise after surprise, so she was going to enjoy her moment as the tables turned on him.

Tilting her head up, she replied boldly, "My father."

"Some father. I'm thinking I'm going to enjoy meeting your father."

Kassandra's chin came up. "That, won't be necessary," she replied, shaky with the thought of Darius and her father ever meeting.

The one and only time she'd had the courage to introduce a boyfriend to her father had been her last year of high school. Her father had taken one look at the boy and declared he was unfit for her, and worse, he'd called the boy a weakling to his face. That had been it. Humiliated beyond words, she had vowed then that her love life would remain private.

"I'll decide what's necessary, sweetlips and if you're thinking I'm afraid to meet this infamous father of yours, you are sadly mistaken. Trust me I can handle myself. Now, I've got some explaining to do, which will hopefully answer a few of your questions that you claim I never answer. So, sit down, get comfortable," he said, patting the spot next to him on the bed, "and listen."

THIRTY MINUTES LATER they, Kassandra and Darius, were both sneaking into Saad's office, while Rylan kept Saad and Rajheb occupied.

Kassandra had liked Rylan much better the second time she'd met him. Clothing did that to you, she thought, enjoying seeing Darius squirm as he tried to handle the overzealous teenager. It had taken him a full ten minutes to convince Rylan he didn't need to come with them into Saad's office. Kassandra knew Rylan had only agreed when she proposed that he could be the diversion to ensure they wouldn't get caught. Highlighting the danger of that position had been a positive in Rylan's mind. A low growl from Darius had told her he wasn't pleased by that idea, but Rylan had pounced on it.

"Are you sure he'll have an undersea map?" asked Kassandra.

"I saw it here when we first got here. He had it opened on his desk. Here it is," he replied, shuffling three books off of a large looking map.

Peering over Darius' large shoulder, Kassandra could make out the light blue circle graphs that showed where large volcanoes appeared to be located on the undersea map. "Why does he have a geological survey map of the ocean floor?"

"Um, there not exactly what you think they are," Darius replied, his fingers moving deftly from one large circle to the other like he was judging the distance.

"Okay, what are they?" she asked, trying to get a good look at the map

"Sink holes."

"What? They are not. That's the undersea floor. There's nothing to sink into except the Earth's crust. That's insane," she replied.

DARIUS' PATIENCE WAS worn thin. He didn't have time to explain to Kassandra what she was really looking at. All he cared about, as he trained his Titan ears to listen to Rylan's voice was ensuring their cover wasn't blown. Finding the sink holes that connected the seven seas would make it easier for him to slip into each sea undetected. Since he couldn't explain what everything else was he realized he was going to have to borrow the map from Saad, without asking for it. And then he'd have to find a wet suit with oxygen tanks for Kassandra because he couldn't leave her behind. Come to think of it, he'd have to get an outfit for Rylan because Kassandra believed the teenager was human. Boy, the kid was just going to love that, thought Darius, stifling his frustrating groan. Having to deal with Kassandra was enough of a distraction. Now, having to keep tabs on Rylan shorted his tight fuse even more.

Shoving the map into his shirt he headed for the door.

"Darius, what is this?" asked Kassandra, holding up what looked like the statue of a two-headed serpent.

Darius' heart stilled. It couldn't be? Barely able to speak, he said, "Kassandra, very slowly, put that down."

"What?" she asked, moving the two-headed serpent so she could get a better look at it.

"Put it down. Now! And, very slowly," he replied, coming to stand next to her, not daring to touch the ancient relic, which he knew would awaken if his Titan hand came into contact with it. How by Hades had Saad come to possess two of Typhon's heads? wondered Darius.

"Kassandra, I'm going to take off my shirt. I'm going to need you to place the object in it and wrap it up. Then very slowly give it to me, okay?"

He watched as she nodded her head, thankful once again she didn't balk at his command or ask any questions. Once the relic was securely covered he took it, careful to keep it from coming into contact with his skin.

"Time to go," he replied, making sure to telepathically inform Rylan they were safe and on the move. The plan had been that he and Kassandra would get the map and then join them for dinner while Rylan delayed them into thinking he and Kassandra were enjoying the pleasures of each other. While his Titan body ached to do just that, the clock was ticking.

"Do we really need to dine with them?" asked Kassandra, a frown causing lines to form on her forehead. He could tell she was less than thrilled by the idea.

"Yes, we do. Once they retire to their...uhm....beds," said Darius, thinking they would probably each be enjoying an Um'elle for the long night, "then we can leave without getting caught. We'll have to stop further up the coast at a friend of mine for two wet suits and diving tanks but then it's the open waters for us, okay," he said, taking her into his arms. "Kassandra, I want you to know I'm really sorry this has happened to you," he said, his lips brushing hers as desire swamped him.

"I'm not," she replied, bravely smiling up at him like he was her knight in shining armor.

Guilt washed through Darius like a cold shower. The only way for him to get the relics was to rapture into his original Titan form, with Kassandra in tow, which meant...he couldn't even think it, the idea repulsed him so much, he wanted to throw her from him and make her run from the beast he really was.

For the first time he understood what his twin had felt that eventful day almost two decades ago. Looking back, he realized he'd been showing off. When he stupidly got caught in a human net, it was the first time in their Titan history that a Titan didn't uphold the harsh sea law. Instead of killing him, his brother had done the unthinkable – freed him,

Shaking his head, Darius realized what he was beginning to feel for Kassandra wasn't something he could describe and it unnerved him. Sure, she was stunningly beautiful and her mind was as complex as an octopus' but there was more to her than those two qualities. There was something about her that called to him like no other woman or Siren ever had. That wasn't good.

In the end he had taken an oath to protect his mardom and he knew his father would not allow him to break another sacred Titan sea law. If Kassandra found out what he truly was she would pay the ultimate price – death.

"You should be," he snapped, grabbing her arm to lead the way to their bedroom where he could drop off the sacred relic and then together they would walk arm-in-arm, like two lovers, into the dining room.

"Why?" she asked, her wide brown eyes shown with innocence.

By the Gods how he hated her innocence. Why by Theyths couldn't he have popped out of a book by a woman used to the ways of men? That would have made things a lot less complicated. As he propelled them towards their room he was sure he could hear the Fates giggling in his head. A sure sign he wasn't about to like the events that unfolded around him next, he thought.

"Why, Darius?" Kassandra's voice broke into his reprieve.

Turning her swiftly into his arms, he cradled her head in his two large hands. "I'm not at all what you think I am. If you knew the real me then you would run, if you could, as fast as your legs would take you in the opposite direction. Trust me on that one, sweetlips. So, don't think of me as your average guy next door because nice I most certainly am not. I'm not the type of guy you want. And, I will do anything. Absolutely anything to get unbound from that blasted book and you. Do I make myself clear?"

"Absolutely. That makes two of us," she replied, twisting herself free, as he released her.

Good, he thought, hating that he had to vent his anger towards her. But, that was better than ever pretending there could be something between them. A human and a Titan, as if, he thought, hating himself all over again.

# Chapter Twenty

Dinner was a silent affair. Tension knotted tighter than a sailors knot between Kassandra's shoulder blades making eating difficult. She had clenched her jaw shut so hard after hearing Darius admit she meant nothing more to him than a chain that had been brokered around his neck that now her mouth ached. She was the chain he was trying to unhook by any means. Which was good, she thought. Still though, after all they had been through together she had naively thought she was starting to get to know the real him. And, the worse she had believed he was starting to like her. His cold, calculated words had dashed whatever hope, whatever dreams she might have harbored deep inside of her. Without a doubt she knew there could be nothing between them.

"What is this called again, Darius?" asked Rylan.

"Chocolate cake," replied Kassandra, giving Darius the grace to finish his large bite that he had forked into his mouth.

On more than one occasion during the long dinner it had been Rylan's comic adventures, or misadventures, depending on how you looked at them, that had eased the strained tension in the air. A few times during Rylan's recounting of a story she had caught Darius' penetrated look at Rylan, as if he was sending him a special silent message he didn't want to share. That was absurd, thought Kassandra, watching as both Rylan and Darius took their third pieces of chocolate cake.

"You look stunning, Kassandra," said Rajheb, eyeing her like she was the chocolate cake.

Muttering a thank you, she could have sworn she heard a low growl from Darius. But, that was absurd. He had made it plain as day he wasn't interested in her.

"Yes, that color suits you. I hope you don't mind that I had Felicia pick out something for you," said Saad, reaching for a drink of his sparkling mineral water.

That remark threw her off. Here she was thinking it was great not having the sultry, exotic Felicia at the table while the young woman had obviously gone out of her way to pick out a stunning outfit for her. Kassandra admitted to herself she had been pleased and her pulse had quicken when she had spied herself in the mirror.

Tonight, she felt regal. For the first time in her life she understood her friend Melissa's motto, "Clothes make the woman."

The dress was a deep shade of green. It was form fitting with a low neckline and while it was long at the back it was cut just below her knees in the front, allowing her legs the freedom to move. It had off the shoulder sleeves tied with small bows and the material felt like silk on her skin. When she had tried it on she had been stunned to discover how well it fit her.

"Tell Felicia thank you," she said, meaning it, as she took a sip of her coffee.

"You were made to wear beautiful things, Kassandra. And if you were mine I would deck you in diamonds and jewels," countered Rajheb.

"Okay, that's it. We're done," said Darius, coming to stand behind her.

Kassandra attempted to take another sip of her coffee, but that wasn't going to happen. Darius yanked on the back on her chair, and took her arm before she could say anything else. Just before he left, he grabbed two more pieces of the chocolate cake and without a word he not-so-politely escorted her out of the formal dining room.

Yanking her arm free once they were safely out of earshot of Saad and Rajheb, Kassandra fought the urge to kick Darius in the shin. "What was that for?"

"What?" he asked, marching ahead of her, acting like nothing had happened back there.

"Why are you behaving like such a brute?"

"Me, a brute. Sweetlips, if you wanted to see a real brute we should have stayed a few more minutes with them because I promise you I would have done something completely brutish...like bash Rajheb to a pulp," he grumbled, marching ahead of her.

"Ohh," she responded, pondering his words. If she didn't know better he was jealous, but again, that notion was absurd.

A few minutes later she was sitting with Darius watching as Reece ate his cake. By the look of rapture on his face she had a funny feeling this was his first taste of chocolate.

Sitting up in bed, with a white starched shirt on, Reece said, "This is the best thing I have ever tasted."

"Oh, come on. It's only chocolate cake. You've have cake before, right?" she replied, watching as he shook his head to indicate no. "Okay, mystery man. You and your Uncle are a pair," replied Kassandra grinning in delight at the two of them.

A stretch of silence was her cue to leave. As it was she felt awkward around Reece. The image of the young child Darius had cradled in his arms was still too fresh in her mind. It was such a huge leap for her to look at him now and see a fully grown man, who was devilishly as handsome as his Uncle, that it pained her. Her rational brain went bleep every time she tried to think how that could be physical possible so like many things that had occurred since she met Darius she tried really hard to ignore the implausibility of it.

"Well, that's it for me. I'm glad you're looking better, Reece. I've got to turn in. Tired day and all, plus I want to be fully awake for that big adventure tomorrow, you know. A girl's got to get some beauty sleep." Kassandra rambled as she headed for the door.

Bad habits die hard. Her father had always said rambling was his cue when he knew she was lying to him or about to get into mischief. Thankfully Darius had no idea her ramblings were a nervous indication of what she planned to do tonight. If he did, she knew without a doubt, he'd tie her up again.

"I'll be there soon," replied Darius, finishing his cake quickly.

"That won't be necessary," she replied, coolly, existing the bedroom in haste.

KASSANDRA WAITED A full hour before she snuck back towards Saad's office. She was positive she'd found a secret door in his office and couldn't let the opportunity pass. What was he trying to hide?

Tiptoeing silently, she made her way unobstructed to his office, which of course was once again locked. How Darius had managed to open the locked door simply with a few ancient Greek words mystified her. Hell, though, she'd try it. Repeating the rhyme word for word she was amazed when the door unlocked. Stepping inside she shut the door as silent as she could and then went over to the side panel wall behind Saad's large chair. Running her fingers along the inseam of the paneled wood, she pushed. And voila!

She almost let out a "whoopee" when the wall moved back and opened. Poking her head in she watched as the long corridor lit-up on its own. Stepping into the secret hall, she paused when the wall shut automatically behind her. Great, no escape, now Mrs. Marble, she thought to herself, forcing a calming breath to compose her thoughts.

Faint voices coming from the end of the corridor alerted Kassandra. Careful to make no noise she inched her body tight to the wall as she walked to the end of the long hall. She stopped when the hall led to a large opening. Glancing around she noticed it was an undersea cave equipped with the most modern up-to-date equipment she'd ever seen. Then the voices started to get louder.

"The injections aren't working. I've told you that."

Kassandra could barely discern two figures to her far right. They were walking towards her. Eyeing a large pink buoy, she crouched low and slunk behind it.

"I've brought someone who will help."

Her breath hitched when she realized it was Rajheb with someone else coming her way. Forcing her panic down, she practically screamed when a large hand clamped over her mouth. Without thought she bite down hard.

"Ahh, sweetlips, you don't listen very well. I told you to stay put and look where I find you. As for biting me, the second time, I'm really going to enjoy paying you back," said Darius, whispering the words into her right ear while his hand covered her mouth.

"Now, I'm going to let go of my hand on your mouth, but you've got to promise me you'll be extra quiet."

She nodded. His voice and erotic words were doing strange things to her body. A throb began to pulse between her legs. It was a wanting she had no time for.

"Good," he said, his body brushing up hard against hers. He was once again asserting his dominance, giving her no space to breathe, letting her know in no uncertain terms he didn't trust her.

She prayed he'd inch back a step to give her more breathing room. No such luck. They were crouched together like canned sardines as they watched Rajheb move to a side door and haul out an old man, who had obviously had the crap beaten out of him. Kassandra heard Darius' gasp and realized he knew the person.

"Who is he?" she whispered.

He motioned for her to be quiet, and she complied, aware he was trying to eavesdrop on the conversation. Not that they had to. Rajheb and the other man, who on second inspection must be a scientist since he wore a long white lab coat, weren't attempting to shush their voices. In fact, they seemed to be having a heated discussion.

"I've told you before I can't fix them. They've mutated because of the plague. They are rogue," said the old man.

Kassandra watched horrified as Rajheb smacked the man hard in the face. She felt Darius' grip on her hand tighten.

Edging back a fraction of an inch, she tilted her head up at him to whisper, "We've got to save him."

"Quiet," he mouthed.

In case she didn't get it, he proceeded to place a finger over her mouth, effectively shushing her. To bad it also caused her heart to race. Worse, she had to clamp her mouth firmly shut so as to keep from flicking her tongue out to lick it. An erotic image of drawing his finger deep into the recess of her mouth to suckle it made her dizzy. God, how she hated this man.

# Chapter Twenty-One

Darius had known the minute Kassandra started rambling she was trying to hide something. It wasn't like her to act nervous, but that's exactly the reaction he sensed from her body as she hastily left the bedroom. If he could have he would have gone after her immediately. However, Reece's innocent question, asking if he'd been intimate with Kassandra yet, had unsettled him so much he queasily realized he needed to explain some very important details about being a Titan in human form to his nephew, pronto. *Great, I'm stuck dealing with the sex talk. You owe me big time, bro,* he thought to himself, thinking how best to respond.

Now, here he was. The urge to throttle Kassandra fueled his cells. What by Zeus had she been thinking? He took that back; she wasn't thinking at all. If she had, she most certainly wouldn't have ventured back into Saad's office and without a doubt she would not have discovered Saad's secret wall panel. The panel Darius had every intention of discovering himself tonight after ensuring all was well with his nephew and that Kassandra was sound asleep.

*The woman never did as told,* he thought, wishing he'd tied her down to ensure her own safety. She could have rated all she wanted but at least she would be alive.

Darius eyed the imposing Red Sea guards who were walking about in human form. They were even wearing black military uniforms. He wasn't fooled. Every Titan sense within his body knew what they really were. He calmed his breathing and reached out to shield both his thoughts and those of Kassandra's. He knew the Captain of the Red Sea guards was probably scanning the area telepathically. There was a dozen of them. Too many for him to take on his own. The warrior Titan he was wanted to fight his way out while the rational part of his brain knew stealth was his best option. Still though it had almost killed a part of him to watch Rajheb man-handle Master Odeon and not barge in and kill Rajheb with his bare hands.

However, Odeon was a master like no other. He was an ancient Titan. Darius hadn't been surprised when Odeon had telepathically told him in no uncertain terms to not interfere. At least he now knew where their chief Titan scientist was. He had been working with Jamie to find a cure for the deadly plague killing his mardom, and Jamie had informed him Odeon had disappeared two weeks ago. Now, he knew where he'd was. Once he was in the water he'd reach out and let Jamie and his twin know Odeon's whereabouts and tell them the strange happenings taking place at Saad's place.

A shrill alarm sounded briefly and then a steel covering slowly opened up to the turbulent sea below.

"What is that over there?" asked Jamie.

He wished he could speak telepathically to her. Her human voice could easily be picked up by the Titans. Darius prayed the sound of the cooling engines and machines drowned them out.

"Sharks," he answered, his eyes narrowing as he tried to reach out with his inherent Titan sense to read the sharks minds. No such luck.

A loud thrashing bang caused Kassandra to grip his arm.

"I need you to fix them. We have one week left and then we need to deliver them. If he can't fix them, kill him," said the scientist looking man to Rajheb.

"Darius, they just said..."

"Shh," he replied, shaking his head.

Darius realized then these were the sharks Saad had mentioned. They were experimenting on sharks for some unknown reason and he expected Master Odeon to fix them. Did it have something to do with the plague? Darius didn't know but he indented to find out. He also needed to find out who was the human. What were Saad and Rajheb thinking to work with a human? It made no sense to him. Deranged, killing sharks...unless, he thought, Saad and the scientist were trying to find a way to control the sharks to use them as their own fighting machine. Still though for what purpose? Those questions he'd have to figure out later, now, he had to get Kassandra out of her before they were discovered. He could only shield their thoughts for so long before the Red Sea guard Captain sensed the influx of Titan power.

"When I move inch back and then we'll make a dart for the corridor," he said.

He watched as the guards flanked Rajheb's side. It was now or never. Darius made his move motioning for Kassandra to follow him back up the corridor. Even though the hall was no longer lit he relied on his other Titan senses to allow him to move at ease. Grasping Kassandra's hand in his they made it back safely into Saad's office. A click told them the automatic shutting mechanism sealed the door again. Safe back in their bedroom, he wasn't one bit surprised to find Rylan there waiting for them.

"The yacht's ready and I managed to get those wet suits and tanks you asked for," replied Rylan, standing at attention like a young cadet.

Darius didn't want to know how the kid did that, he simply wanted to be underway. "Let's go," he said, ushering everyone to the balcony.

"We're jumping?" asked Kassandra, eyeing the eight-foot drop.

"We can't risk being seen going out the front door and this is the quickest way to the dock. I'll jump first and then I'll catch you. I promise," said Darius, taking hold of Kassandra's face in his two hands.

"Okay, Mister, you asked for it," she replied.

Darius didn't like her mischievous tone. Jumping easily to the ground he held out his arms for Kassandra. He watched as she backed up into the room and took a flying leap on top of the balcony railing, her hands briefly touching the rail as she propelled herself forward, tucking in her knees to complete a full rotation to land on her feet, like a cat. The grin lighting up her face was equally amazing.

"Can I just pop...?" asked Rylan from the top.

Darius eyed the semi-god and in no uncertain terms informed him telepathically he was not allowed to pop anywhere while Kassandra was present, and that he'd have to jump. He watched as Rylan eyed the ground.

"He's afraid of hurting himself," said Kassandra, backing up to give Rylan space.

What semi-god can get hurt? thought Darius, all but growling at Rylan to get his ass moving now or never.

"You should catch him," said Kassandra.

"He'll be fine. Jump Rylan. Now!" muttered Darius, as he moved towards the dock, turning his back to the teenager.

"Okay...okay," said Rylan as he jumped awkwardly over the railing. While his landing wasn't perfect he did manage the feat. "I think I broke my ankle," he whined as he shuffled down the dock.

"No, you did not, and stop whining," said Darius, as he ushered them both onto the yacht. "You can still stay here, Rylan or go visit your Uncle, if you'd like," taunted Darius, knowing full well that would spur the rebellious teenager into action.

"I'll manage and guess what my ankle is feeling better already," he replied, jumping onto the yacht to prove his point.

"I just bet it is," grumbled Darius, as he started the engine. "Rylan, take this bag with you, it's got the ancient book with it. I want you to take another look at it and try again to figure out a way to get us unbound, okay."

"Well, do, Captain," said Rylan, giving a mock salute as he grabbed the bag and headed below deck.

"Hey, when did you get here?" asked Rylan, practically yelling at Darius' and Kassandra to see who was on board.

"Thought you could leave without me, Uncle?" asked Reece, lying down in the small bunk.

"I thought I told you to go to the safe house," said Darius, ushering Rylan out of the way so he could make sure Reece was okay.

"I'm fine. I'm coming with you. This is my family, too," he said, trying to sit up.

"Look, Reece, you still need to rest. I need you to be safe," replied Darius, running a shaky hand through his hair.

"Let him come, Darius," said Kassandra, surprising him.

"You don't understand. If one hair on his head gets hurt I will be in big trouble," he replied, bone weary with having to keep everyone safe.

"It's his decision, Darius. It's his family. And, while I don't understand what's going on....I do know the seriousness of the situation. I don't think it's safe to send him back to Saad's house and what better way to keep an eye on him than to have him with us."

Her logic undid him.

"Fine. You can come, but stay there. Don't you dare come out of that cabin. Do you hear me?" he replied, trying to sound angry as he proceeded to tuck the blankets around Reece like he was still a ten-year-old.

Running back up on deck Darius surveyed the scene.

"What can I do?" asked Kassandra.

Darius moved away from the wheel as he replied, "Take the wheel."

"With pleasure," she said. "Ah, Darius we need lights. I can't see where I'm going," she replied.

"Follow them," he said, pointing out the two leaping dolphins to her right.

"Friends of yours?" she replied.

"You could say that," he said, turning his attention to the dock as he eyed Rajheb and Saad running towards them.

"We're not going to get away," said Kassandra, as she watched the two men jump into a second smaller yacht.

"Oh yes we are," replied Darius, telling her to put the yacht in full throttle.

Darius watched as they tried again and again to start the boat.

"You did something to their boats," stated Kassandra.

"I didn't. Rylan did," he said, giving credit where credit was due.

An hour later, Darius ordered the yacht to stop.

"This is the place. Rylan and Kassandra go suit up. I need to talk to Reece alone," he said, moving below deck.

Fifteen minutes later he returned and had to force himself to not laugh at how ridiculous Rylan looked. "Just where did you get the suits?" asked Darius, trying hard not to grin.

"Don't say it. Not a word. I didn't have a lot of time. I just grabbed what I could. I thought this one would fit her, but it doesn't, so unless you'd like me to..."

"Sorry Rylan, it will do," quickly cutting off his prattle, while wishing he could take a photo for future reference of Rylan the semi-god clad in a hot pink wet suit.

"Anyway, this is top of the line. It has a digital driver so we can speak to each other, it also has a crystal silicone seal, an equalization system to fit over any nose and an exhaust valve feature so we won't get any bubbles, and..."

"Okay, I get it. It's top of the line. Just finish getting ready, will you," said Darius, all but gritting his teeth at Rylan's useless dribble.

"Where's your suit? And where exactly are we going?" asked Kassandra, reaching over the deck to test the temperature of the water with her finger.

Okay here's the hard part. For the past hour he had tried to think of a plan that would allow him to get the seven sacred relics and the only way he could do it was as a Titan, which meant the unthinkable. Part of him reasoned, that if he was lucky and got all the relics he'd be able to get his sister, Mercka, to erase Kassandra's memories of what she was about to witness, while the other part of him worried what his father, King Sadok would have to say about it. The truth of the matter was he was running out of time.

"Once you're in the water I'll explain," he said, ushering them to the bow of the yacht.

"How, I won't be able to hear you," said Kassandra, fiddling with her mask.

Darius knew she was delaying jumping into the cold Atlantic water after her recent experience in it.

Taking her in his arms he leaned his body tight up against her wet suit, not missing the feel of her breasts sharply outlined in the suit as they brushed up against his chest. "I promise you'll be okay. I won't let anything happen to you and you've got to trust me on this one okay, sweetlips," he said, tucking in a stray curl under her cap. Darius knew if he had to he would force her but he didn't want that. He wanted her compliance. He ached for her trust. Trust that he had no right too, but still he yearned for it.

He watched as she titled her head to look up at him. "I trust you, Darius, the question is do you trust me?" she asked, staring him bodily in the eyes.

Do I trust you? Hell, yes, he wanted to shout. But, the question really was did he trust himself. Well, he was about to find out just how much.

"Kassandra, please get in the water. We need to be underway," he said, breaking contact from her.

Her meek nod was his answer.

Two minutes later, with the two of them safely in the water, he stripped and dove head first into the sea. Motioning for the two of them to follow him he dove down, prolonging the rapture for another moment as Kassandra got used to breathing oxygen with the tank.

Then in the blink of an eye he allowed the power of the sea to claim him and raptured into his true form. His Titan ears heard Kassandra's in drawn breath, and her heart accelerate while all that Rylan said was, 'Wow'.

"This is what and who I really am," said Darius, using his telepathic powers to invade her mind.

Her thoughts were a jumble and he worried it might all be too much for her. Then he heard her laugh. "You're not a genie, you're a Titan, well that explains a lot," she said, grinning like there was no tomorrow.

# Chapter Twenty-Two

Kassandra wished more than anything she could talk to Darius. He had a lot of explaining. She had wondered how he was going to travel underway through the cold Atlantic Ocean without a wet suit and now, knowing he was a Titan – a mythological creature of the deep, rattled her.

Her father had told her stories about the Titans and Sirens of the under-sea word. As a child growing up those stories had taken on myth proportions. It had been those stories that had spurred her on to become a librarian of antiquity. She loved ancient things. She loved the myths surrounding them and had on more than one occasion gone to sleep dreaming of what it might be like to be a Siren swimming and living in the wild sea, free to roam the ancient ships dotting the ocean floor. A small part of her as a child had secretly wanted those stories to be real. After all, the way her father told them made them appear larger than life. Now, she wondered, was there more to her father than she knew. Did he know they were real? No, that was impossible. They were simply stories he made up for a fanciful child, she thought, forcing her eyes to blink.

Taking another look at Darius she marveled at his changes. His dark hair was fuller and longer and trailed behind him in the current. His upper body was more muscular and his long, tapered torso reminded her of a powerful swimmer. Then her eyes did a double take. A sleek, powerful looking tail, which shimmered with a dark blue color easily propelled him through the water. A ridge of hard iridescent golden scales separated his torso from his lower half. Covering his chest was the unmistakable outline of a sea dragon in vibrant red, orange, and deep green with blues hues. It curled around his chest and Kassandra knew without a doubt that it wrapped around to his back. Two green eyes stared at her. And, for one moment she wondered if it too would come to life.

Her hands itched to touch his body. He was a myth larger than life. She had watched mesmerized as his body began to blur and then a blinding white mist had taken over him and when next she looked he stood before her in all his glory. The only word to describe him was magnificent.

As if he read her thoughts, his body moved towards hers. His powerful tail circled her body and even through the wet suit she felt his heat. Then it dawned on her. She had felt that once before. Just before Darius had left her treading water for what had felt like hours, she had felt his tail touch her skin. He had changed then and didn't tell her. Why was he letting her see him now?

One of her father's myths popped into her mind. Nana, daughter to the river god Sangarius, who was also the mother of Attis. She fell in love with a male human and her father had cast her out of the sea for betraying their race, but not before killing her lover and almost succeeding in killing the child she bore. In the end, Nana was forced into exile on land and ended up begging for food for her child, who later vowed revenge for his father.

Darius' warm hands grabbed her around the waist, forcing her daydream to come to a complete halt.

"Kassandra I know you can hear me, so I'm going to explain a bit of what I am. I'm a Titan belonging to the North Seas. For the past decade while I was trapped in that book a plague has been slowly killing my family and friends. Now, it's up to me to find a way to stop it. I have two days to find the necessary things and it isn't going to be easy. I know you have lots of questions. I'll try to answer them when we are able to communicate together. Oh, and prepare yourself for a wild ride," he said, his thoughts loud and clear in her head.

Then in the next second she felt his powerful tail swoop up forcing them down, fast towards the ocean floor.

"Take a breath, Kassandra," said Darius, reminding her she had been holding her breathe. The feel of oxygen filling up her lungs was a welcome relief.

Where are we going? she wondered for the umpteenth time as they hurdled even faster towards the ocean floor. Closing her eyes in panic, she heard Darius calmly say, "Keep your eyes closed this is going to feel like one hell of a roller coaster ride."

Roller coaster ride? I hate those. What's he talking about? Then in the next instant she felt her body plunge into something so cold it caused her to hold her breath again as every cell in her body fought against the extreme assault. Then warmth rushed back through her as they descended what could only be described as a tunnel that twisted and turned and even went uphill for what seemed like an eternity.

"We're almost there. You're doing great," he said, his voice a soft reassuring caress in her mind. Why it felt so right to hear his voice in her head made her smile. Then it made her mad. How come he gets to communicate...oh, yeah, he's a Titan. A mythological creature that really doesn't exist, she thought, just as they existed the tunnel with one whoosh.

"Can we do that again? Can we? That was the best. The best! The absolute wildest ride I've ever been on," prattled Rylan, practically danced around them in his wet suit.

Kassandra was able to hear him loud and clear because the two wet suits were equipped with microphones so they could talk to each other.

"Okay, Darius. You know, you take all the fun out of things," said Rylan.

Obviously, she thought, Darius could comminute with the teenager. Momentarily, she wondered why the kid wasn't freaking out with what had transpired. Before she could even make a hand motion Darius forced them behind two large boulders.

Her nose immediately wrinkled as a pungent, sour odor like rotten eggs wafted over her.

"Oh, my gawd, what is that smell?" asked Rylan, sounding like he was trying to hold his nose.

"That is something we are going to avoid at all costs," said Darius, motioning for Kassandra and Rylan to stay still.

Kassandra watched in disbelief as the weirdest sea creature she'd ever seen swam past her. Separated by the distance of about two car lengths she marveled the creature didn't spot them. With the body of a large eel it had three menacing looking dog head. It had to be the most ferocious creature she'd ever seen. A black leather leash dangled from its collar. Just as she was about to take another peak at it, Darius pushed her further into the ocean floor.

GREAT, JUST WHAT I need. Tartahounds! What could be better? Darius motioned again for both Rylan and Kassandra to stay absolutely still. The last thing he wanted was to be spotted by the unleashed Tartahound, which was a mystery in itself. He remembered his twin telling him that more and more of Hades' demon dogs were roaming the seas without their masters - Hades' legionnaires. But, this Tartahound still had a leash dangling wildly from its collar and that unnerved Darius. His Titan senses didn't detect any legionnaires but something was not right. From his personal experience dealing with the deadly hounds, any that had lost their master went directly back to Hades' lair. However, this Tartahound was scouting for something. It was the something that worried him.

I don't have time for this, he thought, eyeing where they had existed from the undersea portal. The pull of the sea dragon ran like ice through his veins. Relying on its skill more than his Titan senses, his infra-rayed eyesight spotted the Fad'hal cave where one of the ancient artifacts was safely hidden. Or, he assumed it still was.

Ten years ago, he made a hasty trip to the cave renowned throughout the undersea kingdoms for its special properties. It was there he hid the sacred celestial globe that belonged to Urania he had found stashed in the main foyer of the Duc'alle Palace in Venice. How was I to know the globe belonged in the safe keeping of the Arctic waters?

Darius didn't want to go back into the Fad'hal cave. He had forced himself a decade ago to not look into the torks that hung like stelligalties from the ceiling of the cave. The tork crystals that grew in this cave were sacred and held the special power to show someone seeking their soulmate, their Sokhan, a reflection of that person. The idea had terrified him then and more so, now. However, he didn't have a choice.

Making sure one last time that the Tartahound was gone he instructed Rylan to guard Kassandra while ordering her to stay put. Then he swam to the cave armed with a large canvas net bag which would enable him to carry all the artifacts back to the Court.

Part of him yearned to talk to Kassandra. He knew she must have a million questions jumping around in her head, but again he had underestimated her. Instead of panicking, she'd laughed at him. That wasn't the reaction he'd been expecting at all. But, once again this human woman surprised him. Shaking his head, he forced himself to pay attention to the mission.

Entering the cave, he forced himself to not look at the hanging torks. Remembering where he had stashed the globe he moved a few boulders out of the way. Just as he finished placing the globe in the bag the hairs on his body stood on end. Grabbing the bag, he swam like a tiger shark for the entrance.

"Going somewhere, are we?"

Darius groaned loudly.

"I don't have time for this Muroka. Get out of my way," replied Darius, slowing down as he took in the number of Tartahounds flanking the chief Titan slave driver.

"I think you have all the time in the universe," said Muroka, as he patted the nearest Tartahound with adoration. "Have you met my latest pets? This is Bertha, she's the youngest, and this is Pinky and over there," he said, pointing to the largest Tartahound Darius had ever seen, "is Bull. They are very special pets, aren't you pretties. Daddies got a special treat for you after you take care of our little problem, that's right, cutie, a special treat," babbled Muroka as he continued to pat the two Tartahounds nearest him who were now slobbering green droll down all three of their faces. Worse, Darius could have sworn they were also purring, or maybe growling, he thought, thinking of a quick means of escape.

"Oh, don't even think of it. You see here, Bertha, has been enhanced. Where ever you go she will scent you. Only you. And the same goes for Pinky and Bull. You see after your last escape in which I once again had to explain myself to Hera, I realized then and there that I needed help. So, I approached Saad and yes, I can see recognition is dawning on you. You see he's developed this new vaccine that not only enhances an animal's natural instincts but if that vaccine is coated with another Titan's what did he call it...ah, yes, DNA, then those two elements combined well, let's just say they make for an interesting hunt. I have been tracking you the minute your body came into contact with the sea. And I have to say this has been the easiest hunting party I've ever undertaken," said Muroka, grinning, revealing to Darius that the Titan had only two teeth remaining in his rotten mouth.

"Are you done, Muroka. Let's get on with it. I'm leaving so you're going to have to stop me," said Darius, as he charged with all the force he could muster while holding onto the bag.

The entire time Muroka had been talking, Darius had issued orders to Rylan to get Kassandra to safety vowing to kill the teenager with his own hands if he dared to disobey obey.

As one of the large gapping jaws of Pinky, who was wearing a bright pink collar, came within inches of his right arm, Darius turned to maneuver his body up and to the left to also avoid Bull who was coming at him with Muroka hanging on to his leash. Bull, like his namesake, charged Darius. The result was Darius felt as if a dozen sea boulders had fallen onto him. Catching his breath, he forced his body to move barely avoiding Bertha's snapping three heads. Wishing for a weapon, even a jackknife, he felt a moment of relief when Rylan, who was obviously eavesdropping, popped a large double-edged Triton neatly into his hand.

"Thanks, kid," muttered Darius, charging into his nearest opponent. With years of Titan training, he set to work, hacking away at the three Tartahounds forcing them back, away from the entrance of the cave. Still, though it was hard work. As Bull gathered speed for another frontal attack, Darius managed to swing the Triton up slicing off two of Pinky's heads, just barely avoiding the deadly blood that spewed forth. That moment of hesitation cost him as one of Bertha's heads clamped down hard on his arm. Gritting his teeth against the pain he swung the Triton, managing to force the blade up into the hound's body praying he'd hit a vital organ that would force the hound to release its hold.

"No!" screamed Muroka, as he gathered speed with Bull who was still advancing on him.

Plunging the blade in further, Darius felt the moment when the Triton finally found its mark. In one heartbeat the Tartahound released its grip on his arm and then black ooze poured forth from its body. Darius forced his powerful tail to propel him out of harms way as the deadly toxins from the dead Tartahound caught fire.

Eyeing the now free entrance, he didn't hesitate. Hot, blinding pain poured into ever cell in his body, but still he swam forward, away from Bull and Muroka. It seemed the lost of Bertha had a profound impact on the Titan slave trader who was vowing to make him pay for what he did. Secretly though, Darius knew he was already paying for it. The bite from Bertha had been lethal. The deadly toxins in the Tartahound's salvia were slowly killing him.

"Darius, what can I do?"

Darius forced himself to keep moving while paying attention to Rylan.

"Get Kassandra to safety. I told you. Go!" commanded Darius, angrier than a mad shark at Rylan for disobeying him.

A powerful spasm wracked through his entire body and he forced his teeth together from stopping the scream that was wrenching itself free from his body. Then he collapsed as the poisonous venom made its way to his Titan heart. Failure never felt so deadly, he thought, shutting down his system before it was too late.

# Chapter Twenty-Three

Kassandra didn't think her eyes could get any bigger. First the strange eel-like dog with three heads which resembled something straight out of a Harry Pottery movie. Then after managing to wrestle free from Rylan who seemed intent on moving her away from all the action, she watched Darius emerge from the cave's entrance looking like death-washed over. Her heart had lurched madly and she had to bite the insides of her cheek to stop screaming – not that it would do any good since no one would be able to hear her through the diving mask.

Luckily, when she had forced Rylan to go to him the teenager didn't hesitate. Now, however what was she to do.

"What's wrong with him?" she asked, talking into the diving mask's microphone hoping Rylan would know what was causing Darius' body to slowly turn green.

"I'm not sure. I think he got bitten by one of those...those...I have no idea what those things are called, but let's just call it one Hell of an evil-looking devil dog. I think he must have gotten bitten or something. I honestly don't know what to do. Do you?"

Slowly, Kassandra shook her head. Cradling Darius' body in her arms as the three of them nestled together behind a large outcrop of dead coral, she wished more than anything she could feel his skin with her own hand, instead of the wet suit gloves she was forced to wear.

Then a piercing scream rent the air and the next thing she knew two more of those devil dogs emerged from the cave along with the scariest Titan she could ever dream of.

"Okay, that's not good. We've got to get out of here and fast. That's Muroka and he's got it in big time for our friend, Darius. I vote we run," said Rylan.

"That's who?"

"Muroka. Trust me, not someone you need to know about. Look, I promised Darius I wouldn't do any popping about as he calls it, so we've got to move and move now," said Rylan, attempting to grab Kassandra by the arm.

Pulling Darius' body closer to hers, Kassandra briskly pushed Rylan away. "I'm not leaving without out him." Thinking fast for more options, it was then she noticed one of those brown looking sink holes. The same type that propelled them here.

"Let's make a run for that sink hole. Any luck that thing and those creatures won't be able to follow," she said, hoping that would be true.

"I'll take the bag," said Rylan. "It's what he was looking for."

Kassandra numbly nodded. "I'll carry him." Can you carry that? I'll manage him," she said, with more confidence than she felt. She watched as Rylan's eyebrow's lifted in disbelief. "Trust me I can carry him. Plus, the water will give him more buoyancy."

"Sure, whatever you say. I'll take the light-weight bag and you take the Titan. That sounds fair to me," said Rylan, turning to pick-up the bag like he was about to juggle it.

"Don't even think about it," muttered Kassandra, trying to hook Darius' body over her shoulder.

"How about I help you with that?"

"Okay, if you just push his upper torso over my shoulders I'm sure I can make it."

"I'm sure you will," said Rylan.

There was an odd twinkle in Rylan's eyes that gave her pause. And how does he know Darius is a Titan. I think it's time Rylan and I had a chat. As soon as we get back to the boat, she thought.

Another guttural scream caused her to strain her neck for a look.

"I think our time is up. We've got to go. And now!" said Rylan, all but running for the sink hole, seeming to move with perfect ease in his wet suit and tank.

Praying she was right; Kassandra forced her flippers to move. Realizing that they wouldn't give her enough momentum she reached down to unbuckle them. With her feet clad in diving slippers she pushed herself forward attempting to run while holding onto Darius for all he was worth.

A terrible stench filled her nose causing her to gag.

"Don't look behind you...just run," shouted Rylan, as his body disappeared into the sink hole.

Kassandra had to force herself to not give into the temptation and look over her shoulder. The rotten sulfur smell almost caused her to throw-up. Why isn't Darius heavy? she wondered, as her feet finally found the brown spot on the ocean floor. As that thought penetrated her brain her feet and body sank into the sink hole and she prayed with all her might that the beasts wouldn't follow.

After another horrifying rollercoaster ride, she landed with a loud thud rolling onto the ocean floor which caused her to finally let go of Darius. She watched as his body almost dead-like lay on the ocean floor. Warm water washed over her as she dared herself to look around. Just where are we? she wondered, taking in the rich colors of the ocean floor. The sea was awash with red coral, bright blue iridescent flowers lined what could only be described as a pathway. Angle fish and seahorses darted all around her.

"Welcome, Kassandra, to the Red Sea. We will take care of the Prince," said the most sensuous, sultry, female voice Kassandra had ever heard before. Darting her eyes around she tried to find the source of the voice. It was then she noticed that the angel fish had departed and she couldn't help gasp as the loveliest creature she could ever imagine glided towards her.

"I am Queen Ny'ula from the Royal House of the First Hu'lan. We will take care of the prince. You must leave."

There was a tense note in her voice that gave Kassandra pause as she forced her eyes to blink. The Siren who glided towards her had skin as dark as ebony dusted with a light gold shimmer. Her hair was as red as the surrounding coral and it flowed around her in brilliance. Her tail, yes, tail, thought Kassandra, fighting the urge to stroke it, looked like a mirage of a thousand different colors. But, by far the most striking feature was her eyes. They were honey-yellow and the soft, reassurance look made Kassandra feel safe.

"You must leave, immediately. No human can enter the Red Sea. You don't have much time," whispered the Queen, her voice a light brush inside Kassandra's head.

"Where is Rylan? And, I'm not leaving without him. What's wrong with him," mouthed Kassandra, hoping the Queen understood her.

"I can read your thoughts. But, again, you don't have much time. Trust me; we will take care of him. You must leave." With that statement, Kassandra watched as the Queen made a motion with her tail. Immediately an entourage of six Siren's surrounded Darius.

"Hey, lady," thought Kassandra, "I'm not going anywhere without him." Jealously washed over her as the Sirens, who all had to be spectacular in their own right, touched Darius' body in awe. Not that I don't have a breath of awe for him, but heck, I didn't go through everything in the last few days just to give him up to...up to...oh my, he's a Titan, these are Sirens, and I'm a human, he can't ever be with me. What was I thinking? I was thinking he was my prince in shining armor, a fantasy come to life, but that's not real.

She watched as the Sirens picked up Darius and carried him away. While the rational part of her brain reasoned they might be able to help him that other, more feminine part of her brain, screamed at them to back off. As if they could hear her, and maybe they could, she thought, all six Sirens stopped.

"Where he goes, I go. And just where is Rylan? Kassandra asked again, hoping for a straight answer.

In a language Kassandra couldn't understand, but which sounded a lot like Persian, she watched as the Queen made a motion with her hand ushering the Sirens away.

"You must come with us, quickly," said the Queen, speaking in English inside her head. Just how can she do that? Kassandra felt bone weary. Her head was beginning to hurt and her legs felt like they were led. What's happening to me? she thought, trying to summon the energy to argue, move, do anything. Then it dawned on her. She was still bound to Darius and that blasted book, which luckily was still sealed tight inside the plastic bag which also now housed the globe. All of which were being carried by Rylan when last Kassandra had seen him.

As if on cue, the teenager appeared, except he wasn't wearing a diving mask or suit anymore. In fact, he wore ripped jeans, a white t-shirt and he was barefoot. Okay, I've got the bins. I've gone loony from the lack of oxygen. Tapping the dial to make sure it was working she took a deep breath of oxygen. Okay, that felt like oxygen, but it can't be real. Oh my, I've gone completely delusional, that's it. I must be locked up somewhere and I know, there injecting me with drugs. Yeah, that's it.

It was then Kassandra noticed Rylan motioning to the Queen to come to his side. Judging by the Queen's body language she wasn't one bit happy. She watched as Rylan shrugged and then walked away, now armed with two beautiful Sirens on either side of him.

"You are bound to the Prince. This is not good. You must come with me," said that sultry voice inside her head, again.

Kassandra nodded her ascent. She was still mystified as to Rylan's transformation that she knew she was incapable of forming a coherent sentence.

Then four arms grasped her as two Sirens flanked her sides helping her move through the water.

"You only have one of your human hours left. We must move quickly. There is only one remedy that might help the Prince.

A groan from Darius caused a chill to reverberate through her body.

"He doesn't have much time. There is little hope for him, but we will try to heal him. The toxins in his body are slowly killing him. You will not be able to help him and he would want you to leave. For your own safety you should leave him to his kind. You are human and without skill in this matter. As much as Rylan told me of you, I know you care deeply for him, but the Prince is a Titan and you are a mere human. Again, I must warn you that your safety remains precarious. That breathing apparatus you are wearing has about little oxygen let. After which time you will expire and I will not be able to intervene. It would go against our sea law. Do you understand me?"

There was no mistaking the Queen's harsh tone and as much as Kassandra knew she was being told the stark truth; she didn't care. There was no way she was about to leave Darius.

"I will stay out of your way, please...please just make him better and then I'll leave," said Kassandra, over and over again in her head.

The slight royal nod from the Queen was her cue. Forcing her body to move and follow the group which for her benefit had slowed down, she prayed Darius would be alright.

As the ensemble entered a large cave, Kassandra noticed it wasn't dark. There was a neon yellow glow illuminating the entire dwelling. As they moved to the back of the very large cave, she marveled at the array of different looking crystals that lined the ceiling of the cave. The Sirens stopped and gently laid Darius down in a scallop-shaped bed. His body, as a Titan, fit perfectly into it as his tail curled the outer ridges of the bed.

"What are you doing?" she asked, as the Queen placed three crystals, one bright blue, one flaming orange and the last blood red inside Darius' mouth.

The Queen then sat down, "Now we wait," she said, motioning to the Sirens to leave.

Kassandra looked around for a place to sit. What she really wanted to do was crawl into the strange bed and lie her body down next to Darius' body. And, then cuddle him but that was impossible in a diving suit equipped with a large oxygen tank on her back.

Hot searing pain caused her to gasp at the exact moment that Darius' body started to convulse. Her eyes felt as if they were on fire and if the diving mask hadn't been in her way she would have yanked it off to scratch at her eyes.

"What's happening to me?" she asked in her head, as another flash of pain traveled from her toes to her mid-section.

It was then she felt a pull on her arm. The Queen was trying to get her to sit, but that was impossible as she tried hard to control the pain slicing through her entire system. She fought the urge to rip the entire diving suit off her.

"Rylan, did you find it?" she heard the Queen ask inside her head and then just like that in popped the teenager, still clad in his casual attire.

"I did. I did. Darius won't believe it. He's going to be so pleased that I finally figured a way to get him unbound and then I know for sure he'll let me help him on this mission. Heck, I bet he'll make me an honoree Titan captain. Think of all the fun we'll get into," babbled Rylan, as he waved the ancient book around like it was a piece of loose leaf.

"You must finish it now. The human is running out of time."

"Oh, yeah, sorry about that Kassandra. Okay, on the count of one, and a two, and a three...or is that one, two, three, and then you do it?"

"Rylan, now!" commanded the Queen.

Kassandra could only watch through one eye, the other burned so intently she fought not to scream.

"Okay... 'into the mists of time you dwell, until love conquers this spell, but you are bound together forever if opened without thought, for your actions cannot atone for what was sown by the seeds of time, so you must choose to lose your heart's desire for in three blinks,' this is where you blink three times Kassandra," said Rylan, as he held open the ancient book, "the chain will be broken, your fate unsealed, unbound you will remain to claim your own destiny,' ta-dah! It's done."

A gush of cold current swept through the cave causing everyone to look at the entrance. In a whoosh, Kassandra felt as if a part of her were free. She felt light-headed and dizzy. And instantly she felt a calming relief. Gone was the pain. In its place was a feeling of euphoric that she had someone managed to live through it.

Kassandra ached to use her real voice. It was hard keeping her thoughts straight. And, before she could even begin to question what exactly Rylan really was, the kid proceeded to groan loudly.

"I just don't believe it. I've been called back by my Uncle. Have to go. Tell Darius I'll see him soon. It was nice to meet you, Kassandra. Bye."

Without another word, he was gone. One minute there and another gone. How? She wondered.

The touch of the Queen's satiny smooth hand on her arm broke into her thoughts, "Are you feeling any better?"

She wet her lips, "Yes. I think I am. What about him?" she asked, moving to be closer to Darius.

"We will know shortly if the crystals worked, but you must leave. Now," said the Queen, practically dragging Kassandra down the cave.

"Wait, what about Rylan. I take it he's not exactly your average teenager. What exactly is he?" asked Kassandra burning to discover his true identity.

"That question is best not answered. You need to leave," said the Queen, propelling Kassandra to the cave's entrance. "I promise we will take care of the Prince. You have less than fifteen minutes. You cannot surface here. You must go back to that sink hole you came in and then return to the surface."

"But, when we left there were these weird looking eel-dogs..."

"Tartahounds. I am sorry, but with any luck they should be long gone by now. It is your only chance. Don't worry about the Prince, if he survives we will take care of him, if not his body will once again belong to the sea," said the Queen.

A dozen questions were swimming around in Kassandra's head. She wished she had more time, but she could sense the unease in the Queen. At the entrance, she was surprised when the Queen warmly embraced her. She felt an odd sense of comfort, but that was short lived, as a groan from Darius rippled to the entrance.

"Is he really a Prince?" she asked, the answer to that terrifying her.

"Yes, my dear, I am afraid he is very much a Prince. Follow that path back the way you came and then don't hesitate. My thoughts will be of you. Now go."

Kassandra couldn't argue with that. She had her answer. An answer that caused her to question her own sanity again. While she trudged back down the path she prayed that Darius would be alright. Knowing she'd never see him again she fought the onslaught of tears. Now is not the time, Kas, get your ass in high gear. Worry about him once your safe, breathing that sweet oxygen...the essence of life, once again.

Eyeing the brown sink hole, she jumped on the spot. Instantly, her entire body was swallowed up again. This time she closed her eyes tight, hoping when she finally landed back in the cold Atlantic Ocean there wouldn't be any sight or worse, smell, of those Tartahounds. Then the origin of the word Tarta as in Tartarus, being from Hell, jumped into her mind. *Its times like this that being a librarian of antiquity sucks...I really didn't need to figure that one out!*

# Chapter Twenty-Four

D arius' tongue felt like it was three times its normal size. His eyelids felt like molten led and every cell in his body screamed in agony.

"My Prince it is good to see you again," said the seductive voice in his right ear which caused his Titan senses to jump.

Opening one eye he took in his surroundings. First thing first, he knew he was no longer in the Atlantic Ocean. The warmth of the water alone could attest to that fact but it was the smell of the sea which told him where he really was.

"Queen Ny'ula, why am I here?" The Queen leaned in closer to him. Her tongue darted out to gently lick the inside of his ear. "The human is gone. She was a very brave thing. But, Darius, what do you mean bringing Zeus' nephew to our realm. You know the rules. No gods, or semi-gods in our kingdom. I'm thinking of reporting you," she said, giving his ear another playful flick of her tongue.

Abruptly sitting up he cut her off. "Look, Ny'ula, who brought me here?"

"I just told you that. That ridiculous woman. She carried you here and then Rylan muttered some words that broke that ludicrous spell and now she is gone. Come, let me see if you are one hundred per cent better," she purred the words as she attempted to sit on his lap.

Carried me here. What by...then clarity washed into him. I found the globe, got bitten by a Tartahound and Kassandra brought me here. The notion seemed so far fetch that he couldn't believe it. But, the reality of where he was slammed into him. And, as much as he'd like to think Rylan helped he knew the kid would never leave

Kassandra, too afraid to face his wrath if something were to happen to him. Then the other portion of what Ny'ula said jolted him. He was finally free of that blasted book and Kassandra. Why, however he wasn't entire pleased about that.

He pushed the Queen off his lap. "How long have I been out?" he asked, hoping it wouldn't be a repeat of the last time.

"Not long. Only about two crests," she said.

Two crests. That's only about twenty human minutes. Kassandra couldn't have gotten far, he thought, grabbing the nearby bag with the globe.

"She has left you Darius. Isn't that what you wanted?"

"Well, yes, of course, but you see..." he paused. "It's complicated. I have to go. Look, Ny'ula thank you for healing me. I'm not sure what you used. I thought Tartahound bites were fatal," he said, watching as she gracefully moved away.

"They usually are. Lucky for you I have recently discovered a cure."

"How recent?"

"You were my first specimen. So now, I know it works," she smiled smugly up at him.

The idea of being Queen Ny'ula's goldfish didn't sit well with him, but heck, it wasn't like he could complain. "I need to go. I promise to come back sometime soon," he said, gliding to the entrance, as he threw the bag carefully over his shoulder.

"By the way where is Rylan?" he asked, turning to watch as the Queen gathered her composure to follow him.

Looking up at him with her iridescent eyes she blinked at him, as if he were crazy for asking the obvious. "Gone. I banished him from this realm, of course. And, Darius," said the Queen.

"Yes," he answered.

"If you are not happy being unbound do something about it. You are after all a Prince of the North Sea and a renowned Titan warrior." She taunted him with a provocative smile before she turned and disappeared into the depths of the cave.

I am happy about being free at last. Right? He recalled how Kassandra had handled every situation in a way that made him look at her twice. She wasn't like ordinary women. And she certainly wasn't like any Siren he'd known. Yet, still why he wasn't enthusiastic, jumping up for down about being unbound, he wondered. Wait a second.

"Ny'ula, how many others know a human came to the Red Sea?" shouted Darius.

Without bothering to show herself, Ny'ula answered. "I told her to leave the minute she entered our waters. And I told her that she didn't have much time. I am sad to say that all of them...all of them know" her voice sounded weary.

"Does that mean..." he couldn't finish the sentence. You should have told me at once."

"Why? What is the life of one mere woman if she can put our entire existence at risk? You know the sea law, Darius. You knew the risks. What will be done, will be done," she replied, her voice echoing off the walls.

Without looking back Darius darted for the sink hole, praying he wasn't to late.

Fear, clenched tighter than an eel wrapping its slippery body around his heart. He prayed to all the gods that Kassandra had made it safely to the surface, but deep down he knew that would be impossible.

'They all know,' Queen Ny'ula had said. The "they" being all the rulers of the seven seas, which meant if she had made it to the sink hole with enough oxygen left in her tank than she would once again emerge in the Atlantic, which just so happened to be ruled by his father, King Sadok.

Things couldn't get much worse, he thought, swimming faster. The last Titan he wanted to face was his father. While they had managed to patch their frayed relationship, he knew allowing a human female into their realm would not go unpunished. From what Darius had learned his father had been looking forward to stepping down as ruler, but the plague had made that impossible. When his twin, Seth, started to show symptoms of the illness it had forced his father to hold off on retirement as he had joked to Seth. Not that Seth would be any more lenient, he thought.

However, being forced to deal with his father face-to-face over the life of a human woman was not going to put him back in his father's good books. If he'd ever been in it, he thought. Then his brother's joke that since he was born seconds after him that meant, he, Darius, was next in line for the throne. A shudder passed through his body at that thought.

Emerging head-first from the sink hole he honed his body for battle half expecting to see Muroka and his enhanced pets. Heck what else could top off this day. What he ended up seeing was his father along with two other Titans. Warrior Titans he had trained with for centuries. One was trying to remove the oxygen tank from Kassandra's back. He could see she was fighting them, not that it would do any good. He actually smiled when she managed to kick, Balarius in the most sensitive spot on a Titan's body. He reasoned Balarius had always been a sore looser so it didn't pain him to see the Titan double over for a good reason. Then Galagan, the younger warrior, grasped her arms tight behind her back while his father, King Sadok moved in.

Darius had to admit his father was a sight to behold not that she would think that in a minute as his father gently pried off her diving mask to remove the regulator from her mouth.

Why by Tethys isn't she thrashing around or screaming? And why aren't I rushing to her rescue? He watched spellbound as

Kassandra calmly reached out and touched his father's cheek. Okay, now I know I've seen it all. Then his father turned his way and eyed him.

"Finally, you have decided to come back to us, Darius. It took you long enough," said his father, in a reproachful tone causing him to cringe. Steel green eyes vivid with an intense emotion he couldn't read stared at him, waiting for an explanation.

Darius thought quickly. What could he say? Now, did not seem the best time to explain all that had happened to him in the past decade.

"Father, let her go," he said.

"Darius you of all Titans know our rules. Rules that were designed to keep our realm safe. I don't need to explain the consequences to you, of all Titans. But, why...why did you allow this woman to enter our realm. Surely, you did not think she would be allowed to return to her world."

What choice did I have? he wanted to say to his father. Instead he forced his mind to turn to the situation at hand. "What did you do to her?"

"She has been enthralled. It is a state of bliss which makes her quite unaware of what is happening. To her mind this is all a dream."

"Then you will let her go," he said, swimming closer, pushing the command into his voice.

His father's grin. His penetrating look said it all. "Don't try your tricks on me, son. I am still ruler of this realm."

There was no way he was going to say he was sorry. After all, it wasn't like he thought his subtle push against his father's will would do anything. Yearning to reach out and touch her he asked, "Is she breathing?"

His father moved away from Kassandra and turned to him. Darius didn't move. He wondered what his father was up to.

"It is good to see you again, son," he said, embracing Darius in the tradition Titan way.

The gesture shook Darius. His father had never been an emotional Titan, but he sensed a turbulent of feelings running wild through him. And, for the first time that he could remember he really looked at his father. Still one of the most powerful Titan's he knew, his father had aged. Fine lines etched his face and there was a streak of white in his long black hair.

"Ah, now I see what has happened to you. I think I'll have a talk with Zeus about that nephew of his. He's always been up to no good, but this goes beyond what is acceptable. Now, I must finish taking care of this sad business. Your mother..." his father's voice actually choked, "your mother...she is unwell."

Darius shook his head. It was uncanny how his father could discern everything that had happened to him by a simple embrace. Then, again, he long ago discovered there was nothing simple about his father, one of the longest rulers of the North Seas.

"Father, I didn't know, but Kassandra, she...let her go," said Darius, fighting the panic he felt when he looked at her. Her eyes were glazed, her pupils dilated. While her chest was moving it unnerved him this power his father held over her.

"Do not ask that of me. This is a responsibility that could be yours someday. Seth, he like your mother, is infected with this terrible, dreadful calamity that is destroying our race."

There was a harsh tone to his father's voice that caused Darius to back up.

"Surely, you don't think I could ever...that I would ever," his eyes quickly transfixed themselves on Kassandra. Her chestnut brown hair was streaming wild behind her while she floated directly in front of them. "I have no idea how to enthrall anyone. I'm not looking to take the throne. Seth and mother will get better. The Court of Cabiri said if I find all seven artifacts from each of the seven seas than there's a chance we can stop this plague."

"The Court of Cabiri actually said that to you... that doesn't seem possible," muttered his father.

"King Sadok, Tartahounds are in the vicinity. We must move and get you to safety," said Balarius, finally recovered from his painful contact with Kassandra's foot.

Darius was actually grateful for the interruption.

"Blast those things. Hades and I are do for a long talk about his pets. Yes, Balarius, it is time we left this place. It reeks of death," said his father, turning his back on Kassandra.

"What about her?" asked Darius, hoping he'd have the chance to take Kassandra to the surface.

Casually gliding away his father's voice sounding like a booming aftershock in his brain he clearly heard him say, "The choice is yours, son."

# Chapter Twenty-Five

*The choice is mine, what does that mean? What choice.*

"Darius is that you? Help me," garbled Kassandra, her eyes blinking wide as she kicked her feet in an attempt to propel her body to the surface.

For one millisecond he did nothing except watch. He knew exactly how she would be feeling about now. With his father's enthrallment obviously worn off, she was swallowing mouthfuls of salt water. Once the water filled her lungs her brain would start to get fuzzy and she would stop fighting, stop attempting to breech the water to the surface. The lure of drowning was just that, it wasn't painful. The power of the sea once it claimed a victim thankfully did it with a loving caress. Eventually the pressure of the water would cause her heart to stop and that would be it. Kassandra would be dead.

That thought sobered him into action. Without thought and relying on instinct he swam after her. Grasping her ankle, he yanked her into his embrace. She fought him as was expected. Pulling her in tighter so that she couldn't thrash around he did what his heart desired – he kissed her for all he was worth.

The brek'ah, the kiss of life, was not to be taken lightly. It was the one and only gift a Titan or Siren could give. Once given, a part of their essence was forever tied to that person. Once that person died so to them.

Darius deepened the kiss. Forcing her head back he breathed into her mouth willing a part of his essence to fill her, praying he was doing the right thing.

The words ingrained into his being since the beginning of time rolled around in his head. He wanted to shout them out to the sea, but he couldn't. He had to continue kissing her until she was able to kiss him back. Then and only then would he be sure she was safe.

Continuing to breath into her he felt the exact moment when awareness rushed through her. Her hands clasped his head and she returned his kiss, greedily. Knowing this was the time, he released her mouth and unclasped her arms from his head. The simplicity of the ancient words rolled off his tongue.

"You are mine for all of time. Neither sea, nor land will separate thee from me!" he roared the words into the water. He felt the power of the sea claim him filling him up with a renewed sense of energy.

Then Kassandra's scream of agony sliced through the waters causing him to grit his teeth.

SEARING PAIN RUSHED through every cell of Kassandra's body. She knew if she opened her eyes her body would be on fire, because that's exactly how she felt, as if she was being burned alive. Her skin blistered and she felt the uncanny desire to rip it off her in shreds. Anything to alleviate the hot, blinding pain consuming her body.

Thrashing around blindly she screamed again this time sounding more like a wounded animal than human, even to her own ears. Something was happening to her. Something so painful she knew she couldn't take much more before she passed out.

"Take a breath of sea water. Let the water heal you. It will be okay."

Darius' calm voice penetrated her consciousness, cushioning her pain for a millisecond. How could his voice sound so nonchalant while she was on fire? Then it dawned on her. She was drowning.

"You are not drowning. Trust me you will be okay."

Again, his voice, with that husky, rumbling candace that sang, 'I am male' rang inside her head and for the briefest of moments she felt as if his calm was soothing her burning pain.

Then a new eerily unfamiliar feeling crashed into her body. She felt as if her leg bones were melting. Her scalp itched and she could have sworn her hair was growing, but that was impossible, she told herself. A warm sensation washed through her and she blinked, finally feeling the worse of the searing pain ebb. She took a deep gulp of sea water. She had lived through whatever had happened to her body.

A gasp from Darius caused her to stare at him.

"I had no idea you would be so beautiful. I mean you were beautiful before, but now, like this, you are perfection," he said, gliding around her.

"What are you talking about?" she asked. The sound that came out of her mouth was like nothing she'd ever heard before. Just who was this person speaking? Her stomach was doing nervous flip flops and she didn't care one whit for Darius' perusal of her.

"Take a good look at your new self, Kassandra."

His voice was soft and seductive as he glided closer.

She lowered her head and looked down. Gasping, she stifled the terrifying scream rising inside of her. Gone were her legs and in their place was a long, graceful tail. She was a Siren.

*How did that happen?* She bit the insides of her cheeks, hoping the stimulus of pain would wake her up from this all-to-real nightmare. When she looked at her naked breasts that were now bobbing about in front of her, she couldn't help the small hysterical giggle.

Self consciously she ran a shaky hand over her new body. She realized then that somehow her diving suit had disintegrated as her fingers took in her new form. Large breasts gave way to a slim torso and then a gilded edge gave way to a sleek, velvety smooth tail. She could see her hair cascading around her body in long wavy streams. Hair that was now as long as she was.

This time there was no escaping the lunatic laugh bubbling within her. If she didn't laugh she'd probably end up screaming until Hell froze over.

The feel of Darius' warm hands on her waist pulling her in tight forced the laughter away.

"It's okay Kassandra. I'll explain it all to you," he said, his fingers skimming the raised edge of her tail that separated her mid-section. The sensation was sinfully erotic.

A look of pure possessive passion and something else flared to life in his eyes causing those nervous flip flops in her stomach to jump into over drive.

With his lips a whisper away from hers, he asked, "Are you okay now, sweetlips?" There was genuine concern in his voice.

Kassandra nodded, afraid to open her mouth again. That weird sound that had come forth before sounded not human and she hadn't liked it one bit.

"You can speak telepathically to me now, but you can also speak out loud. The rapture inherently converts your mind. I will be able to understand you no matter what you say. In your new form, which I have to say makes you the loveliest Siren in all of the seven seas, rely on your instincts. And, yes, darling, I can read your mind," he grinned such a masculine smile she blushed.

His sexy grin grew and a tingle cascaded up her spine directly to her enlarged breasts causing them immediately to peak and stand at attention.

Great, that's just great. Now, he can read my mind and all I'm thinking about is sex and I'm not even sure how to... how Sirens...okay, that's it. Darius stop it. I know you're listening so stop pretending you're not amused by this situation. I think it's time I got back. So, do whatever you have to do to make me human again, okay, she said, pushing his body away from hers attempting to put some breathing space between them.

"Kassandra, I..." he paused and she watched as he ran his hands through his long hair. Hair she yearned more than anything to run her fingers through. "I can't."

"Can't what?" she practically shouted inside her mind.

"I can't make you human again. Ever. I had to make you into a Siren or you would have died."

"Darius, this isn't funny. You're a Titan, surely you can make me human again."

She watched as he crossed his arms over his chest. The look reminded her of a wild, untamed warrior. The startling colors of his tattoo did nothing to diminish the fact he was a mythological god that was very much real. The idea should have terrified her. Instead it thrilled her. However, without a doubt she knew if he could turn from a human into a Titan than he could make her back into a human.

"You're looking at things from a human perspective," he said, obviously reading her mind.

"So," she replied, happy that at least her sarcasm was alive and well.

"You're not, anymore. And I never was," he replied, so matter-of-factly that it came out sounding smug.

"I've read everything there is about Titans and I know you have powers so don't kid yourself, Mister. Turn me back, now!" she said, wishing she had something to cover her breasts with.

The sight of them kept shocking her. She never had her friend, Melissa's, cup size and used to envy how she could fill out a sweater, but she guessed glancing again at her enlarged chest that these beauties were off the charts. Then she recalled a lecture by Melissa telling her in no uncertain terms there were more cups sizes than the simple A, B, C & D that lined the shelves in the department stores. What would that make her, now? A definite F, she thought.

A ripple in the water warned her that Darius was moving closer. She let him grab her arms, bringing her in closer to his chest. Heat flowed off him, causing all of her weird hormones to quicken.

"Kassandra, what you've read about us is nothing but the skimming of the truth. And, sweetlips, while my powers are profound, I can't change you back, ever." He paused, his hand moving up to cup her chin, forcing her to look at him. "In fact, the only way to make you a Siren was to give you the kiss of life, which, I'm afraid means you and me are once again bound together...only this time it's for a very long time."

"Kiss of life." Her brain screamed with the unsettling truth of his words. All of the old stories her father had told her, and all of the myths she had read over the years streamed through her consciousness.

"Darius what have you done?" she asked, tears filling up her eyes.

His cold stare caused her to shiver. "I did what had to be done. And, now we've got to go." His voice was back to its usual gruff, commanding tone as he propelled her unyielding body through the ocean waters.

It was then the putrid smell she was becoming to familiar with assaulted her nose and all of her other newfound senses. "Is that what I think it is?"

"Yes. Except it's even worse."

A swish from his powerful tale had them both darting through the ocean at top speed.

"You need to move your body, Kassandra,"

What, what is he talking about? Aren't I moving my body? Looking down she noticed he was right. She was attempting to swim with her arms not her entire body. Moving her lower half, she was surprised at her own agility as her stroke picked up. With Darius' hand still on her arm it didn't take her long to match his stride. Or is that called stroke, too?

A grin lit up Darius face. Her heart accelerated in response. He looked completely boyish, charming in fact and that wasn't good. Not good at all, because she wasn't sure about her current situation. "Ah, Darius, just how long were you talking about?"

"Hopefully at least a couple more centuries," he said, not once breaking his break neck pace.

"You mean, me and you...we're um...bound together for centuries," the words sounded weird even to her own ears.

"Oh, and that's not all," he said.

She had to blink a couple of times to stop staring at the undersea kingdom she was now in. The myriad of colors, sea animals and fish were truly breathtaking.

"You're my mate. For life." He darted a quick glance her way.

Oh, Darius, what have you done? thought Kassandra.

Kassandra knew that Darius thought he had done the correct thing by saving her. She wasn't so certain. The Darius she knew as a human valued honesty, and his family above all. Combine that with his strong sense of ethics and viola, here she was – a Siren, bound for ever until she drew her last breath to a man who didn't have any feelings for her.

He was a direct descent of a God, a mythological figure that shouldn't exist, and even though the librarian she was knew that most myths were based loosely on facts, that didn't make her feel better. She knew without a doubt he would for the rest of his life regret what he had done to save her. Then she realized she still thought of him as a man, when her heart knew he was much more. Could she live with herself, knowing she had doomed this Titan, this man, to a fate worse than death. She shook her head trying to sort out her jumbled thoughts. Without a doubt, she knew she couldn't.

Somehow, some way she had to find a way to make things right for him. He deserved that much.

Finding the courage to chart her own course, to undo the wrong that had befallen her living, breathing Titan, eased the ache deep within her heart and soul. She would do it. She'd find a way to set Darius free. If it killed her in the process, she'd at least take pride in the fact she had done the right thing.

# Chapter Twenty-Six

Once again things weren't going Darius' way. Muroka was still after him, only now he was armed with enhanced Tartahounds and by now both Saad and Rajheb were probably after them also. And to top it off his mate didn't want him. He could tell by the sad, weary tone in Kassandra's voice once she learned he'd changed her into a Siren that she wasn't pleased about it.

What could he tell her? I had two choices; let you die or live. The thought of all her beauty and her inner spark fading into eternity had been to much for him. I did what my Titan nature demanded, I claimed you. Only thing is, as his eyes tried hard to stay attuned to the surrounding waters and not stare at her new sexy form, he wanted more than to just claim her with the ancient words. He wanted what he now knew she couldn't give him. He wanted her love. He wanted the ancient mating ritual to claim her sexy Siren body. He wanted to fuse their two souls together for eternity. The emotion coiled deep an ugly within him. The realization of what he wanted had swamped him the minute he gave her the kiss of life. Now, he had no one to blame but himself. Once again he had messed things up for her because he gave into his Titan essence.

"Don't be so hard on yourself, brother. Give your mate time. She will adjust. You forget that it took Jamie time, too. Show her our world and for once in your life, woo her," said his twin's voice, still sounding weak to his own ears.

By the Gods, even his sick brother was giving him advice. Him, the so-called Prince of Sex, who'd been with more women and Sirens than he could recall, was getting a lecture from his twin who'd been celibate for over a decade before he met Jamie. "You forget, brother, that I am not so weak that I can't best you at your own game," said Seth's voice.

Darius knew his brother was really trying to reassure him that all would be well. Sadly, he didn't think that was so.

"What's the matter?" asked Kassandra, her hands reaching out to touch the fish as they darted between them.

"Seth. He thinks I should..." Darius paused, maybe he's right. Maybe I should try wooing her for a change. When? First, I've got to finish this quest and then I'll deal with Kassandra, he thought, setting his priorities straight.

"You're able to talk to your brother. Can you talk with anyone else?"

"Yes, I can talk with my immediate family but it's always been easier with Seth because we're twins. We're connected on a different level. He thinks that I should finish this mission so we can all get on with our lives." The lie slid sickly off his lips. He knew his tone was clipped, but if she wanted distance from him, he'd give her that.

Together they darted over a large coral reef teaming with a cluster of male sea horses.

"Oh, my god, they are so beautiful. I didn't know they stayed together in a group," stated Kassandra, stopping to admire the perky fish.

Sea horses? The woman, no Siren, his brain screamed, was awed by sea horses. He all but humpfed at that. "That's nothing. Wait until I show you the continental reefs, they have clusters of fish that humans have never discovered and then there's the ...." He paused, realizing she had stopped moving.

"Thank you," she said.

The simplicity of the words crushed him.

Realizing they still weren't safe until they reached the first outer barrier of his kingdom he pulled her along, "For what?"

"For trying," she replied, her voice strained and weary.

Pulling her closer to him, he replied, "Look, Kassandra, I didn't have a choice. Would you have rathered I let you drown? Is that what you wanted? To die. I did what had to be done. We're almost there."

"That doesn't make it right Darius and you know it. I never asked for this and you've gone ahead and bound us together when I swear you don't even like me," she said, stopping abruptly again with a downward swish of her tail.

Not like her. By all that was created from the dust of times. She's mad. How could she think that? I've had to fight against my nature not to claim her as a mere human, and now, he groaned...I'm doomed.

Pulling her to him he had to stifle another groan as the feel of her breasts came into intimate contact with his chest. More than anything he wanted to taste her, feel her and make her lush, Siren body scream in climax. He could give her pleasures the likes she'd never imagined. A vivid image of him claiming her caused his heart to speed up and his erection to jump to life. Blast it! he thought, wishing he could assert control over that piece of his enlarged anatomy.

"Darius, I thought you said it wasn't safe here," she said, pushing her arms in between them to break his hold.

"It isn't sweetlips and I've got news for you... you ain't safe from me, either," he all but growled the words as he once again grasped her arm and sped away.

SAAD WAS TIRED OF HAVING to deal with his half brother, Rajheb. They had never seen eye-to-eye before and things certainly hadn't improved over the centuries.

"Why don't you send the sharks after them?" His brother asked for the fifth time.

Saad stalked away from the cave's platform. Eyeing the three sharks that were kept in the large holding tank he had to fight the urge not to throw his brother into the waters to give him a taste of his own medicine.

"You are not listening, Rajheb. Father wants us to get the ancient book, not Darius. If we let these things out," he pointed down to the sharks with an exasperated sigh, "then no one is safe. Once Master Odeon finds a cure for the enhancement, which I'm sure he will with a bit more persuasion then we will have the upper hand."

"What are you talking about. I want Darius' head on a platter and I want that human female and no one is going to stop me. You can tell father to go to Hell," said Rajheb, shedding his clothes as he got ready to rapture.

"You are not going. Do you understand me?"

"Try to stop me Saad...if you can?" taunted Rajheb, diving headfirst into the open underwater compartment that was an outlet to the Atlantic.

Saad simply sighed. He yearned to stop Rajheb but new it would be futile.

"You should have stopped him," said a soft, melancholy voice causing shivers to travel down his spine.

Spinning around he tried to pinpoint the voice.

"Why don't you use your powers Saad?"

"Whose there? What do you want?" he asked, trying once again to find the source of the voice, which echoed off the walls of the cave.

Then the person behind the voice materialized and he felt the full force of her power.

The word was a mere whisper but he couldn't help it, "Mother?"

"Is that how you know me?"

Saad bowed low in reverence to the entity he'd been told over the centuries was his mother.

"Father said someday you would find me?" he said, his voice sounding strained to his own ears.

"Yes, he would know that." There was an audible sadness in her voice when she spoke of her mate, his father.

"Your father thinks to outwit me in this game, but I am sad to say it is not a game of chance. I will not deny you are of me essence."

A smile lit up her face, causing goose bumps to form all over his sensitive skin. "They call me the Sister of the Future. I was named by the Creator. I am Sesta."

Saad tried hard to blink but in her presence it was all but impossible. Her eyes were like looking into a pool of shimmering clear water that seemed to mirror the surroundings. Lithe and tall she stood in regal grace with hair as dark as ebony. Her body was unearthly pale. She was beautiful yet frightening all at once. The force of her power vibrated like a static aura all around her.

"I need you to help me, Saad. Will you do that?" Again, the voice echoed off the walls of the cave to resonate deep within his being. He had to fight the urge to not reach out and touch her.

As if she read his thoughts he felt the moment when her fingers caressed his cheek. His skin prickled in acute awareness of her ancestry, her power and her awe of him. Him, her one and only true son. The knowledge hit him hard.

"You are of my essence but I am sorry to say the Creator has taken my memory of you away from me. The time has not come for me to know...no do not think that, the Creator does know what is best for us. When the time is right, which is ironic for an entity such as myself to say, all will be revealed. But, Saad, I need you to help Darius, not fight against him. Rajheb seeks to destroy him as do many others, including your father, for varied reasons, but if they succeed then all will be lost for all of you. Trust your instincts when it comes to Darius. You can help him."

Saad was about to ask how and why he should do what she asked when he'd never known the loving embrace of his mother, but she vanished as quick as she had materialized. A feeling of loss and loneliness overwhelmed him. He had many questions he yearned to ask his mother but once again she was gone.

Turning around he looked at what he'd created over the last decade and for once he saw it through another's eyes. This is not something to be proud of, he thought, eyeing the menacing looking sharks, swimming in their crazed circle in the holding tank. He had enhanced them without thought to their own natural killing instinct.

Moving to a locked door at the back of the cave he opened it speaking in the tongue of the ancients.

"Master Odeon, I need your help if we are going to save Darius," he said, helping the old Titan to his unsteady, wobbly human feet.

...

An hour later and they were making progress. A buzz in his head was the only warning before he was blinded by the yellow haze of power.

"She was here. I felt her," said a sing-song voice.

In his head he heard Master Odeon clearly tell him not to move, or say anything. The warning should have been enough for him, but it wasn't.

"Who is here?" he asked, his voice sounding loud to his own Titan ears.

"Ahh, we materialized in real time. I told you before not to do that, Bella," said the voice, coming from his immediate left.

Saad tried to turn his head but he couldn't. His body felt like lead. "What have you done?" he asked, thankful he could speak.

"I told you not to move or say anything, freshling," grumbled Master Odeon, clearly feeling the same as him.

"You could have told me why," snapped Saad, frustrated beyond measure.

"Is that Odeon...ooh he's changed so much, still handsome in his Titan way, but he's aged."

"Well, you would too, Ava if you were still a Titan," mumbled Master Odeon.

The haze dissipated as quickly as it came. Standing to Saad's immediate left was a creature very much like his mother, power and beauty resonated around her. He felt the pull of her deep within his cells.

"Saad, met Ava the Sister of the Past and Bella the Sister of Today. They are your mother's loving siblings," sarcasm laced Master Odeon's words.

"Saad....the son," said the creature named Ava, her face unearthly pale, as her long blond hair cascaded to her shoulders.

"We could use him," replied Bella, reaching out to touch him.

"I wouldn't be doing that girls," said Master Odeon. There was an odd twinkle in his eyes, Saad didn't like.

"Did that Titan...that pleblite...that creature just warn us to stay away from Saad, as if?" said Bella, haughtily

"We will take him. We can use him, as bait."

Bait? What did they want with him, thought Saad, eyeing the two women now hovering above the floor while they discussed him like he wasn't there.

He watched as they reached out simultaneously to touch his arms, which were still frozen. Panic welled tight within his chest. He had a sinking feeling he wasn't going to like where they took him.

However, the minute they touched him, they backed away. Fear had jumped to life in their eyes before they could mask it and they both had reacted like their fingers had been burned.

"He is...."

"Do not say it. I can't believe this. Why does this always happen to us?" whined Ava, her celestial face contorting in anger.

"Did you know, Bella?"

"No...but let's review the past and find out how this could have happened?"

Then the two of them were gone as quick as they materialized. Relief pooled into Saad's limbs. He sank onto the cold concrete floor. With the help of Master Odeon, he gathered his strength to stand, hating he'd let fear of the unknown mark him.

"What just happened?" he asked, not quite believing the two powerful beings were gone.

"History just happened," replied Odeon, walking away to check on the latest batch of vaccines they'd been working on to reverse the heightened affects of what he'd done to the sharks.

Saad rubbed his weary eyes. Something wasn't right. First he gets a visit from his mother, and now her sisters. Things weren't making sense and why would he be bait. His mother wouldn't come after him.

"Don't be so sure about that," replied Master Odeon, reminding Saad he'd forgotten to form a shield to protect his thoughts. Feeling more like a freshling than he had in a long time, he raised his shields.

"What just happened here?" he asked, walking over to where Odeon stood.

"This vaccine should do it," replied Odeon, as if he'd never asked the obvious. "Did you never wonder, Saad, why you were different?"

Ancient Titan eyes stared at him. The intensity of the knowledge glimpsed in those eyes, momentarily startled Saad. He blinked. Sure, he had wondered. Who wouldn't? It wasn't as if the mystery around his birth was a secret. But, what did that have to do with who he was?

"It might be time for you to ask your father some really personal questions about just how you came to be," replied Odeon, turning his back to Saad.

Saad watched as the old Titan picked up a vaccine and then as calm as a could be walked over to the holding tank and without flinching jabbed the needle deep into the first shark that scented him.

"Now we wait," said Master Odeon.

Saad had a sinking feeling that Odeon's words weren't referring to the shark. He didn't like that one bit, he thought, rehashing what had just happened him today for the umpteenth time.

# Chapter Twenty-Seven

Kassandra admitted being a Siren was cool. That childish thought did nothing to diminish the magic of Darius' undersea kingdom. After swimming away from the deadly Tartahounds he had taken her into the deeper realms of his kingdom. She had felt a tingle deep within her soul as they breached the outer barrier, and she had listened spellbound to Darius as he told her how the barrier worked to keep humans out of their world. She had also noted his fear, however brief the emotion was, when she had pressed about the use of technology and its impact into his world. He had assured her the Titan warrior guards...the same guards she had shyly passed in awe, were constantly vigilant for any attempts from human technology to breach the barriers.

That should have brought her comfort. It didn't. "You mean to tell me that not once in the past century humans have ventured into your kingdom."

"No, what I'm telling you is those that have either were claimed by the sea or they were killed. It's that simple," he replied.

There had been a wealth of information in that one simple statement. "Was that what happened to me? Was someone trying to kill me because I...I saved you and took you to that other undersea kingdom?

"Yes," he replied, matter-of-factly.

"Who?"

"My father."

That stopped Kassandra cold. Darius father was the one who had tried to kill her.

"You mean to say that your father tried to kill me and yet you saved me. Why?"

"Leave it," he grumbled.

"Ahh, we're back to the beginning. You saved me because of your honor," countered Kassandra, as she glided over to a large red flower that resembled a tulip. "What do you call these?" she asked, wanting to change the conversation back to a more neutral one.

His shout, "Don't touch that!" froze her.

"Humans call it a red-gilled nudibranch, while we call it the eye-flower, and this one is breeding," he said, gliding closer.

She eyed him. Never tiring of seeing him in his natural Titan form. His hand reached out to rest on the small of her back and it did more to warm her than she thought possible. It took a lot of willpower to force herself to pay attention to his words.

"When this plant breeds it can release prickles that dig deep under the flesh and cause the person to hallucinate for days. And trust me you don't want to hallucinate the life of this plant."

She giggled. "You mean you actually hallucinate what the plant's life?"

"That's it. The prickles are memories from the plant of it's growth, change and anything that happened around its surroundings and take my word on this, it is not fun."

"Darius is that you?"

The shrill voice caused Kassandra to shiver.

"Who is that?" she asked, barely able to discern the fast approaching shape zooming their way.

"Brace yourself, that's my baby sister, Mercka," he replied, pulling her in tight for a hug.

It seemed Darius couldn't keep his hands off her. At every opportunity he either reached out to stroke her backside, arm or heaven forbid her very sensitive tail. She would never have taken him for the touchy-feely type, but had to admit it felt damned good.

"It is you. I knew it had to be you. I told Mother you would come back and not to worry, but did she once listen to me. Father was just by to check on her and he told me you had returned. Darius it is so good to see you and I know you've got a good reason for being away for so long," babbled Mercka, embracing her brother in an unusual manner.

First she kissed him over both eyelids and then in the middle of his forehead. Vaguely, she heard Darius' voice inside her head telling her this was the formal greeting between Titans and Sirens.

As if she'd just noticed her, the vivacious Siren turned to smile sweetly at her. Kassandra noted she had the loveliest hue of orange hair she had ever seen.

"Oh... sorry about that. You are? No let me guess. Give me your hand," said Mercka.

"That's not necessary, Mercka. This is..."

"No, it's alright," interrupted Kassandra, holding out her hand. She caught the guarded look from Darius and wondered what could be so wrong about letting his sister touch her.

Mercka didn't hesitate. She practically pounced at her outstretched hand. The contact of her warm hand on Kassandra's caused a shiver to pass through her.

"You were human. And a Seeker. That's great. Darius you've finally found your Sokhan," said Mercka, pulling her in for the formal embrace.

Out of the corner of her eye she watched as Darius moved further away from her. His eyes had narrowed to slits. She could tell by his no-nonsense stance and the tick in his jaw something was now troubling him. Before she could even begin to ask questions, Mercka once again took the led.

"So, Kassandra Delong, welcome to our family. This is just great. First, Seth finds Jamie, and you are going to looove her. She's a Sensitive Siren and of course of royal blood, not that you need that, and now Darius' has found you – a Seeker. You know the only other Seeker I have ever met was..." here she paused finally taking a breath.

"Darius what's her name? She's the Queen of the Red Sea who came here last year for the Reign of Titles. Now, that was a great party. It was when Jamie was crowned as Queen of the South Seas, anyway, what was her name? I'm sure it will come to me in time," babbled Mercka, gaily swinging her arms back and forth in the water.

"It was Queen Ny'ula," replied Darius, his voice sounding so cold and menacing to Kassandra that a prickle of unease crept through her body.

"Mercka, I need you to leave us for a few minutes," he said, his arms crossed over his chest, his body tense and controlled.

Still darting between them Mercka stopped. Mimicking her brother, she turned towards him, "Look, Darius don't get upset with her. She probably doesn't even know her own talents. It's not like she could have told you before. Right?"

Then Mercka's eyes stared at her. "Okay, that is my cue to leave. It was nice to meet you Kassandra. Don't be to hard on her, Darius," she said, darting away as fast as she had appeared.

Kassandra licked her lips. She felt uncannily nervous. Darius' stare was making her anxious. She actually backed up when he glided forward.

His hands grasped the upper side of her arms. "Let me go."

"Why didn't you tell me?"

His voice was a soft, controlled hush, which did more to make her feel threatened then if he had of yelled at her. She knew he was fighting for control.

"Tell you what?" she asked, knowing exactly what he was talking about. After all it wasn't like she hadn't been warned. Even Saad when he had found out about her special talent had warned her that it would be in her best interest to tell Darius as soon as possible.

She hadn't realized they were moving until her sensitive tail hit a wall. Somehow in her frenzied state of trying to sort out what she should tell him he had propelled them into an undersea cave. His hands left her arms as they moved to claim her sleek bottom pulling her in tight to his chest.

"Oh, I don't know, Kassandra, that you can find lost things," he said, his voice a husky whisper as he nuzzled her neck, all the while his thumbs padded her silky bottom. It was an incredibly erotic feeling. His thumbs continued to span her bottom, in a slow tortuous circle. She bit the insides of her mouth to stop herself from squirming more into his hands.

What is going on? She could tell he was mad. Deep down, boiling angry at her. But his actions, the slow, seductive feel of his tongue traveling down her throat were doing strange things to her mind and body. She was craving something. Something she couldn't describe, something that seemed just out of reach. Something she feared would only get her in more trouble.

"I want you to know something, Kassandra. You are mine and I intend to claim you," he said, reaching out to tweak both nipples. Pain and pleasure clashed like a thunderous wave deep inside of her.

"Look, Darius, I know you're angry with me," she tried to push him away, but all it ended up doing was freeing his mouth from her neck so he could claim a breast. The sensation was like being speared with a hot iron poker. She felt as if she were melting. His tongue rolled around her pebbled nipple causing her to silently scream in pleasure. She could feel his hands holding her bottom seeking something and then she felt it. He found her opening. Without any preamble he bodily placed a finger deep into her wet opening.

Then her body acted on its own. Her tail wrapped around him, drawing him in tighter to her. Her breasts swelled even more and she thrummed with a deep craving that shook her normal, shy resolve. It was a real physical ache. Her breathing was becoming labored. She shook her head hoping for clarity.

"Darius, we can't," she croaked out the words, not even sure what they couldn't really do. After all, she didn't even know how Sirens did it.

He spun her around so fast her hair swirled into her face.

"Face the wall."

There was nothing gentle in his voice. The commanding tone of it terrified yet secretly thrilled her at the same time.

"Spread your arms."

When she hesitated he briskly positioned her arms into place with her palms flat up against the wall of the cave. Her backside was to him and when she attempted to look over her shoulder he turned her head back to the wall.

Kassandra tried again for reason. "Darius, whatever you're doing, stop it. I can explain," she said, trying not to give into the wriggle her lower half wanted to.

Even though he was being his overbearing, commanding self she didn't feel afraid. She felt strangely exhilarated, which scared her even more than his actions. She realized she should be fighting him more, but that wasn't what her body really wanted. And, it would appear her brain had long ago shut-down. She silently hoped it would reboot soon, otherwise she might end up regretting what she was doing or about to do.

The hot feel of his breathe on her neck caused her to moan and then all rational thoughts fled.

"Oh, sweetlips, I am positive you can explain it, and I will explain all of this but sometimes actions speak louder than words."

His words were a soft, light caress as he nibbled on her earlobe. Who knew earlobes could be so sensitive? thought Kassandra, wondering momentarily what other delights she'd discover about her body if she let Darius have his way with her.

Then both of his hands slid down her bare back. She felt the tips of his fingers scale down her backbone, touching and teasing as he went. Then the tips of his fingers glided over the hard ridge separating her waist from her tail. She felt him move, his heat leaving her backside left her feeling beret. Then the moist feel of his tongue licked her hard ridge and she couldn't stifle the groan. She was so incredible sensitive in that spot she couldn't stop her body from wriggling. She felt her tail bucking on its own as if it was anticipating something. Then his tongue moved lower. His two hands pushed on her bottom forcing her painfully aroused breasts up against the cool, rough wall of the cave. She felt sinfully wanton. The rough feel of the wall on her nipples only served to heighten her pleasure.

Momentarily she wondered what he was going to do but then she felt it. The feel of his tongue deep inside of her wet opening overwhelmed her senses. She keened out a note that sounded foreign yet alluring all at once. Then she was mewing, groaning and grinding her body for more.

Swiftly he moved up and the hot, hard feel of his body flanking hers scared her.

"Darius, you've got to stop," she groaned, realizing how ridiculous that even sounded to her own ears.

His hand moved to her front to play with her already pebbled nipple, while his other large palm cupped her breasts. Her body was being bombarded with so many new sensations she felt overloaded. When she was sure she couldn't take anymore of it, she felt him release her breast. Then his throbbing erection rubbed up against her sensitive tail.

She yearned to look. To see all of him and hold him in her hand, but sensed he was barely able to hold on to his control.

The realization of what they were about to do slammed into her. She didn't want it this way. She couldn't let it happen.

Pushing her arms against the cave's wall she managed to spin herself around. She panted from the effort and from the sexual stimulation her body was acutely feeling. She titled her head up to look at him. There was a heated look in his eyes that scorched her soul. And, then it was gone. He blinked and she watched as the awareness of what they had almost done washed over him. Before she could say anything, he darted from the cave. Her body almost sung for him to come back to finish what he started, but she knew better. It was for the best he left, but like her friend Melissa would have said, "How come the best things in life sometimes hurt so damn much."

# Chapter Twenty-Eight

Darius didn't stop until he was far enough from Kassandra that he could no longer smell her scent. Even though if he was honest with himself, her scent was now fully engrained in his being. She had tasted as sweet as the morning dew as it gathered on the lily pads he drunk in delight during his travels in Ireland. It was a heady mix of innocence and wantonness. He shook his head, angry at himself for what he had almost done. The ancient words that would have bind not just her soul to his but her body and heart had rolled around in his brain until the beast within him had tried to force him to chant them, to give into the urge to claim all of her. But he hadn't. Even in his frenzied, state of achingly wanting to brand every inch of her tantalizing body with his, he didn't dare utter them.

By Tethys he was glad she had pushed him away. Never in his existence had he ever taken a woman or a Siren in anger. He was the Prince of Sex, who lived to pleasure his lover senseless. He had prided himself on his controlled love making. It would seem that finesse and all he'd been learned over the centuries mattered little when he was around Kassandra.

*Why by the Gods didn't she tell me?* he muttered to himself, hardly paying attention to his wanderings, until the soft ripple of water alerted him he was no longer alone.

"Why did you leave her alone?" asked Mercka, darting past him at lightening speed.

Darius realized he had wandered into the Titan stadium, which was uncannily empty. "Leave it," he replied, noticing almost immediately that all of the warrior Triton's still looked as if they could use a good cleaning. *What was going on?* It frightened him that his *mardom* could have fallen so quickly into a state of decay.

"You need to go back and get her. You turned her into a Siren. You can't just leave her," said Mercka, not bothering to ignore him.

"She'll manage fine on her own. She always does."

A hard yank on his arm stopped him. He could have easily shrugged off his little sister, but he didn't.

"Darius, what's wrong with you? You seem different. The Darius I knew would never just leave his Sokhan. I'm not sure what's really happened to you, but I don't like it. And, let's be honest," here his sister paused. "I'm sure you haven't told her everything, either. Go back, apologize and talk to her. Father wants to see both of you," said Mercka, finally leaving him in peace.

Go back and apologize...if Tartarus froze over he might, but not until then.

Part of him wanted to shout he was different. Ever since the sea dragon had healed him he felt different. The knowledge that he was no longer a Titan in his prime, and that his eyesight would never be the same were the facts of life he'd have to live with. He'd be damned if he was about to share that morsel of information with anyone yet, let alone his baby sister.

"Fine," he mumbled more to himself than to acknowledge that his playful, baby sister's words had their desired affect on him. Swiftly turning about, he made his way back to Kassandra, not liking the conversation they needed to have. If only she knew just how close she'd come to being fully tied to him, she'd kill him. That idea immediately caused a part of his anatomy that remembered every feel of her silky skin to buck to attention with a mind of its own. By Zeus! He hated she had fueled his fantasies when as a woman, but now, as a Siren, he knew being celibacy was going leave him hard an on edge.

He spied her the moment he crested the last outcrop. She was sitting regally on a large boulder and talking to a young Titan warrior as if it was a normal, everyday occurrence. Relying more on scent he recognized the Titan warrior as none other than Galagan, who had been with his father when they had tried to kill her.

A red haze of jealousy slammed into him. Did she have no idea how alluring she was? Her wild untamed chestnut brown hair streamed sensually around her body, and even though she kept her arms firmly crossed over her breasts, he knew, without relying on his poor eyesight she was looking up at the warrior with those chocolate brown eyes of hers that were a deadly mixture of sex and innocence. He didn't like her talking with the Titan, at all. The realization of that hit him hard. She was his, whether she knew it or not. Every cell in his body knew it and that blasted young Titan was about to find out.

"Like what you see." The words were a low growl meant for Galagan's ears only. He could have used his telepathy to push the young warrior away but he played by the books.

Darius watched the young warrior bow his head in acknowledgement of his status. "Prince, it is not as it appears," said Galagan.

He crossed his arms over his chest as he moved closer. "It appears to me that you are talking to Kassandra...is there something else I should know."

"No...no...that is to say, yes, I was simply talking with her."

Darius took great pride in watching the formidable Titan trip over himself.

A motion behind him told him that Kassandra was now standing. "Stop it Darius. Galagan was simply looking for us and he came to personally apologize to me for what he was forced to do. Thank you, Galagan," said Kassandra, reaching out to touch the warrior's arm. In doing so she could no longer completely cover her chest. That meant she was now bare to Galagan's gaze.

"If you so much as bat an eye movement lower than her nose I will break you in half," said Darius, pushing his telepathic thoughts loud and clear into the young warrior's mind. So much for going by the books, he thought, hating the intense range of emotions Kassandra made him feel.

Immediately Galagan turned his back. "It's...it's...I've got to go. Have to relieve the outer guards. See you around, Prince," said Galagan, swiftly existing.

"Well, that was very princely of you, Prince," said Kassandra, mockingly. "So, you are a real, Prince, right?"

He nodded. Already he felt bad for his brutish behavior towards Galagan. Not that he had any intention of doing anything about it. "We need to find you something to cover up with," he snapped, fearful he'd smash the next Titan he saw to smithereens simply because he eyed Kassandra's chest. While Siren's didn't normally wear anything, the Titan he was, didn't think he could stand it if she didn't. That was an oxymoron if he ever heard one. The Titan he was shouldn't care, but maybe the man he had been forced to be, did. Whatever, he didn't like the possessive feeling and he certainly didn't want to go off half cocked wanting to smash any Titan who simply dared a glance at the lovely Siren by his side.

"That would be great. Then we can talk," she said, sweetly, flanking his side. He breathed a sigh of relief that the idea of covering up didn't phase her. Then he realized she was still thinking like a human, but for once, it didn't matter.

They didn't have far to go before Mercka showed up again. "Here this will make you feel more comfortable," said the perky Siren, as she dangled a bright red swimming bra in her hand. "I think I judged the size correctly, but if it doesn't fit, let me know. Darius, father is waiting." Then as quick as she came she vanished.

Darius grumbled as he helped fasten the small hook of the swimming bra in the back for her. He wondered where his little sister had found the material and why by Tethys couldn't she have used another color, say a dull grey. No, instead Kassandra was now sporting a bright red swimming bra that left enough to the imagination to cause him instantly to harden. He had hoped having her covered would make him feel less like tossing her to the ocean floor and having his way with her – it would appear that was not the case.

"I'm sorry, Darius, I should have told you sooner."

It took him a moment to realize they were already having the conversation he was hoping to avoid. "Yes, you should have. How long have you known you were a Seeker?"

She shrugged her dainty shoulders, the movement causing her hair to spill around to the front. He watched amused as she pushed it out of her face.

"Since I was a child. Actually, it was my brother, Geoff, who discovered it. Whenever we used to play hide and seek I could always find him. Then he started to hide objects around the house. At first I couldn't find them but if I touched him and saw the objects through his eyes I could find them. Sometimes I can find things simply by thinking about them. I know it's weird and for me it's very unnerving. Geoff used to tease me and say I could find anything I put my heart too," she admitted, twisting her long hair into a knot to keep it in place.

Her admission broke through his hurt that she didn't trust him and his anger. "You sound like you were close to your brother," he said, gliding away.

Her soft answer stilled him." Yes, but he was wrong."

He looked at her. Her eyes had filled with tears. "What's wrong?" he asked, moving closer, hoping she wouldn't start to cry. He'd never been able to deal with crying females of any sort.

He watched her regally compose herself and gave her credit for that accomplishment. "It's nothing," she replied, darting away.

As much as he'd like to pursue it, he couldn't. His father wasn't a Titan you kept waiting. "Father wants to see us." He grasped her hand. He was surprised she didn't shake it off. Instead she gently squeezed his hand, causing him to smile.

"Thank you," she said, a sad smile lighting up her face.

"For what?"

Wide, brown eyes assessed him. "For coming back and for not asking me more than I can give you at the moment," she replied, her honesty cutting him as deep as any Triton.

Again, he felt like a heel. "Sorry about that. It won't happen again."

"No, it won't," she replied, evenly, looking him squarely in the eyes. "So, prepare me. What type of Father is yours like? All I know is he was the one who tried to kill me, which I have to say makes me on edge already. If he's anything like my father, Mr. Commander, Mr. In-Control, then I'm sure we'll get along famously – not!"

He noted how she shielded her hurt and anger through her casual sarcastic comment, as if it didn't mean anything, when he knew it did. That bit of information he'd store for another time to ponder.

Bringing her body closer to his, he said, "Kassandra, your father is a pup compared to mine. Picture a King used to having his way, his orders followed and who believes in the sea law more than his own family. Picture a man who wouldn't bat an eye at following those rules even if it meant destroying his own son. That's my father," grumbled Darius, moving past her.

She glided past him and turned her head to look at him. "Is that what happened to you?" she asked, scratchily.

"It's a long, complicated story but let's just say that if my mother hadn't interfered than I wouldn't be here," replied Darius, a grin lifting the corners of his mouth.

"Somehow that doesn't comfort me. So, let me guess, big commanding men...I mean, Titans, run in your family. Great, that's just great," she mumbled, more to herself than to him.

He knew she was analyzing her options, which weren't many. He watched as she huffed out a long breathe and then bravely said. "Okay, let's get this over with."

This was the Kassandra he liked. She had mustered her courage to face the unknown and he was proud of her... more than proud of her, he admired her. Together they glided through the waters to his father's Palace. He wished he could bottle her confidence for a bit of it himself.

# Chapter Twenty-Nine

"You did the right thing. I am proud of you, son" said King Sadok, speaking the words to Darius but looking solely at her. Kassandra gulped. Before her was the Titan who had tried to kill her. He embodied everything she had read or scene in the ancient textbooks she had studied. He was handsome, muscular, regal and the ancient knowledge she saw in his green eyes terrified her. Immortality and wisdom oozed out of every pore of his being making her feel unconsciously small and mortal.

"He is not immortal, Kassandra? We just live longer than your average human lifespan," said Darius, interrupting her wayward thoughts.

"I must say I like what your mate thinks of me," replied King Sadok, his eyebrow lifting somewhat in a small salute.

Kassandra watched as Darius huffed. She noticed how the tick in his jaw had resumed. "Stop reading her thoughts," he commanded.

"You will need to teach her how to shield them. But, first come, have a seat," said the King, ushering them both forward.

Kassandra tried hard to stop looking around the palatial throne room. It was like nothing she had expected. A large round marble table held most of the King's works. The floor was black granite, as were the walls. They had entered the large dwelling which only had walls, no ceiling. There were two round windows on each side of the room which made it look bigger than it was. The centerpiece of the room was a large fountain, with massive Titans arching their Triton's in the middle. Water gurgled neatly up to sprinkle into the surrounding pool. She wondered absentmindedly how water could bubble up when they were fathoms of leagues underwater. Then again, if it was like her being able to breathe water like it was oxygen it made sense in a weird sort of messed up logical way, she thought.

"You are a true delight. It gives me great pleasure to welcome you, Kassandra Lily Delong, daughter of Ivan, direct descendent of Sangerious, River God of the Balta."

"What!" bellowed Darius, flying out of his chair.

Kassandra was stunned. Then she started to laugh. Really laugh. After all what else did they expect her to believe. When she was finally able to compose herself, she noted the patient look on King Sadok's face and the hard set of Darius'.

"That was funny. Really funny. Next you'll be saying I'm a princess," she said, smartly.

"Actually, you are," replied King Sadok, his clear emerald eyes bore into her.

"You could have told me," demanded Darius.

Kassandra watched the King cross his arms over his chest. "Why? What would it have mattered?"

"I could have let...you know what I mean," said Darius, darting his eyes from her to his father.

King Sadok shook his head.

Kassandra felt she was missing important parts of the conversation. "Look, King Sadok, really, in all honesty, my father's name is Ivan but we're not royalty of any kind. He's not a Titan or a god or anything like that."

"He was," said King Sadok, softly.

"I can't take this anymore. I'm going out for a while. When you've sorted all this out, let me know...after all it would appear that I am just your humble servant doing your bidding, Father. For now, I'm out of here."

Darius brushed past her like there was no tomorrow. Without as much as a goodbye, see you later, he was gone. And, she was left alone with his father, King Sadok, ruler of the North Seas, who was assessing her like she was a specimen. She didn't like it one bit. Then again she didn't like what he'd made Darius do to her.

"I didn't make him do it. The choice was always his," said the King, obviously reading her thoughts.

"What choice? You were going to let me drown. He did what he thought was the right thing to do." Kassandra gulped. She couldn't believe she was having this conversation with Darius' father and worse he was treating her like an equal.

"There you are wrong, Kassandra. He always had the choice. And, well he knew it. Darius knows more about our sea laws than he has let on. But, that is his tale to tell you. I did what was right. If the Fates wanted you to be who you are now, then I had to play my part, as did my son. I will admit to being surprised to discover you were a descendent of my good friend, Ivan, but even that would not have been enough for me to turn my back on our tradition. It has been what has kept all our kingdoms safe from prying humans," said the King, as he rose and moved towards the marble table.

"Do you recognize this?" he asked, holding a gold heart. The words, "For Military Merit," shined at her.

"Yes. It's given to our soldiers when they are injured in the line of duty or for their heroic deeds," she answered.

"I know. The only thing I know about this solider is his name. This is from your world war one era. His ship was blasted by one of those human weapons that shook our kingdom. There weren't many survivors but this man, this soldier, was alive when I discovered him. When I gave him the choice of life or death he chose death. Everyone has the choice, Kassandra. This man knew his. As did Darius. He wouldn't have given you the brek'ah unless he knew deep within his soul that you were his true mate."

"You're wrong. Darius' sense of integrity and his ties to his family are what made him save me," she said, fingering the purple cross. The knowledge that Darius' father had offered to save this soldier touched her in a strange way. "You really would have saved this man?"

"Yes, I would have commanded one of the Sirens to give him the brek'ah."

"See, that's just what I mean. You would have commanded someone else to do it, just as you commanded Darius too. The act was not yours to give." She couldn't believe she was standing up to the formidable King. She watched as he considered her words.

"You are so much like your father, it hurts," he said, sadly.

Wow, talk about changing the topic." My father really isn't royalty, you know."

"Actually, he is. Once you have settled in, I will send Jamie, Seth's wife to take you to the reflection pool and that will help you learn more about who you really are. For now, I must go check on my Sokhan, Helem. I will have Mercka escort you to Darius' dwelling." There was genuine concern in his eyes.

"Thank you," replied Kassandra. "What's a Sokhan?"

"It is the least I can do. There is no term in the human language but Helem would say she is my wife, but the word means much more than that. She is my Sokhan. She is the other half of my soul, as you are the other half of Darius' soul. We will talk more, later."

The King reached out and took the purple cross from her hand and gently, almost reverently, placed it back inside a cubby-hole in his marble table. Kassandra knew she was dismissed.

"I do hope your wife...I mean, your Sokhan, will be okay. Please let me know if I can do anything," she said, on her way out.

The King's words brushed her mind, leaving her all but gasping at the intensity of the power that skimmed the surface. "I am counting on you too," he said.

What did that mean? she wondered, passing four Titan guards on the way out. Not one paid her any attention. They were obviously in a hurry to talk with the King.

"Kassandra, I will show you Darius dwelling. It's not much to look at I'm afraid. When he left the kingdom a decade ago he had barely been here so it's quite sparse. Mother would say it needs a Siren's touch," said Mercka, materializing in front of a towering Titan warrior who didn't even blink when she swayed by him.

They twisted and turned throughout the kingdom. Kassandra noted that very few Titans and Sirens roamed the area and so far she hadn't spotted any that looked like children.

As if she read her thoughts, Mercka answered her. "All the freshlings, the young Titans and Sirens are either in their various schools, or working on the play they are soon going to perform. Most everyone else has been assigned to their task and many, I'm sad to say are sick and recovering in the crèche."

"Crèche?" asked Kassandra, trying to keep pace with Mercka.

"This is Darius' place," said Mercka, moving to glide in front of a non-descript dwelling. Like the rest she had seen it had walls but no ceilings. Unlike the rest it had a light-weight marble door.

Mercka motioned for her to move inside. "The crèche used to be the daycare and academic school for the Titans but it's now used as a make-shift hospital for our sick. Both my mother and brother and many of my friends are now there."

The emotion that poured from Mercka into Kassandra caused her to gasp. Then as quickly as it came the intense pulse vibrated away.

"Sorry about that. If I think about what's happening to our kingdom and my family and friends I tend to forget to shield my emotions. That won't happen again. I really am happy that you've joined our family. I'm not sure what's really happened to Darius but he needs you."

"The last person your brother needs is me. Trust me on that score. But, let me know if there's anything I can do to help in the crèche. I really didn't realize the sickness was so wide spread," said

Kassandra, cautiously entering Darius' dwelling. She felt like an intruder and wished he was the one showing her his place. Sadly, she realized, maybe this was better. It was hard for her to think rationally when he was around. All that naked, polished skin called to her.

"See, you're thinking of my brother. That's good," chimed Mercka, causing Kassandra to blush deep red. "Don't be embarrassed. You're his mate, that's to be expected."

Moving to the centre of the large living area, Kassandra said. "Thanks, I think."

"Okay, I've got to go. I promised I'd help Jamie in the crèche. Once she's finished she'll come to take you to the reflection pool. In the meantime, poke around. I know I would," joked Mercka, darting away.

The last thing Kassandra wanted to do was poke around, not that there was much to poke into. The place was beyond sparse. It was empty. The living area was large and there were a number of beautifully carved stones placed around it. A large ledge ran around the perimeter of the room. Making her way to the back she found what had to be Darius' bedroom. Heat pooled to her core. A large scallop shaped bed rested dead centre in the room. It called up a number of fantasy's that made her hastily exit it. The living room was safe so she'd sit there until he found her. In the meantime, she tried to recall every single thing she'd read about Titans and Sirens and the legends of the Gods. There was no way she was going to sit idly away the opportunity to free herself and Darius from what he'd done to them.

A few minutes later, a knock on the door interrupted her thoughts.

"It's me, Jamie. Darius' sister-in-law. May I come in?"

Kassandra opened the door to a beautiful Siren with black hair neatly arranged in a long braid that ran down the length of her back.

"Yes, please. I'm Kassandra. It's a pleasure to meet you,"

"I bet you're feeling completely overwhelmed. I know I did when it happened to me," replied Jamie.

Instantly Kassandra knew she and Jamie were going to get along famously. If anyone could understand how she felt about being a Siren it had to be Jamie who'd spent the first part of her life as a woman.

After all the niceties had passed, Kassandra asked what had been on her mind since Mercka mentioned the sickness. "What's wrong with Seth?"

That stopped Jamie cold. "Didn't Darius tell you? Of course, he didn't. These Titan like to keep everything bottled up inside them. Seth has been afflicted with the plague. We've been trying for over a decade to find a cure. If we don't I'm afraid..."

Kassandra realized Jamie couldn't continue.

"I didn't mean to pry," she said, swiping at her long hair that kept billowing into her face from the undersea currents.

"No, you have a right to know. I just had hoped Darius would have told you," she said, sadly.

"Is this the same thing that is affecting the King's wife?" asked Kassandra, wanting to switch the conversation away from Darius.

"Yes, it's affecting all the Royal Blood Titans and Sirens, some more so than others. That's why we sent Reece to find Darius. Now, I'm not sure we did the right thing."

Gliding forward, Jamie stopped, turning to face Kassandra she said, "Kassandra, it isn't easy learning who you really are. And, it can be especially hard to realize that all your human notions and ideas have to be discarded if you're ever going to be happy here."

"And are you?"

"Happy, you mean? Yes. I love Seth with every cell in my body and my son, Reece, is a true wonder," Kassandra noted Jamie's worried expression.

"He will be okay. He's a very handsome young man," replied Kassandra, trying to alleviate Jamie's motherly concerns. After all, they were valid. Not every mother could claim to let her ten-year-old son leave the safety of what he'd always known to venture to land only to somehow go through an exceedingly painful process and transform from a boy into a full-grown Titan.

"Thank you. I trust he will be, but until I see him with my own eyes, I won't be able to stop thinking about him. I thought, we thought..." Jamie, gulped, a tear trickling down unheeded.

Mustering her courage, Kassandra watched her regain her composure and continue. "We thought sending him from the North Seas would keep him safe from the plague and when Seth realized his first awakening could happen at any moment we realized our options were limited. When Darius finally made contact with us we viewed that as a sign and proceeded with our plans. Now, I'm wondering if we did the right thing."

"You did what you thought was best. I should tell you, Jamie, Darius never left his side. He sat with him through that long night and used his healing powers to help him. Even when they didn't seem to work, he wouldn't budge. If he could have he would have traded places in a heartbeat with your son. That's how much he loves him," said Kassandra, awed at her own speech.

"He stayed with him through the awakening?" Jamie asked, clearly confused.

Kassandra nodded.

"But, Seth said... it doesn't matter, thank you, once again. It seems, Darius is constantly surprising us with his actions," said Jamie, a small fleeting smile awakening her weary face.

"I hope you don't mind but I'd like to wait until tomorrow or maybe even another day to go to the reflection pool. I'm just not up to anymore surprises," she admitted, sheepishly.

"Actually, I think that's best. I should be going, anyway. I don't like to leave Seth to long and I'd like to share with him what you told me Darius did to help our son.... it will mean a lot to him," said Jamie, making her way to the door.

"Ahh, Jamie, before you go. I was wondering do you happen to know if there's a way for Darius to reverse what he did to me?"

She watched as Jamie slowly thought about it. "The only thing I can think of is the ritual blood oath but that might be different since he gave you the kiss of life. To be truthful I don't think it can be reversed."

"Thanks, anyway," she replied, as Jamie closed the door behind her.

Left alone with much to think about Kassandra realized she felt exhausted. Eyeing the strange bed, she approached in warily. Overcome with fatigue she swam into it only to discover it was surprisingly soft and comfortable. Her tail curled up along side her and in no time she was asleep. Since she did some of her best thinking during rem sleep she prayed that would be the case. Nothing would make her happier than to wake up knowing she'd found a way to break free from Darius for once and all. She hoped it turned out to be an easy, uncomplicated formula.

# Chapter Thirty

Sweet pored off him. He wielded the large double-edged Triton and plunged in again into the hot coals of the underground fissure. The heat almost blinding his sensitive infra-rayed eye sight. Once heated he then pounded the sharp edges into place, dipped it into a pile of crystallized oblats that would reinforce the specialized metal. Then he grabbed a large piece of dead reef he could use to carefully sand the sharp edge of the Triton until they gleamed. Two down only twenty more to go, he thought, eyeing the large rusted Triton pile.

"Thought I'd find you hear, son."

Darius didn't even bother to turn his head to acknowledge his father. He watched as his father looked at the Triton's.

"I hadn't realized they weren't being taken care of," he admitted.

"Well, you should have," snapped Darius, picking up a third Triton to repeat the task.

His father's large hand on his shoulder stopped him. "When you disappeared, we searched for you. It wasn't easy. I knew you weren't dead but your mother couldn't find a trace of you. We had no idea you were involved with Zeus' half-nephew. If we had...well, let's just say things would have been different. Now, that you're back I can rest assured you will make everything right," said King Sadok.

Darius plunged the rusted Triton into the heated fissure. "You shouldn't" he grumbled.

"Shouldn't what? Trust you. You are my son and you are our only hope. I sense the Fates hands at play so I wanted to warn you," declared his father, stepping away from him as he pulled out the glowing Triton.

"The Fates can go to Tartarus," he said, eyeing the glowing edge of the Triton.

"Yes, well some would say that is where they originated from."

Turning the Triton over, Darius plunged it back into the heat, his arm muscles bulging as heat from the fissure danced up his arm. "Why didn't you tell me?"

"I wasn't sure at first, but it wouldn't have mattered...she is your Sokhan," said his father, turning to leave. "Darius, if I were you I'd claim all of her. Love her like a Titan. It will make it easier for her to accept her fate."

"I don't need..." Darius didn't bother to continue; his father was gone as quick as he came. Claim her like a Titan. Love her. He ached to do just that, but could he...or should he? What if his father was right? If the Fates were playing them maybe all this was pre-ordained. That notion didn't sit well with him.

First thing first, he'd finish getting all of these Triton's back to their top shape. Then he'd seek out a member of his father's personal guard, a Titan he could trust, and have him oversee picking a bunch of new Titan warriors for training. The last thing his kingdom needed was to become completely defenseless.

A HIGH WARM TIDE WASHED through the kingdom. Every muscle in Darius' body ached. He could barely glide to his own dwelling. He had avoided Kassandra all day but that didn't mean one minute went by when he wasn't thinking of her. He figured giving her time alone was something she needed. The last thing he expected was to see her curvaceous Siren form cuddled up in his bed.

She looked incredibly sweet, innocent and vulnerable. Her long brown hair was draped around her front. Her hands were folded pray-like under her head. Then his eyes caught sight of the red swimming. His breath hitched, he hardened painfully and the beast that simmered below the surface broke free. She was his. This was his mate. This was the other half of his soul and he wanted all of her. Not just a piece, but all of her. And, by the Gods he was going to have her.

He had no notion of moving to the bed until his fingers touched her warm velvety smooth tail. Heat spiraled from her skin to the tips of his fingertips.

"Darius, sorry I fell asleep," muttered Kassandra, attempting to sit-up in his bed. That he couldn't allow. She looked tussled. Her raw beauty was a beacon to his soul.

Swimming over her he positioned his body by holding most of his weight on his arms so he could angle his lower half over hers. He didn't want to scare her but he wanted to assert his control and need for dominance.

"What are you doing?" she squeaked, squirming under him, which only excited him more. The feel of her breasts brushing his chest caused him to see stars.

"You are mine," he whispered the words into her ear and then swirled his tongue in her earlobe. She shivered and arched her back up. "And I intended to make all of you mine."

"What...."

He didn't bother letting her finish her sentence, instead his mouth devoured hers. He messed and molded her lips until she caved and parted them on her own accord. Then his tongue plunged into her wet mouth. She tasted like an orange, tangy and sharp but sweet to the core. And he planned to eat her all up.

With one arm he repositioned their bodies, so that he was lying next to her. He yanked the red swimming bra off her in one swift motion, causing her eyes to flare uncertainly. He liked that. He sensed she did too.

Her heartbeat matched his, and when he trailed a line of kisses and nips with his teeth from her mouth, her long pale neck to her chest he felt her indrawn breath. She wanted him as much as he did her. The knowledge tore through any lingering doubts he'd had about claiming all of her, and the beast within him growled low in triumph.

"I'm going to make you scream in pleasure. I'm going to brand you so that you'll always know you need my touch."

"Show me," she taunted, tilting her chin up at him. Her chocolate brown eyes were sex drenched with a heated need but her challenge spurred him on.

"With pleasure," he said, claiming a peaked nipple. He brought the dark colored nipple deep into his mouth and then flicked it with his tongue while his other hand tweaked and pinched the other. Her moans of pleasure were a delight he'd thought never to hear.

But it wasn't enough.

"Place your arms above your head and don't move them. Or else," he commanded, moving so he could lie directly on top of her. His weight settled into her curves. They were a perfect fit.

"Or else what?" she asked saucily doing as he instructed.

"Or else...I won't kiss you here," he dipped his head lower hating to leave her lush breasts but knowing her mid-section would be highly sensitive.

"Ohh," she breathed the word out, as his tongue licked the hard ridge. He placed both of his hands on the swell of her sleek bottom to hold her in place and then he moved lower.

"Or here," he said, lazily parting her opening so he could taste her sweet Siren nectar. Again, her innocence wrapped around him, reminding him that's he'd be her first and last, he thought, the notion causing his erection to jump proudly, in eager anticipation of what he planned to do.

"Darius I don't know..."

He moved his lips lower and licked her opened folds, loving how she stilled for him as her head lolled back in ecstasy. "This sweetlips is all you need to know," he said, plunging his tongue into her sweet opening, loving how she squirmed in pleasure as he licked her wanting to absorb all of her taste within his essence. Again, his senses were overwhelmed by her heady taste of innocence a deadly combination of fresh water dew, sun kissed apples and roses. She was tangy and he lapped at her like there was no tomorrow.

She arched into his mouth; her hands kept his head in place as pleasure crested inside her. Her folds swelled more as her opening grew wet and slick with a need for more.

He could barely control himself, as his muscles bunched as the Titan lush roared through his cells.

Without words he spun her around, so her sleek bottom was positioned where his mouth had been. She tensed but didn't say anything. He liked she trusted him in their love making and he fully intended to use that to his advantage.

Pushing her up on the scallop-shaped bed he told her again to keep her hands up. Then he smacked her bottom. She bucked under the assault but he knew she had liked it. He kissed the hurt away on one cheek and then smacked the other, ensuring enough heat to cause her to squirm with need. Again, he repeated his actions. A smack, kiss and nip.

"Darius I need," she wriggled lower, trying to position herself against his bulging erection.

"Yes, sweetlips, what is it that you need," he asked, his voice sounding breathless with passion to his own ears.

He took out his painful erection, letting the weight of it settle and then he rubbed it over her wet opening, loving how she inherently knew to position her bottom higher. She panted with need, and he took delight in the fact she was barely managing to keep her hands over her head, her need for him was that great.

"You didn't answer me," he said, smacking her exposed bottom and then nipping her hard. He suckled it away, loving the feel of her Siren skin.

"Darius, I can't breathe...I need...of for god sakes, just do it," she said, bucking wildly against him, trying to aim for his erection.

"This is going to hurt," he said, wishing he could edge the pain away from her.

"What..."

The large tip of him entered her tight sheath. She stilled. He moved his hands under her, forcing her bottom up higher, allowing him more room for penetration. He was large even by Titan standards, so he tried to go slowly, allowing her Siren muscles to get used to the fullness of him.

The last thing he expected was for her to push back with her hands forcing all of him to penetrate her barrier. She screamed. Her agony quickened his heart. Immediately he used his powers to ebb the sting of his penetration.

"I didn't realize it would hurt so much," she said, softly.

"Only the first time," he said, pulling out slowly. He felt her muscles relax and then grip him. He pushed back in, giving a little and then pulling out, going slow with his pace letting the rhythm be set by her need.

"More," she commanded, grasping his bottom tight to her.

"With pleasure," he said, pounding into her.

She was a Siren and when she pushed back against his hard trust her muscles clenched around his shaft. The friction of movement and her clenches almost caused him to spill his life-seed then and there, but he fought it, wanting her to climax with him.

Moving his hand to her front her found her jewel and pebbled it until she bucked like a wild shark, grinding her bottom into him as need for release screamed through her. But it wasn't enough. He wanted and needed to claim all of her.

Still pounding into her, the ancient words spilled forth. "I claim thee. You are mine for all of time. Neither sea nor land shall separate me from thee." The simplicity of the ancient binding words crashed into him and spiraled in awareness into her. They merged fully, two souls as one, two heartbeats as one, two minds as one. Intense pleasure the likes he'd never experienced before washed through him like a tsunami, claiming him and her in one final sweep. Wisps of ancient energy expanded around them and time seemed to stand still as pleasure after pleasure crested through them. He no longer knew where he began or ended. Her memories seeped into him. Glimpses of her life, her father, mother and her brother poured into his mind, as he experienced her pleasure. With one final thrust when he filled her to the hilt he let his life-seed spill, knowing he'd claim his mate for life. He clamped down hard on her neck, biting her as was his right to mark her as his.

He felt the moment when she relaxed into his hold, blissfully exhausted. He hated to withdrawal, but he knew within a moment she'd sense a change within her body. Moving to her side he gently stroked her back, loving the supple lines of her.

Then he felt her awareness that all was not right. She turned, her face pale and drawn.

"Darius I don't feel well. In fact, I think I'm going to be sick," she said, trying to sit up.

"Lie still. That feeling should pass in a minute," he said, forcing her back into the bed.

"No, really...this is so embarrassing. I really feel like I'm going to be sick," she said, and then she gasped. Pain caused her to double over. "Darius there's something wrong with me. There's something moving within me."

Panic was tightening up her muscles and it would be better if she relaxed. He flicked his eyes to her belly and sure enough a large tennis size bulge appeared to be moving around in her stomach.

He reached out and touched it, willed the pain away and watched it settle.

"What was that?" she demanded, her eyes clear and focus.

This was the part he was dreading. He probably should have told her ahead of time, but it was too late now. "That's our baby," he said, moving to kiss her.

"Like Hell it is," she countered, doubling over in pain as the bulge moved again.

Things were never easy when it came to Kassandra. "Really it is, Kassandra. I claimed all of you. You're my mate and when a Titan mates with his soulmate he gives her his life-seed and that's how we reproduce." He hated he'd made it sound technical when it was a gift of the gods.

"Then I suggest you figure out a way to get rid of it," she snapped, angrily swimming out of the bed as she snatched up the ripped swimming bra.

Get rid of it? He hoped she was kidding, because there was no way by Hades he'd get rid of a child of their union. Before he could say anything, she doubled over onto the floor and threw up.

Guilt washed over him. He'd done this to her and like before he'd taken her choice away. Even though the Titan he was said let the consequences be damned, the man he'd been knew no woman liked to have her choices dictated by a member of the opposite sex. To bad that's not how things worked in his undersea kingdom. Using his telepathy, he summoned Jamie and quickly explained what happened. A moment later his sister-in-law swam into the bedroom. With a practiced eye she took in the scene. He shifted in place, not liking her accusing glances.

"Take this Kassandra it will make the nausea go away," she said, forcing her to ingest two green crushed up oblats.

He watched her swallow and then she pasted a tired smile on her face.

"I feel as if I've ran a marathon. I'm wiped," she admitted, trying to position her tail underneath her. In a blink he scooped her back into his arms. Thankfully she didn't fight him. Gently he tucked her back into his bed. Before he'd backed away her eyelids had closed and she was sound asleep.

"You should have told her," said Jamie, gliding in place, letting him know she wasn't happy with what he'd done.

"It's none of your concern," he snapped, bristling with her interference.

"It will be. You still need to find the remaining artifacts and she doesn't even know who she really is and now you've complicated matters."

Darius crossed his arms over his chest. "This is not your concern, Jamie. I will find the artifacts, don't worry."

"You don't understand...I am worried...not just for you but for her. We have no idea how this plague works and for all I know you or she could fall prey to it at anytime. Now, she's pregnant with twins and that complicates things."

Darius yearned to push his brother's wife out his door, but then what she'd said penetrated his brain. "Twins?"

"Twins, Darius. I Titan and Siren and she has no idea what she's in store for," said Jamie, quietly exiting his place.

Darius sank on the ledge in his living room. His heart thundered in his ears. Twins. He was going to be the father to twins. A Titan and a Siren. The idea overwhelmed him. Then the other parts of what Jamie said stilled him. The notion that he'd somehow placed Jamie and his children at risk terrified him.

Taking a second to check that Kassandra was still asleep he gathered the few personal items he'd stored at his place and then left. Now more than ever he had to find the other six items before his Sokhan and his children succumbed to the sickness that was killing his mardom.

When he got back he vowed to explain everything to Kassandra, even though he knew he was taking the coward's way out as he forced his body into the sinkhole. He adjusted his sight to infra-rayed but all he could think about was his Sokhan's lush Siren's body, how the pleasure they had shared had boggled his mind and soul and the knowledge that he'd lay down his life in a heartbeat to ensure her happiness. Somehow, he highly doubted she'd see things his way.

# Chapter Thirty-One

Darius hadn't realized he had gone to his secluded cave until the heat of the underground fissures caused him to sweet. Complications. And lots of them were piling up around him. First thing first he still had to get the relics the Court of Cabiri wanted. Time was running out. His mardom was on the brink of disaster. From what he'd hastily seen things had deteriorated quickly in the ten years he'd been trapped in the ancient book.

"Reporting for my mission. All set and eager to go," said Rylan's voice.

Why wasn't Darius surprised. The semi-god teenager never failed to not listen to him. "Get out of here, Rylan. You know your not allowed in the undersea kingdoms. As it is I'm sure Queen Ny'ula reported you to Zeus."

"No, she didn't for your info."

"Um," said Darius. "Just how did you convince her not to." Darius was afraid he'd be left with sorting out another mess the young semi-god had inadvertently spewed up.

Grinning his most devilish smile, Rylan answered, "She likes me, and it's as simple as that. What can I say? I'm a lady's man."

"She's a Siren," snapped Darius.

Rylan shrugged his shoulders. "Whatever...so what do you want me to do now. You're finally free from that woman... so now it's just the two of us. Want me to pop us somewhere?" The kids' hopeful tone caused Darius to sigh.

"Things are a bit more complicated than before," said Darius, running his hands through his hair.

"Like how?"

"Like I'm bound to Kassandra for eternity or until she dies...that's like how. As for popping us somewhere. No. You've got to go before my father finds out you're in his kingdom and trust me no amount of sweet talk will save you."

Darius watched as the kid digested what he'd said. "You might be right. Your father can be quite cranky. Look, if you need me just say the word. I should probably report back to my Uncle, anyway," said Rylan.

Before he could say anything else, Darius grabbed the kid's arm. "Report back to your Uncle. Do tell me that isn't the case, because if it is...well, let's just say I'm in the mood to kill someone."

The kid shook his head. "It's not like that. I've got to report back in once in a while to make sure he doesn't get worried. He's kind of weird that way. Very cautious about his family. Not to worry...I won't breath a word of our mission to him. You can trust me, Darius," said Rylan.

*As about as far as I can throw you,* thought Darius, releasing the semi-god god.

"DARIUS, I ..."

That was all she managed to say, as the full force of his throbbing erection entered her. He didn't hesitate. Plunging deep inside of her, she felt a momentary tightness and then her maidenhood gave way. Instead of pain a pleasure so blinding soared from the tip of her tail to the roots of her hair. Giving in to the urge to wriggle, she felt him pound into her with a ferocious need that caused her to claw the wall.

"No more secrets, Kassandra. I claim you. You are my Sokhan. My mate. For now, and all of time. Do I make myself clear?" he said, his voice a husky whisper as he pounded faster and deeper, again and again, inside of her. He was driving her mad with a passion she couldn't describe. His words were an erotic promise that thrilled her to the core and she was sure his pounding rhythm would brand her for life.

A warm tingly sensation crawled through her. Coherent thought was almost gone, and she could barely discern his passionate plea.

"Answer me."

"Yes," she breathed the word and then it hit her. A wash of awareness. Her body blurred as it merged one with his as the full force of the mating ritual claimed them both. Attuned in a way like never before she felt his breathe, his heart beat and his sense of victory of finally being able to give into his Titan nature. The clash of his senses and the turbulent build up of pleasure caused her to reach even further for that elusive peak.

She felt his teeth bite her neck and realized he was marking her, claiming her in a way that was preordained from the beginning of time. She felt wisps of energy bind them together and it did more to arouse her than she thought possible. His fingers continued to tweak her nipples and then just when her body felt shattered he stretched even more inside of her. His size was huge but comfortable. He fit perfectly. Together they were a mold that merged to perfection. The hot feel of his seed seeped into her being and she screamed her way to bliss. Vaguely, as if she was no longer connected to her body she heard his roar of satisfaction, of the beast claiming him as he merged fully with her. She shuddered as climax after climax claimed her. Muscles she didn't know she possessed milked him even more and she felt pure feminine satisfaction when he shuddered his last release, panting heavily.

Still he did not release her. His grip on her was tight and calming at the same time. Nor, did she ever want to be released again, she thought. She sighed. Her body was truly loved and satisfied with a feeling of such delightful pleasure she didn't want anything to interrupt it.

"Ah, sweetlips, will you forgive me?" he whispered the words into her ear as he gently kissed the side of her neck.

Instantly she felt aroused again. How is that possible?

A small chuckle from him reminded her that nothing with Darius was ever going to be private, again. "You are now a Siren, and Sirens were made for passion."

Then an unfamiliar sensation surged through her as he finally withdrew. She felt his hands on her waist as he turned her. Finally face to face she looked up at him. Sea green eyes glazed with passion and something unfamiliar stared at her.

"Kassandra, I need to explain something to you …"

Before he could continue she doubled over in pain. What's happening to me? she screamed inside of her head as a warm sensation pitted itself deep inside of her stomach.

Darius' warm palm on her stomach caused the pain to immediately dissipate. "You will feel better in a few minutes. In the meantime, my healing powers will take away your discomfort," he said, eyeing her waist.

She looked down. What the Hell is that? She eyed the small round lump, about the size of a golf ball that was now poking out of her mid-section.

"In another minute it will settle and you will be fine," he said, sounding not so nearly convincing.

Brushing his hand away she felt the lump, which was rigidly hard. "What is it?" She gasped and blinked all at once as the lump disappeared.

"See, now you will be okay," he said, grinning.

"Darius, I'm not so sure. What was that?" Then she groaned. "I feel really sick," she said, ashamed of herself for feeling nauseous at a time like this.

She watched as he ran two hands through his long hair. It was a nervous gesture on his part, which made her even more anxious. "That will pass too."

"Okay, enough with the secret language. I have no idea what you are talking about. Back to basics. What was that lump in my stomach? Where did it go? And, why do I feel the urge to throw-up?" she said, with her hands on her waist.

He glided towards her. His lips claimed her in a passionate kiss. It wasn't the response she had been expecting. But, then again, nothing about Darius was normal.

"That lump is our child and that feeling in your stomach is what humans call morning sickness but I am sure it will go away," he said, his lips trailing a hot, passionate path from her throat to her already peaked nipple. Her body arched on its own to give him better access to her aching breasts. Then his words penetrated her desire drenched brain and she laughed.

"You can't be serious," she said, pushing him away.

The devilish grin on his face said it all. He was.

*There is no way I'm pregnant. That's not possible. Then again, there's no such thing as Titans or Sirens and oh my...I'm really going to be sick.* She turned her face away from Darius as she threw up all over the undersea cave's floor.

After the fifth throw up there was nothing left in Kassandra's stomach. She felt limp, weak and exhausted. Even her eyelids hurt. The feel of Darius' warm hand on her backside wasn't helping her mood at all.

"I don't know how this happened. Or what exactly happened to me. But you are going to fix it. First I don't want to be pregnant and secondly, I want my life back. You, mister, are going to have to just turn me back into a human again. Do I make myself clear?" she screamed the words at him as exhaustion gave way to anger.

Then she collapsed. Her body finally unable to cope with all that had happened to her within the last twenty-four hours.

# Chapter Thirty-Two

The edge of the dark brink of madness and hurt that had engulfed him was gone. Cradled loving in his arms was his mate, his Siren, Kassandra, and the mother of his child. Guilt wedged a deep slice through his honor. He should not have claimed her in anger. But angry he had been. She was a seeker...a being that could find lost things and boy did he have a list of things that were lost and needing to be found, he thought, fuming once again. The hurt part was that she knew what she was, that evidence had been written plainly all over her pretty perky face the minute his baby sister, Mercka, had stated the obvious. Just why the Hell hadn't me?

A small moan from Kassandra squelched his thoughts. What a fool he was. He had revealed his true essence to her and she hadn't been able to tell him that one little secret she had when she knew he was looking for seven relics. Looking for...as in not found, he thought, wanting more than anything to keep that hurt, angry feeling scratching his skin. Because if that was gone all he'd feel was shame.

He had never taken a woman or a siren in anger before. Part of him wished he could say he was ashamed of his actions, but regrettably it had been beyond his expectations. Pure bliss had surrounded his heart and soul with finally being able to claim his mate. A mate he knew he was going to have a hard time to handle, but control he must. No way could he allow his true feelings to show. Two can keep secrets, he thought to himself. He should have trusted his first instinct – never trust a female, whether they are human or Siren.

Now, however what had been a bad situation was only getting worse. Or as his father would point out to him, he'd made his bed and now had to lie in it. Deep down he knew he was at fault. He hadn't been exactly honest about himself to her, but still that did nothing to lessen the hurt. She had known he had to find the seven relics and it was a race against time. The stakes just got higher, he thought, realizing his act of foolishness now placed Kassandra's life in jeopardy. And, worse she was pregnant with his child.

He had claimed her. Even though the brek'ha bound them together for eternity, only the ancient mating ritual of claiming ones true Sokhan enabled his seed to fertilize her producing a child. It was another blessed gift bestowed from the Gods and he had to fight with himself to not give into the urge to stroke her soft, belly.

He admitted to himself he had been alarmed to see a lump, but once he realized what it was, it had warmed his heart. Then she had screamed at him to turn her back into a human and get out of his life.

For a Titan who was suppose to be sea guardian for his mardom and used to giving commands he was utterly speechless.

"Give her time. Explain to her what is happening. Bring her to us," said Seth inside his head, just as he had watched Kassandra's energy run its course.

Now, here he was about to bring his Siren home.

"What about the plague?" asked Darius, hating the sickness that was rotting his undersea kingdom.

"Jamie said that it's already too late for you two. If you are contaminated the symptoms will show themselves soon. You might as well bring her along to meet everyone. I'm about to get my daily dose of medicine and trust me brother, this is not something you ever want to have to digest," said his brother groaning more for show than anything else, thought Darius.

Kissing her gently awake, Darius let Kassandra's body slide down his. But he did not let her go. When she was finally awake, and he felt physically she was alright, he told her. "I want you to meet my family. I promise to explain all of this, Kassandra." Her beauty was surreal and his body thrummed with an immediate hot, hard need to thrust into her silky wetness simply by looking at her.

"Fine. Then you'll make me human again, right?" she said, her hands rubbing her stomach.

Stifling the urge to pull her in tight to him he said, "I explained that to you all before. You are a Siren. I can not make you human again, but...my mother might know of something to help you get rid of..." he couldn't bring himself to say it. The thought of killing his child settled like muddy water deep within him.

"Darius, I'm really tired. Can I meet your family another time," she muttered.

Scooping her up into his arms again he took his fill of her. Less than two hours ago she had been a human. Then she had to endure the first rapture, which is always the most painful, and then I had to claim her, what was I thinking? Not only does she have to cope with being a Siren, which I have to say she is taking pretty well, but now she's pregnant. Silently he vowed to keep his hands off her. To give her space. After all it was him giving into his Titan nature that caused all of this.

"What happened to her?" demanded his father, as he carried Kassandra into the crèche which used to be the Titan school and was now used as a makeshift hospital – something his race had never needed before.

Darius took a look around. There were five scallop-shaped beds and in them were three Sirens, one being his mother, Queen Helem of the North Seas, looking just as unconscious as Kassandra. The feel of Jamie's hand on his shoulder brought him instantly back to the moment.

"She will be okay, Darius. Seth explained what happened to her and you did the right thing," she said, ushering him to place her down in the empty bed by his mother.

Forcing his hands off her he sat on the edge of the bed, "Does she have the plague?"

"No, I don't believe so. She's simply exhausted. It's not every day that a woman gets to rapture into a Siren and then..." here Jamie smiled and paused.

"I know..." he muttered the words low not actually talking to anyone in particular.

"This has been ordained since the dust of times. You have found and claimed your Sokhan and we are proud of you. Give her time, she is a strong one. She will do you proud," said his father's loud voice as he joined Darius to watch as Jamie took over.

"You knew all along," accused Darius, pinching his nose in an attempt to sort out what to do next.

"I had my suspicions, but I am not always right, as your mother would kindly point out if she could," winked his father, causing Darius to blink. Did my father actually wink at me? Just what is going on here? He took a long, hard look at his father – the Titan feared and awed for his power. Slumped shoulders and for the first time he noticed the age lines around his father's eyes. When did this happen? When did my father become old? The vulnerable look on his father's face hit him hard. His father's love for his own Sokhan, Helem, his mother and Queen of the North Seas, ruled his father's heart more than he let on. Sighing, Darius, asked, "Is that why you gave me the choice?"

"I never once doubted you would do the right thing. Not all Titans find their Sokhan. Count yourself lucky, Darius," said his father.

Why is everything a test with him and why don't I feel lucky. He turned his back to his father and eyed Kassandra's limp form. When

Jamie motioned them away from the bed, together they watched as she held up a small, green oblat over Kassandra's forehead. Gently, she swiped the small, powerful crystal over his mate. An audible groan from Kassandra caused him to grit his teeth.

"It is okay, Darius. Trust Jamie, as we have come too. She will be fine. Why don't you go talk to your brother while Jamie tends to her," said his father, his eyes pointing out Seth in the far corner, who was propped up in the bed.

"Is he..."

"He seems to be getting better, as does your mother. Before Master Odeon left he and Jamie had been working on a vaccine and it does seem to be dulling some of the effects of this plague, but I am afraid it might only be a temporary reprieve. I must leave you and go to Helem," said his father, gliding away to sit on the edge of his mother's bed.

"Father about Master Odeon," said Darius, reaching out to stop his father.

"I already know. But, all is not lost. Master Odeon is a far more powerful Titan than you or I could ever imagine. Trust him as I have come to over the long centuries," said his father, gently patting Darius on the arm.

It was on the tip of Darius' tongue to ask exactly how long his father had know Master Odeon who was thought to be one of the oldest Titans in the North Sea, but the pat on his arm confused him. Did he just do that? When did the iron-fisted Titan who lived to follow the rules of the sea law become compassionate?

Darius shook his head to clear his thoughts. Taking a long look at Kassandra he forced himself to leave her. After all she was in good hands. Gliding over to Seth he grinned.

"You picked a very pretty one," said his brother, grinning that devilish grin he was all too familiar with.

Instant jealously raged through him. "Keep your eyes off her brother dear or you will quickly find yourself having a relapse," he said, turning his head to catch Jamie giving him a penetrating look.

"Ahh, I had to see for myself. It is true. Finally, my brother you have found your Sokhan. As for my eyes looking at your mate, you need not worry. I only have eyes for her," said Seth, winking at Jamie, who was gliding towards them.

Jamie sat next to Seth's lap. "Did you know before you turned her?" she asked.

"Know what?" asked Seth, reaching out to stroke his mate.

Running a tired hand through his long hair, Darius answered. "No."

"As I thought. She has a very unique gift, Darius, but she might not be able to help you in your quest," she said, tousling Seth's hair with her fingers.

"Will the two of you cut it out," said Darius sharply, already tired of seeing his brother and his wife flirting. Then Jamie's words sunk in. "What are you talking about? Does she have the plague? Is she going to die?" Saying the words was extremely hard for him. The idea of losing Kassandra ripped his heart and soul in half.

"No, I don't believe she has the plague, but she's pregnant you know," said Jamie, but there was an odd twinkle in her eyes and a strange gleam in his brother's that caused him to worry him.

"I know. I already said I was sorry about that. And brother, it's not as if you weren't in this position yourself," he said, longing to return to Kassandra.

"No, you are right, but..." here his brother paused, "tell him the rest, Jamie,"

"The rest," he said.

"Ahh, she's carrying twins," blurted out Jamie, as his brother grinned.

He almost fell off the bed. "What?" he bellowed. "Twins?" Quickly he wracked his brain. The only other twins born in the North Seas had been he and Seth. That had been over two hundred years ago. The idea of twins, of two babies, quickly filled him up with pride.

Wiping his hands with his face he fought like the devil to not grin. Twins, I am the father of twins, he thought, wanting to shout it out to the entire kingdom.

Then a loud groan from Seth pierced through his thoughts. He watched as his twin fought against the pain. Instantly he was there lending his brother his healing powers, but he knew within moments it was doing no good. "What's happening to him?"

Jamie motioned for him to move as she grabbed a large blue oblat. "Sometimes the medicine works and sometimes it doesn't," she said, forcing the crystal into Seth's mouth.

Another groan of pain filled the room. "Mother?"

"Maya, give her the extra strength oblat and then a shot of the solution," said Jamie, as she motioned a young Siren forward.

"You should leave Darius this is not a pretty sight," said Jamie, darting between Helem and Seth as fast as a tiger shark.

"No, I'm staying," he said, moving to his mother's bed. Her once beautiful skin was green and pale and parts of it looked to be molting. The tired, weary, stance of his father slumped over her tore into him.

"Darius, where am I?" said Kassandra, finally coming to and attempting to sit up.

"You should take her to your dwelling. She shouldn't be in here to see this. It will frighten her. And, Darius, she needs to rest," said Jamie briskly.

Gliding to Kassandra's bed he scooped her up without protest and quickly glided to his own dwelling. Once inside he gently laid her on his bed. A bed he hadn't slept in, in over two decades. A peripheral glance around told him nothing had been touched. His mother had probably insisted it stay the same until he returned.

"Darius, I think I'm going to be sick again," croaked Kassandra, attempting to slide her body over to the side of the large scallop-shaped bed.

"Jamie said to give her two of these daily. It will help with the sickness," said the Siren called Maya as she darted into Darius' dwelling.

Taking the small vials from her he said thank you. Then it dawned on him. He was going to be the father of twins, but were they Sirens or Titans.

Speaking telepathically to Jamie he demanded an answer.

"Both," she replied, with another stern warning to make Kassandra take it easy.

Both. A Siren and a Titan. The idea terrified him while warming his heart. Secretly he longed for the Siren to look exactly like her mother, his beautiful mate. The Siren who was currently forcing herself to not get sick all over his bed.

"Take this," he said, tilting her head back as he forced the green crushed crystals into her mouth.

He watched as she diligently chewed and then swallowed them. Then her eyes lit up.

"They tasted minty and thank God they seem to be working. Darius, I want to go home," she said, her eyes misting over.

More than ever he wanted to pull her into his embrace. Instead he sat beside her on the bed. "Kassandra, I tried to explain this to you. I really can't turn you into a human again. You are going to have to come to terms with being a Siren. Is it really that bad?"

He watched as she rubbed her stomach and had to force his hands to keep still.

"Am I really pregnant?" she asked, her eyes filled with awe.

"I am afraid so...and," he paused, not quite sure if he should tell her the rest.

"And?" she said, her hand reaching out to grab his.

"They're twins. Jamie said one is a Siren and the other is a Titan. You know the only other time twins were born was well over two hundred years ago."

He watched as she flopped back into the bed, her hand absentmindedly rubbing her stomach and then reaching down lower to stroke her tail. He squeezed his eyes shut . Torture. It was pure torture watching her hands on her own body. His body ached to repeat her actions. Deep down he felt the beast start to raise its ugly head and he fought against his Titan desire.

"Twins...I really can't believe this. Tell me this is all a dream and that when I wake-up everything will be alright," she said, her voice sounding weary to his own ears.

"Kassandra, what do you want me to say. If saying sorry will make things better than I will do it. But, I can't change or undo what has been done," he said, running his hands through his hair. "Once you meet Jamie, I am sure she will help you understand better."

"Jamie? Did I meet her?"

"No, unfortunately you were unconscious, but I promise to introduce you soon. Are you going to scream again at me?" he asked, reaching out to move her hair off her shoulders.

"No, I don't think so."

Then she started to laugh and cry all at once.

Not sure what to do he relied on his instincts. Grabbing her to his chest he cuddled her on his lap while rubbing her back. "Ahh, sweetlips, it will be okay. I promise," he said.

"Like you promised to get those relics," she said, turning her eyes up to face him.

The relics? In all the confusion of the past few hours he had almost forgotten his mission. He still had to get the relics if there was going to be a chance to save his mardom.

"I can help you, Darius," she said, stilling his thoughts.

There was no way he was going to let the mother of his children help him. No way at all. He didn't care if she just happened to be a Seeker. She was carrying his children and he would not put her or their life in jeopardy.

"Absolutely not!" he said, his tone commanding leaving no room for arguments of any sort. "You are staying here. And in no uncertain terms are you coming with me."

"So, the He-man has returned," she replied, tartly, her eyes all but narrowing to slits.

If being He-man meant keeping Kassandra safe than so be it, thought Darius, ignoring her protests.

# Chapter Thirty-Two

"**D**on't judge Darius to hard. He is a Titan who will give you all of his heart but he feels the need to prove his worth to me and that is another tale, for another time. Did he tell you where he was going?"

She gulped. "Going? What do you mean?"

"I thought as much. He left the North Seas in search of the relics the Court has asked him to find, but all is not right with the Court at the moment," sighed Sadok. "I find it hard to believe the Court would set Darius on this course. I am going to look into the matter myself. In the meantime, I thought you should know that it pained him greatly to leave you in your present condition, but I trust his judgment. As should you. I must leave now, but before I go, I know my Helem would tell you to go to the reflection pool to see for yourself your heritage. I will send Mercka to guide you."

With a flourish King Sadok left. A dozen questions burned bright in her mind but she realized with his hasty exist that he wasn't the question and answer type. He simply commanded, much like his son, Darius.

Thinking of Darius filled her with an intense longing. She closed her eyes. Haunting images of his warm hands gliding over her body caused her skin to tingle in anticipation. Ugh, she groaned, shaking her head to get a grip on herself. She wasn't happy with him at the moment and tried hard to keep that in mind even when her traitorous body all but screamed for his touch.

The silence in Darius' dwelling threatened to suffocate her. Shaking her head, she made the thousands of questions looping around in her brain halt. While the tale seemed implausible she knew Darius' father told the truth. As the fog started to burn off in her panic-stricken brain she mentally listed the oddities of her father.

The fact he could speak ancient Greek was something she had always wondered at. The fact he had been Commander of an elite special naval forces group trained in underwater reconnaissance, something she only found out about by accident when her brother joined the same naval group, hadn't seemed unusual at the time. The unusual tattoos on his body he attributed to his early yeas with the navy. His devotion to her mother was something she was used to now, but as a teenager her friends used to point out how unusual it was for two married people to always be touching hands, or kissing. But, somehow learning the man who tucked her into bed at night, the man who sat and cuddled her when thunder and lightening rained down from the heavens was capable of killing his own grandfather unnerved her. Did she really know her father? Did she even know herself?

Then another more pressing thought popped into her head. King Sadok didn't trust the Court that told Darius he needed to find seven relics that would stop the plague. Is Darius being sent on a wild goose chase? Kassandra chewed on her lower lip, ignoring the rumble from her tummy. She was ravenous. Taking two huge mouthfuls of seaweed salad did the trick for the moment of settling her stomach.

"Father said you wanted to go to the reflection pool. Can you tell me what he said? Can you?" asked Mercka, darting to and fro.

"Mercka, that's not polite. I can show Kassandra the way, plus I'd like the chance to talk with her. Would you mine checking in on your mother for me and giving her another small green oblat. Maya had to run an errand for the King," said Jamie, ushering Kassandra forward.

"Sure, no problem. Catch you later, Kassandra," replied Mercka, darting away.

Together, Jamie and Kassandra made their way around the reef. "Did the King tell you anything about the reflection pool?" asked Jamie, pointing out the nearby cave where the pool was located.

"No, not really. He simply said it would help me understand my heritage. Have you been there?"

"That's one way of looking at it," replied Kassandra, absentmindedly rubbing her stomach.

"I know his actions have surprised you and I'll admit even us, but Darius would never have claimed you as his soulmate unless he felt that. As much as the idea probably terrifies you...I know it did for me...well, let's just say that these Titan's have a way of making all logical thoughts flee, if you get my meaning," winked Jamie.

"I'd like to believe that was true, but the Darius that I know seems more bound to his honor of what's right and wrong, that to be truthful, Jamie, I think he gave me the kiss of life because he felt letting me drown was wrong and that he was the one who had put me in danger in the first place."

"I don't believe that for one minute. And, neither should you. Darius has genuine feelings for you, you'll just have to decide if he and this life are what you want to pursue. Here we are," said Jamie, as they crested a large outcrop of boulders and came face-to-face with a small cave entrance. "Would you like me to accompany you into the cave?"

"No, thank you for the offer, but I feel I must do this on my own. And, thank you Jamie, you are right. I've been so preoccupied with myself I really haven't taken the time to get to know the real Darius, as you say," said Kassandra, leaning in to give Jamie a hug.

"Good luck, Kassandra."

Kassandra took a deep breath. Did she really want to know her heritage? Shaking her head, she realized she did. She had never lacked courage, but for the first time in her life, she faltered. Looking back, there were things about her childhood that did seem strange to her. Maybe now, she would finally get some answers. She squared her shoulders and glided to the back of the cave.

There surrounded by four perfectly round boulders was a small pool of blood red water. Is that the reflection pool? The urge to place her hand in the water overwhelmed her. Giving in she was surprised to feel a small electrical pulse travel through her hand and into her body. Cozy heat settled into her bones, causing her eyelids to feel drowsy. Then the images spiraled into view, causing her heart to accelerate.

A Titan whose face she recognized immediately as her father sat holding an old woman in his arms. The woman had long silver-grey hair. Her figure was slim but had a wasted look about it that made you realize she had been sick with an illness for quite a while. Her father howled out his anguish, as he cradled his mother's dead body. She watched as he took the body into the sea and gently released it to be claimed by the ocean.

The scene shifted. She gasped. Her father was chained to an underground cave. Blood dripped onto the sea floor from fresh lash marks across his chest. Another Titan came into the cave. Taking what looked to be a Triton he branded her father. The smell of burning flesh filled her nostrils and even though her father was gritting his teeth he did not cry out. The taunting words of what the Titan said were loud even to her own ears.

"You are not one of us nor will you ever be. I disown you today and for eternity for your existence. Tomorrow at low tide your worthless hide will be cast to the sharks." And then the massive Titan glided away. Kassandra shivered. She knew the burn marks had hurt but it was the words she realized that had come from her great-grandfather that marked her father for the rest of his Titan days.

Again, the scene changed. This time she saw her father plunge a serrated blade into the back of his grandfather. The old Titan evilly grinned and then his skin turned a sickening shade of gray. Then her father's words rang out loud and clear from the pool. "I avenge you in the name of my mother, your daughter, princess Nana. Today you die!" The echoing words of her great-grandfather chilled her to the bone. "Today and for all the days to come you will live in misery."

Kassandra wanted to pull her hand out of the bloodied water. She felt her great-grandfather's words clench her heart with fear, while another part of her yearned to learn more. The sight of her father – the man she knew who ruled his life in precise order giving into passion to kill his own grandfather completely unnerved her. It bothered her more than what had happened to her. Funny that should be the case?

A third scene quickly filled the space around her. This time she saw her father, a humbled Titan kneeling before what had to be the famous Court that King Sadok had talked about. While she couldn't hear what was being said, she knew things hadn't gone well for her father. Then King Sadok step forward. He was handed the same serrated blade her father had used to kill his own grandfather. The King bowed his head and then the scene shifted again. Kassandra moved closer to the pool. King Sadok was talking with her father but again the words were hidden from her. Then the King plunged the blade into her father's heart. Kassandra couldn't help gasp. What is going on? She watched her father crumble to the sea floor; she saw the King place his own hand over her father's heart. A blast of white light encompassed the two. Then the King lifted her father up out of the sea and carried him to a beach. While she wanted to hear what Darius' father was saying, she was moved by his gentle touch. Without a doubt she knew this was how her father came to be human. King Sadok left out the fact that the Court had appointed him with the burden of killing her father.

Wrenching her arm free from the reflection pool she stumbled back into a boulder. Her body and mind felt drained. The hard, cold impact of granite on her back brought reality rushing back to her.

"I can't do this. I can't. I don't want to know. I don't." Tears ran unchecked down her cheeks.

A hum inside her head caused her to still.

"What is wrong, Kassandra?" Darius' voice was silky smooth but she had grown to recognize its varying shades. Concern was etched deep and light in his tone.

"I'm okay...I think," she replied, wiping away tears, wishing vehemently he was with her in person.

"Why are you sad?"

What could she tell him? Learning the truth about who exactly was her father was killing her. And, now knowing what his own father had been forced to do to his friend caused her to flinch. Instead she mustered her courage. "I'm fine. Really. Where are you?"

"Don't try to change the topic, sweetlips. What's wrong?"

Kassandra sat up on the boulder as she pulled her eyes away from the blood red water in the pool. "Darius, I don't want to talk about it...I'm," here she paused, "I'm just confused."

"You should be resting. Why aren't you resting?

Gone was the concern, and back was Mr. Commander.

"Leave me alone, Darius," she muttered.

"Never, sweetlips. Never."

"Kassandra?" asked Jamie, hesitantly gliding into view.

Kassandra all but growled in fury. How dare he? I can take care of myself. "Darius you shouldn't have sent Jamie after me. I can take care of myself." She had to take a deep breath to calm her nerves after that admission.

"It would appear you can't. Don't push me, Kassandra. I want Jamie to take you home."

Home? "It would appear that she can't take me home and I'll never get to go home, again," she replied, sarcastically.

She felt his sigh.

"Don't push me, Kassandra. I will make you leave with Jamie," he said, his voice gruff and unyielding.

Make me leave? What the Hell was he talking about? Was he able to make her do things she didn't want to? The idea repulsed her. But, she wouldn't put it past him.

Frustrated and angry at her situation she fought against the urge to scream. The last thing she wanted Jamie to witness was her waging a battle of wills with Darius. "Fine. I'll go home, but whose home? Yours. Not mine, Darius. And don't you ever forget it," she replied flippantly, her tone ice hard.

"You're upsetting the twins."

What the hell? So, now he can read my vitals? Even as she thought that her stomach almost heaved up the contents of her lunch.

"Go rest, Kassandra, please," he said, his voice almost pleading.

It was the please that did her in. "Fine," she replied, taking Jamie's outstretched hand.

With a slight pull she glided from the boulder. Together they made their way from the cave's cool interior to the outer warmer waters. Kassandra was thankful that Jamie was blessedly silent.

"I knew I should have stayed with you," said Jamie.

Before she could further blame herself, Kassandra cut her off. "How did he know I was sad?"

Jamie stopped. Her tail swaying in the gentle waters. "He is your Sokhan. Your soulmate. What you feel, he feels and vice versa. Think of it as two souls finally finding each other to become whole," replied Jamie, smiling. "Of course, if Darius tries to shield his feelings from you, you might not be able to feel his. That used to drive me nuts when Seth did that. Sorry, the last thing you need to hear about are my troubles. I've sent Maya ahead to fix you up something special. Um..." Kassandra watched as Jamie actually fidgeted. "Um, Seth and I were wondering if you made your decision."

"No. I still need to think about it," replied Kassandra, twisting her tail in the sand at the bottom of the ocean floor. She couldn't quite meet Jamie's eyes. Even after learning all about Jamie and her own confusions when Seth had claimed her, Kassandra didn't feel comfortable expressing her fears or desires. Part of her yearned to have Darius' children while the other part of her screamed that was absurd.

She had to force herself to pay attention to Jamie's words. "I know it's an extremely hard decision. Has anyone explained the process to you?"

With her eyes wide, she replied, "No."

A sigh from Jamie caused her to look up.

"I take it, it's nothing like what I thought," she said, wishing for once things could be simple for a change.

Yes, simplicity had its merits. She actually wished her days of working at the library and then having to rush home to get ready for her weekend shift with the reserves was all she had to worry about. She had another sinking feeling the talk Jamie wanted to have with her wasn't one she would relish.

# Chapter Thirty-Three

Would figure, thought Darius, forcing himself to not give into the shiver his body desperately wanted to. How could anyone live here? He was convinced if it got any colder his body might actually start to shut-down on its own forcing him into hibernation. That thought alone made him move faster. Forcing his body to move at breakneck speed he dove head-first for the fifth and last portal that would take him to the cursed Arctic waters of Thorgeir's seas.

He had succeeded in getting two of the ancient relics and after discovering the third was resting in Thorgeir's inner ice chamber he was determined to get it, then go home and work things out with Kassandra. The fact it happened to be a Trident crafted of Poseidon's own hands didn't faze him one bit. And, the fact that Thorgeir would never let him have it willingly disturbed him less. This was a mission he had no intention of failing. After the entire outcome didn't bear to think about, he mused, vowing with every cell in his body to keep his Sokhan safe.

He was still fuming with the knowledge of what his father had told him. Kassandra's father was the fabled son of Nana. An ancient Titan who had done the unthinkable – killed his own grandfather. No wonder he wanted to end his life. Darius understood his rightful need for vengeance but knowing it and actually doing it were two different things. Personally, he couldn't imagine giving into that type of passion.

As his body finally emerged from the portal he stilled. All of his Titan senses had jumped into overdrive.

"Fancy seeing you here?"

Darius swiveled his head to the right as his eyes tried desperately to make out the shapes in the dark, murky Arctic waters. Not that he needed to see the Titan who was casually leaning against the gate to Thorgeir's inner ice chamber. The voice was a dead give away.

"You are so predictable Darius it truly is pathetic," spat Rajheb.

"And you Rajheb are like a bad sea urchin nice to look at on the outside but rotten to the core on the inside. Oh, but you knew that already," taunted Darius, wondering why Rajheb was here.

"You know I've always hated you and your noble attitude. You're just like your brother. Except your brother was better than you and that's a crying shame because you'd like to be just like him...oh wait....isn't he dying of that deadly plague, so after I'm finished with you, you'll finally get what you want, to be just like Seth – dead!" spat Rajheb as he dove at Darius.

Moving swiftly aside, Darius dogged Rajheb's attack. "Come on Rajheb do you really think you can kill me? This should be fun," taunted Darius, playfully ducking his way around Rajheb.

"You said I could have him," whined a scratchy voice to Darius' right. The sneer on Rajheb's face told him he wasn't going to like what he saw when he turned his head. Sure enough, he thought, eyeing the Siren who could have passed for Medusa. Instead of snakes, eels slithered where her hair should have been. Yellow reptilian eyes stared hungrily at him. That he didn't care for one bit.

"Oh, come Darius, don't tell me you've never head of Salina?" sighed Rajheb, pretending to buff his finger nails.

Darius wanted more than anything to throttle the annoying Titan. Oh yeah, he'd heard of Salina all right. Medusa and Poseidon's love child. Only thing, it was suppose to be a myth, one of those stories other Titans told to each other to scare the scales off the freshlings in warrior training. So much for myth. He watched as a forked tongue flicked out of her mouth as if she was scenting him.

"You said I could have him all to myself. That he would be my pleasure toy," whined the creature, her forked tongue continued to flick in and out.

"Oh, I did didn't I. Sorry, Darius, seems like I can't kill you after all. But, trust me after Salina's done with you you'll wish I had," said Rajheb, sarcastically, turning to go through Thorgeir's inner ice chamber. Slyly he opened the gate.

"I don't have time for your theatrics, Rajheb. Either kill me now or get out of my way," demanded Darius, darting for the inner ice chamber door. A hard yank on his lower half stopped him cold. One of Salina's eels had wrapped its body around his.

"Don't think you'll be joining me, Darius, old Titan, but I promise to make sure Thorgeir knows you were here," taunted Rajheb, darting away.

Darius let the rapture happen. One instant he was a Titan and then in the next he'd changed into an electric eel. All of this Rajheb missed. Part of Darius would have enjoyed seeing the Titan's look of disbelief. Not every Titan could rapture into other sea beings. In fact, it was a unique talent that only Royal Blood Titans and Sirens from the North Seas possessed. A hand with a death grip grabbed his eel-like body. Even as he strained he could hear Rajheb's chuckle.

You are going to pay with every cell in your tainted body once I get rid of this hideous creature, thought Darius. He knew all of this was a diversion providing Rajheb with enough time to get the Trident and take a portal back to who knew where.

Desperate to break Salina's grip, he raptured into the smallest thing he could think of – a snail. He knew he'd have to undergo a quick rapture again into a Titan before he floated down to the ocean floor.

A loud boom shook the sea just as Darius managed to rapture back into his true form.

"You there. Stay true!"

Even though it had been well over a century since his last visit with Thorgeir there was no mistaking his commanding voice. Turning he faced the ancient Titan who ruled the Arctic seas with an ice fist.

Maybe diplomacy would have been better? thought Darius, hating the fact that maybe his father's approach might have worked better. Down deep he knew that to be untrue. King Thorgeir would never willingly relinquish control of Poseidon's Trident. No, the only way to get it was to steal it quickly and then send an orb back explaining why they desperately needed it.

Other than Master Odeon, Thorgeir was the only other Titan Darius knew who sported a long, white beard that flowed well past his jutting chin. The ancient Titan still kept his hair untied. He looked very much like a Viking of lore, with his long white hair bellowing behind him. Light blue eyes assessed him, keenly. His towering seven tail form was impressive.

Darius watched as Thorgeir crossed his arms over his chest, a clear sign he was angry. "This can not be the son of my most trusted friend. By the gods I do not believe mine own eyes. Why Darius? Why did you come to steal what is mine?" demanded Thorgeir.

Darius wanted to deny the accusation but Thorgeir wasn't finished with him yet.

"At first I did not believe Saad, but I see I sorely misjudged that Titan. So, where did you put it....where is it, son of Sadok?"

Part of him wanted to tell Thorgeir the Trident really wasn't his, while the other warrior-trained part of his brain planned an escape route. Bloody Tartarus. Saad is here. That just figures. Those two are worse than two sea cucumbers. I should have known where one is the other follows, go figure, mused Darius.

"I didn't take your blasted Trident, at the moment, Saad's brother, Rajheb did," said Darius, using his most commanding, but persuasive voice.

He watched Salina snake her body towards Thorgeir. He knew by the look in Thorgeir's eyes that whatever the Siren said caused his old teacher to be under her spell. The idea repulsed him. Worse was the knowledge that Thorgeir wasn't about to listen to any of his reasoning.

"Salina hear tells me you grabbed the Trident and hid it. She was lucky to catch you before you departed. Darius you fostered with me for one cycle, why would you betray me?" asked Thorgeir, motioning to two of his guards to approach.

Me betray you? Darius wanted to shake his head at his own predicament. Yes, he had come to take the Trident but it was necessary if his mardom had a chance at ending the deadly plague and by the gods I didn't actually take the thing. Darius thought fast. There was only one option left open to him.

"Thorgeir I have captured another," said a voice from the inner chamber, before Darius could say or do anything.

Could it be? He prayed he was right and that they had indeed captured Rajheb. Finally, that Titan would get what he deserved! Instead he watched as Saad was hauled out of the ice chamber.

"What? Saad, I told you to stay where you were. Just when I was beginning to trust you, I get it now...the two of you are working together. Guards take them below!" bellowed Thorgeir.

Darius, all but rolled his eyes at the situation. The only thing that could make it worse would be if Rylan showed up. As if on cue, the hairs on his nape stood on end. Stifling a groan, he eyed two guards hauling Zeus' nephew none to gently out of the ice chamber.

"Well, it would seem that we have found another of your cohorts," said Thorgeir. "Saad I know, but who are you?" he asked, motioning to the guards to bring Rylan forward.

Before Rylan spoke, Darius broke in. "He is a nephew of mine. Rylan this is Thorgeir, King of the Arctic Seas. Thorgeir, Rylan." Darius prayed the teenager half-god kept his mouth shut for once.

Finally, Salina left the king's side to slither to a squirming Rylan who was being held by two guards. Her tongue darted in and out, while the eels on her forehead shrank back into her skull. She looked even more frightful bald.

"This is no Titan. He smells not like a Titan," she spat, snaking her way from Rylan back to Thorgeir.

How the Hell does one smell like a Titan? wondered Darius.

Then Thorgeir moved towards Rylan. There was a look on Rylan's face Darius didn't trust.

"Darius make them stop pulling on my arms," whined Rylan, trying to squirm out of the guard's grip.

Darius wanted to speak telepathically to the kid but didn't dare. He knew both Saad and Thorgeir were expecting that. Through clenched teeth, he muttered, "Just stay still."

"What so they can kill me? I don't think so," muttered the kid.

Darius wanted to laugh at that. They couldn't kill him. He was a semi-god and the last time he looked Zeus had never allowed one of his own to be killed. So, in all likelihood maybe things were improving if Rylan was here. Now, I know I'm sick. Struck down with that blasted plague if I'm actually beginning to think having Rylan is going to help me get out of this situation. And, why exactly is Rylan here? And what's with Saad?

"Take them to my special chamber. I will deal with them later," said Thorgeir, motioning to the guards to take the ensemble below to his infamous deadly ice circle.

Great, just what I need... to be even colder than I already am, thought Darius, allowing his body to be dragged by the guards down into the bowels of the ice chamber, silently trying to communicate with Rylan to stop fighting.

In Titan form Rylan lacked his finesse but evidently he made up for that with his squirming. Somehow he managed to land a sucker punch on one of Thorgeir's massive guards. Not a good thing, thought Darius, moments before he heard the guard's fist impact Rylan's face, knocking the semi-god teenager unconscious. Darius prayed he'd remain that way until they were safe from Thorgeir and Saad.

All three of them were dumped onto the cold, marble-like floor. There was barely enough room to maneuver. The three of them were packed in tighter than sardines in a can, he thought, forcing his body into a half sitting position, which meant he had to bend his head to keep it from scraping the ice ceiling.

"Ahhh, that thing punched me. He just punched me. I can't believe it. Was I unconscious," babbled Rylan, coming fully awake before Darius was ready to deal with him. "Wait until I get my hands on him. He really shouldn't have messed with me. Boy is he ever going to regret that. So, what's the plan?" asked Rylan, slouching against the wall.

"You must use your inner will to warm up, Darius," said Saad.

Darius immediately bristled. He hated Saad's holier than thou voice." Shut-up Saad. And why by Tethys are you here? Seems like it was your brother that got us into this mess," replied Darius, scuttling over to peer out the small slit of an opening carved into the ice door. Two guards flanked the door and another two were on full alert at the end of the corridor. Great, Thorgeir's not taking any chances.

"I came to save you," replied Saad, sitting regally as if the cold didn't matter one bit.

Darius' eyed him. He didn't trust the Titan at all. But, there was something unusual about Saad and Darius' seventh sense told him something had changed. Through gritted teeth he said, "You do that...go right ahead. Because once you save us, I'm going to sweep you and your brother's worthless body into Tartarus as a special gift to Hades. The two of you are poisonous leeches that deserve each other. To think you were tinkling with nature and look what it got you – demented sharks, crazed Tartahounds, ah,...I see you didn't think I knew about that. Too bad Muroka had other ideas. Not that he succeeded." With that admission Darius turned his attention back to formulating a plan of escape.

"You know if I could just pop..." said Rylan, seeking out Darius' private channel of communication.

Darius answered, all the while keeping his barrier up, not daring to let Saad overhear this conversation. "Shut-up, Rylan. You can not pop anywhere. If they discover who you are all of Tartarus will break loose and I mean that literally. No gods, and that includes semi-gods are allowed in the undersea kingdoms. Didn't Zeus explain that to you. And that's not a question. Just sit still until I figure out how to get us out of here." He took another look out the small opening in the door, wondering if the guards were getting bored.

"Okay I am not going to pop anywhere, but I am certainly going to heat things up in here. Just how do Titans live in this environment?" answered Rylan.

Darius noted that for all the kids' brash talk he was afraid. He watched as Rylan's eyes darted here and there, probably trying to adjust to the light. It was times like now, when the kid was under stress he forgot he was a semi-god and could simply at will make his eyesight adjust to the darkness, or for that matter heat up his own internal temperature. As for Darius his tattoo was starting to really itch and burn his skin. Instinctively he knew he was relying more and more on the gift the sea dragon had bequeathed him. It should have unnerved him, but it didn't. Without it he knew he'd be blind. A helpless Titan wasn't a Titan at all. Without a doubt, though, he knew darkness was not an impediment for Saad.

No, it was the blasted cold, locked door and bloody guards that made escape almost impossible. Almost, thought Darius, refusing to believe there wasn't a way out. He sighed in frustration. Then the hairs on his body stood on end. A quick look around informed him that both Saad and Rylan had felt whatever he had.

"You did well, Saad. I am proud of you."

The voice was a soft whisper almost a caress of undefined power.

"Mother?" said a startled Saad, attempting to sit up straighter in the confines of the tight space.

"Mother, who exactly is your mother?" asked Darius, afraid he wasn't going to like the answer.

"So untrusting as you should be, but Saad has proven his worth to me today and I need for you to get out of this place to get something very special. Something that will not only save you and your mardom, but save my future and my son," said the voice.

Darius didn't say anything. He waited for either the voice to explain itself or for Saad to answer his initial question. When nothing came he pushed his thoughts into Saad's mind.

"My mother is Sesta, the Sister of the Future," said Saad, loud enough for all of them to hear. His eyes dared Darius to say anything.

"No way....that is way cool, way cooler than having an uncle whose a God...I mean the Creator created her, ohh my gawd when I get back to my Uncle's palace he is going to be so amazed that I met...does this count as a meeting when I haven't actually seen her...I mean, do you even have a figure, well, dah, of course you have a figure I mean otherwise how could she be your mother..."

Darius placed a calming hand on Rylan's shoulder to stop his prattle.

"Why are you here, Mother?" asked Saad.

"To set things right, Saad. I was summoned by the Creator after I left you and he has filled me in on my future...on your future...on us, so I am about to make things right. Prepare yourself."

With that slight warning the ice walls started to vibrate and shimmer. The water started to flow in slow motion around him and Darius watched spellbound as time seemed to suspense itself. Then in a heartbeat he felt his body transported through time and then as abruptly as it started it was over.

Looking around he realized he was back at the fourth portal, the last one before he made it to Thorgeir's seas.

"You will need this." And before his eyes Poseidon's Trident materialized.

Darius took the offering reverently with outstretched hands staring at the glowing celestial being that shimmered in front of him. "Why are you helping us, really?" he asked, dubious of the real reasons behind Saad's mother's help.

Then before his eyes her shimmering form crystallized into that of a beautiful Siren. But, there was no mistaking that this creature was made by the Creator and that she was the Sister of the Future. She was beyond the description of worldly beauty, but there was an edge to her expression that immediately radiated power, fury and something more, something he couldn't name.

He watched her hand reach out and touch him. He forced himself to stand his ground. Deep down he knew this was a test of sorts.

"You are a noble creature, Darius, Prince of the North Seas, descendent of Oceanus. He would be pleased. Integrity, and loyalty are ingrained in your heart more than you will ever know but beyond that you are passionate and that is what I want. That is what I crave. I am helping you because if I don't your race will die. This is my last interference with time. Saad and Rylan will have no memory of being in Thorgeir's seas and the events of the future have been wiped clean. Do not trust the Court. Now, I must go. Time is a precious commodity but remember without love...time means nothing."

"The Court...what about it. Don't leave," shouted Darius, seeking more answers.

The words were subtle and washed over him slowly. "The Trident you will need for another reason. What you really seek is Gaia's tears."

Then in a blink her presence was gone. That was it. Once again he was left on his own. Only thing was doubt about his mission caused him to see red. Was the infamous Court playing with him, causing him to go on a wild goose chase, all for not. The idea infuriated him. To think he had let them play him like a pawn. Grasping the ancient Trident tightly in his hand he turned for home. Now more than ever he felt the yearning to be with Kassandra. Why that was he couldn't fathom? All he knew was that he needed to see her. Needed to feel her next to his skin. And kiss those sweetlips of her. Anything to drive the pounding anger away.

# Chapter Thirty-Four

"So, if I digest these two oblats today I will abort. That's what you're telling me, right Jamie?" asked Kassandra, forcing herself to say the word as her stomach clenched in fear and her mouth dried up.

"Yes. Basically, you have twenty-four hours to make the decision, after that it will be too late," answered Jamie, holding out her hands.

"To late for what?" asked Mercka, gliding unannounced into Darius' dwelling.

The last thing Kassandra wanted to explain to Darius' little sister was her current dilemma, so she tried for a diversion.

"Any idea when Darius might return?" she asked, quickly taking the two small black oblats from Jamie and tucking them inside her bra.

"He's home now. He just arrived. He seemed pretty excited about getting the Trident. He was on his way here a minute ago but Father wanted a word with him, which means you won't see him for hours," declared Mercka, flouncing around as she twirled her tail and then darted to and fro around Darius' living quarters.

Kassandra knew her face had drained of color. What if Darius had overheard her and Jamie talking? That idea terrified her. She wasn't quite sure what choice she was going to make but the last thing she needed was to have to deal with Darius.

"I think I'll go take a walk..."she laughed, "okay...a glide around," she said, hoping they'd both get the hint that she needed privacy.

She watched Jamie whisper something to Mercka and then they were both giggling.

"No way! She wouldn't want to see that," said Mercka, all but swishing herself in one space, her eyes were wide with excitement.

Curiosity got the better of her. "See what?"

"I think I'll let Mercka explain, but in truth it's something you have to see with your own eyes," said Jamie. There was an odd twinkle that unnerved Kassandra. She was sure she was missing something.

"Okay let's go," said Mercka, grasping her arm to lead the way.

"Guess I have no choice," answered Kassandra, waving goodbye to Jamie.

DARIUS WAS FUMING MAD. Stealthy he had hurried home intent on seeking out Kassandra, only to discover she wished to abort his children. The thought sickened him. Worse was the knowledge that his brother's Sokhan, Jamie, was consorting to help her.

"Will you stop pacing, Darius," roared King Sadok, as he looked up from his examination of Poseidon's Trident.

Darius stopped abruptly. "Well did you find anything?"

"No nothing. None of this makes sense. Maybe you should take it to Kassandra to see if she's able to figure out these strange etchings," said Sadok, leaning back in his chair. His hands lazily waved away the green orb vying for his attention. "I am amazed that Sesta sought you out. Are you absolutely sure she said to seek out Gaia's tears?"

"Yes," answered Darius, for the umpteenth time. Even in his agitated state he noted that was the fourth time the green orb had attempted to reach his father. "Answer that bloody thing, father," said Darius, his teeth clenched in frustration as he took possession of the Trident again.

Darius watched as his father waved the orb away again, reminding him he was King and still ruler of the North Seas, and he'd answer the pestering orb on his own time and not a minute before. "I have no idea what she meant by Gaia's tears. Go ask Kassandra, she is after all a scholar of ancient things. She might be able to shed more light on what these etching translate into also. In the meantime, I will send a missive to a Court clerk I know who owes me a favor and see if he can shed some light on what's going on behind the scenes with the Court. For now, we must be extra careful, Darius. I can not tell you our defenses are down as you know that to be true. We should be at least thankful that Hades' isn't up to his old tricks with those blasted Tartahounds of his."

"Ahh that reminds me, Father. I forgot to tell you about some very unique Tartahounds, Kassandra and I met before we came here," said Darius, interrupting his father.

Sitting back, regally in his throne chair, Darius watched as his father plucked the orb from the water. "Tell me everything. And, Darius, I mean everything," demanded his father, motioning for him to take the seat opposite him.

Great, that's just great, grumbled Darius, careful to keep his shields up, wishing he'd kept his mouth shut, knowing he'd be interrogated until his father had gleamed every ounce of information he thought might be helpful.

What felt like hours later, Darius leaned back in his chair, feeling spent. His father had a way of draining him of his powers.

"Are we done?" asked Darius, rising from the hard, uncomfortable seat, knowing full well his father had made it that way on purpose.

"For now. Seek out Kassandra. And Darius try to be patient. Her life as she's known it has been completely altered and changed. She needs time to adjust," he replied, grasping another flashing orb that was now darting in front of him.

"What she needs and wants, I can not give her," grumbled Darius. With that realization his heart constricted.

Darius watched his father raise his head, ignoring the pulse from the orb. "Are you so sure, son? Look inside your heart. What she needs and wants, you of all Titans, can give her. In fact, you are the only one that can make her whole."

Great now I'm getting a love lecture from my father. Well, there's a first for everything, he thought. "That's not how she sees things. She wants her life back. She wants to be a human again and you know that's not within my power. Plus, I'm not sure it's safe for her here. Maybe I should have let her..." Darius paused, unable to even say the words. "Besides, this plague is destroying our mardom. Seth seems to be getting worse and mother..."

"Do not talk of your mother. She will recover and be fine. I will not loose her," said Sadok, motioning it was time Darius left.

Darius knew he was dismissed. I hope you're right, father, he thought, darting from his father's dwelling. In his haste he almost slammed into Jamie.

"Ahh, there you are. Kassandra was wondering when you would be finished?" said Jamie, cradling a bundle of newly matured oblats in her arms.

"I just bet she is," snarled Darius.

"Ahh, you overheard us. Darius don't judge me too harshly. This is a decision only she can make. But it is a decision you can certainly help sway," said Jamie, transferring her bundle to her other arm, offering him a tentative smile.

Having a sister-in-law who is a Sensitive is a bitch, he thought, wanting to remain angry at Jamie. Deep down he knew exactly where the fault lay – with him.

"Mercka took her to see the freshlings play of Sleeping Beauty. I thought it might be a good chance for her to see the freshlings play for a change. You know she's never seen or held a newborn. Why don't you join her and then take her to see Ferra's newborn?"

"Ferra has a newborn?" Darius tried hard to picture the young, perky gardener with a freshling.

"You've been gone for quite some time, Darius. Ferra has three freshlings. A little more than five years ago she and Aaron mated. A week ago, she delivered her latest Siren. She's a delight. It would do Kassandra good to see the freshlings. She's still thinking in human terms and to be truthful, the idea of carrying twins terrifies her."

That's her and I both, thought Darius, alarmed at one moment with the idea of being a father while proud the next.

"Thanks, Jamie. I'll do that," he said, almost escaping.

"And, Darius, let her use her brain. Don't be afraid of her powers. Encourage her to embrace them. Trust me it will makes things go a lot smoother for you both," she said, once again rearranging her bundle of oblats before gliding away.

...

"I will save you my love," said the freshling Titan. Instead of a sword, the young Titan brandished a Triton and instead of clothing as a costume he was adorned with a shining shell necklace. His upper body was painted in tattoos that he proudly showed off at every chance.

Kassandra openly laughed at the young Titan's antics. Bravely he surged forward to kill the evil witch. And since none of the freshling Sirens could be convinced to be the evil witch, their guardian – the primary teacher who looked after them during the day – had gamely undertaken the task. Bedraggled with ugly mops of seaweed covering her face she bent over in pain when the young Titan playfully jammed at her.

"You are no match for me ugly witch. Be gone!" shouted the young Titan, delivering the witch a fatal blow.

Kassandra couldn't take her eyes from the stage. Rigged up on what looked like a sunken pirate ship, the young cast of characters had eagerly embraced their roles.

She caught his masculine scent moments before his arms circled her waist to possessively bring her body close to his. She hadn't realized how much she had missed his touch, his scent or his body until she allowed her own to be molded to his. The soft, feather light feel of his breath against her ear caused her to shiver.

"Enjoying yourself?" asked Darius, gently nipping at her ear lobe.

"Shh! Don't interrupt," she snapped, with more force in her voice than she meant. She didn't like how he seemed to take over her body, her mind and her heart with just one touch. It unnerved her. Made her feel vulnerable. And the last thing she wanted was another complication in her life. She wanted more than anything to remain mad at him but with his body holding hers clarity and reasoning were fleeing.

"As you say, no speaking." The words were a light breeze in her ear and then he boldly kissed her exposed neck. She couldn't help the full body shiver. Without a doubt she knew she shouldn't have challenged him.

"When this play is over I want to show you something." Again, his words burned a promise of something decadent. His husky voice was a low sexy note playing in her mind. Kassandra had to forcibly place her hands on her lap to keep her tail from moving in anticipation.

A few minutes later the entire cast of young Titans and Sirens assembled in front of the ship. Swaying in motion to the current they bowed low. The entire audience made up of family and friends briskly moved their tails. It was Darius' voice inside her head telling her this was part of their custom. The brisker the current made from the audience's lower-half movements was a measure to how much they liked the performance. Considering even Kassandra was starting to feel the wake of the undersea waves she gathered it was a huge success.

"Come," he commanded, pulling her up with him when he rose.

She bristled from his commanding tone of voice. Before she could say anything to Darius, Mercka gave her a fierce hug.

"I have to go Kassandra. Thanks again for coming with me. I promised to help clean up the mess when the play was finished," she said, winking at Darius, as she darted away.

Kassandra wasn't amused. "Did you make her leave?" she asked, careful to keep her back to him. She wasn't ready to see his face or those haunting emerald green eyes of his.

"Maybe," he replied, and she could have sworn she saw his grin in her mind.

Turning her body around he took the choice away from her. "Please come with me. I want to introduce you to a good family friend."

The tender look in his eyes undid her. "Sure. That would be nice. And then Darius we can..."

But Kassandra didn't get to finish her sentence. His mouth came down hot and hard on her lips. Demanding. His hands pulled her in tighter. She could feel his heart beating in time with hers. She yearned to run her fingers through his long silky hair and realized she was losing her inner battle. It was like going against the current. Useless. With a will of their own she felt her fingers grasp his head, bringing him even closer. His ragged groan shook her.

As abruptly as it started it ended. It was only then she realized they weren't alone. The audience, some fifty Sirens and Titans had all stopped their talking to watch. Mortified Kassandra felt her face burn in shame.

"This is not your fault, Kassandra. It is mine. I am their Prince and they have never seen me with a Siren before. By openly embracing you they know you as my Sokhan. And that is what I want to talk with you about soon. But for now, let's leave before I forget my true intentions," he said, nodding his head to the few Titans who openly grinned at them.

Leaving sounds good to me, she thought, letting him pull her along, not missing the possessive feel of his arm around her mid-section. After a short glide they came to what looked like a large garden. At one end of the garden was a small dwelling.

"Ferra, may we enter?" asked Darius. Kassandra knew he asked the words out loud for her benefit.

"Darius, I can't believe it's you? Please come in," said the sweet, very feminine voice on the other side of the dwelling, causing Kassandra to feel instantly jealous.

Like most of the dwellings she saw there was no door to keep out intruders. Only Darius' family had incorporated the human concept of a formal door, not that it was needed living in a society that tended to use telepathy more than their voice.

When Kassandra glided inside the sight caused a lump to form in her throat.

"Kassandra this is Ferra. Ferra meet my Sokhan, Kassandra," said Darius, embracing the young woman in the traditional way.

Did he just introduce me as his soulmate? Why that made her insides feel like jelly scared her. It was only once the woman backed away Kassandra noticed the very small bundle cradled at her breast.

"Is that...." she couldn't finish her sentence. Her hands moved protectively over her own stomach as the twins chose that moment to move. Immediately Darius was at her side. Concern was etched throughout his features and in his voice. "Are you okay?"

"Yes. When I get nervous or excited they like to do flip flops in my belly," she admitted, pasting a smile on her face.

"Where are my manners. Please have a seat Kassandra. I know exactly how you are feeling. This is Tina, our latest freshling. She's a week old and can't seem to get enough milk and here comes Trisha our three-year-old and Tashya our one year old is still sleeping. Please have a seat," said Ferra, ushering them both forward. "Aaron should be back soon. He would love to see you Darius," she continued, placing sliced sea cucumber in front of them.

Kassandra couldn't pry her eyes away from the young mother. Without thought she moved the newborn from one breast to the other, while giving a snack of fresh sea urchins to the demanding three-year-old. The newborn was beautiful. Dark black hair framed her small head which was the size of a grapefruit. The thought of holding an infant terrified Kassandra. A screeching wail from the back chamber told them that Tashya was awake.

"Would you mind, Kassandra?" asked Ferra, gently depositing the newborn into her outstretched arms, before she could utter a protest.

An immediate sense of warmth radiated throughout her system. Instinctively she brought the young freshling close to her beating heart. Then the baby woke-up and two piercing emerald eyes appraised her. A soft coo from the newborn melted her heart.

"Darius she's so soft," said Kassandra in awe. She watched as he moved forward.

"Just think Kassandra you are carrying two of these special beings within you. Do you have any idea how much the idea of being a father thrills me? I want to teach them the magic of my undersea kingdom, but first I need to find a way to stop this plague. Jamie said I should trust your powers so I'm asking for your help," he said, reaching out to gently stroke the baby's soft, downy cheek.

Tears slid down her face. Her emotions were rubbed raw. It's just my hormones, she tried telling herself. She forced herself to take a calming breath. Seeing Darius like this. A Titan awed by the beauty of newborn. Hearing his yearning to be a father. And most importantly him asking for her help opened the flood bank she thought she'd held at bay.

"Don't cry my love. I didn't mean to upset you."

Kassandra knew Darius was clearly puzzled by her reaction. As was she.

"So sorry about that. I'm going to have to stay with Tashya for a bit so I'll take Tina. Thanks again for holding her. And, Darius you really don't know anything about pregnant Sirens do you. We cry at anything and everything. I'm sorry I don't have more time to chat but I'll try to come by tomorrow to see you, Kassandra. Aaron said he's going to be late, but that'd he'd touch base with you tomorrow, Darius," said Ferra, efficiently taking the baby from her arms.

"Thanks again Ferra. That reminds me Jamie asked me to see if you might have any more milata green for the soothing balm she's been making for Seth and Mother," asked Darius.

"Most certainly. I'll gather the herb and bring it along to her tomorrow."

Kassandra watched as the newborn immediately latched onto one of Ferra's breast. Absentmindedly she let Darius lead her away from the domestic family scene.

"There's one more place I'd like to show you," he said. The glint in his eyes should have been her warning.

A short time later they arrived at a strange looking undersea cave. The outer walls of the cave had dark blue crystals, which shimmered as the current from the sea moved over them.

"These are the lava waters that flow throughout the kingdom. They help relax the muscles. Let's soak and talk for a few minutes," he said, drawing her deeper into the cave.

Kassandra let him drag her into a pool of warm water. Talk? I just bet, she thought, to herself. Letting her body slide into the warm water, she immediately began to relax. She watched as he moved to the other side. His emerald-green eyes lit-up. It was a look she recognized. Sexual hunger clawed at him. Kassandra shook her head. She was determined to not give into the bone-melting desire to touch him.

"So, will you help me?" he asked, lazily licking his lips, as his broad shoulders spanned the back of the pool.

Did I have to notice his lips? Why couldn't I have been looking at the bubbling water that would have been better? Anything but those lips of his which are so good at kissing. Not that I'm thinking of getting kissed or anything like that.

In a blink Darius closed the space between them.

"You forget my love..." he licked his lips slowly as he eyed her. "Your thoughts are now in my head. Your desire is in my heart and you have no idea just how hard it is for me not to make love to you," declared Darius, leaning his head in close, his mouth an inch from her.

He is such a tease, thought Kassandra, not giving into the desire to tilt her head up. No, no, no. That's just what he wants.

"You bet it is, sweetlips," replied Darius, moments before his hands cupped her face forcing her mouth up to meet his.

"Let me love you like a Titan. Let me give you pleasure you can't imagine."

His words were creating erotic images inside her head causing her breathing to come hard and fast. Then his mouth claimed her and she lost track of all her rational thoughts. There was nothing like it. He demanded and took, never once letting up. Forcing her mouth to comply and open wider, forcing her tongue to duel with his, and forcing his breath to merge with hers. The wildness and ferocity of it drew her in, heightening her own sexual pleasure all the more.

"That's it sweetlips, let it happen. Let the Siren you are come out to play."

Again, his words taunted her while she fought against the new bubbling desires that threatened to swamp her body. She could feel her breasts swell even more. She felt wet with desire as her body all but opened to his words, practically screaming, come take me, take me right now. She felt wanton. And ached to take control. She yearned to do the taunting, but she wasn't sure how to go about doing that. Pushing him back against the pools' polished stone surface, she brazenly rubbed her aching breasts against his chest. His answering guttural groan told her she was on the right track. His enjoyment gave her the courage to do even more.

With one sweep from her powerful tail she moved to tower over him so that her breasts now were a hair's breath away from his lips. Looking deep into his eyes she took her own breast in her hand and cupped it into his offering mouth. The look of pure desire that flared in his eyes gave her a momentarily sense of panic.

Maybe I'm asking for more than I want. Then he took a long hard suck on her breast and she was sure she saw stars. She had always had sensitive breasts as a human, but now, as a Siren, they were aware of everything. Having Darius' hot mouth sucking and his tongue licking her pebbled nipples caused her to whimper in ecstasy.

Her head fell back in bliss when his other hand went to play with her other nipple.

"Ohh, Darius, I didn't know..." she tried to finish her sentence but it did no good. After pebbling her other nipple hard with his free hand, he moved his mouth to it and took a long hard suckle bringing her rosy colored nipple deep into his mouth. At the same time, he reached lower to finger her mid-section.

She felt hot and cold at once. The hard ridge of her mid-section that connected her tail to where her belly button was almost rippled in mind-shattering pleasure.

"That's it Kassandra, give into your nature, don't fight it."

He said the words as his tongue lazily licked her neck. She had to fight the urge to buck against him. Her body ached for his. Shyly she moved her own hands lower seeking the rock, hard bulge that was now pressed hard against her mid-section.

She felt his hands move lower over hers and then she felt all of him as he fitted her hands around his throbbing erection. Both of her hands closed tightly on him.

"You're killing me," he groaned

"I'm sorry," she instantly replied.

He laughed. The rich, timbre of his voice sending shivers down her tail.

"You're killing me in a good way, sweetlips, don't stop," he said, drawing her hand back to his rock-hard erection.

New to the game of seduction and sexual play, she let him set the pace.

Kassandra's eyes darted lower. She really wanted to see him – all of him. As if on cue, Darius grinned wickedly and then brazenly raised himself up onto the edge of the pool. In Titan form he was magnificent. Unabashed she watched as he leaned back, which provided her with an amazing view of his complete eye-full anatomy.

He's huge, bloody huge and just how the hell can and did that fit inside me. Even as Kassandra thought that, her body began to pulse with an answering cry to his desire. The sight of him, gloriously aroused to the point where she could actually see the veins of his shaft standing out calling for her attention undid her.

Moving forward she took one last look into his passion-stricken eyes before her courage faded and then without hesitating another second she moved forward and calmly took the tip of him deep into the recess of her mouth.

She revealed in the taste of him. He was male. Musky and salty and so much more than she fought to find a word to best describe his unique taste. She yearned for the taste of him to be absorbed into her cells.

"By the gods Kas, you're good," said Darius, his voice husky with need.

That was all the encouragement she needed. Using her tail to keep her in place, she was able to take most of his shaft into her mouth. Darting her tongue around the large tip of him, she wickedly licked her way down and then back up. Then she cupped him. His ragged groan caused an answering pool of wetness to form within her own body.

"I can't take much more of this, sweetlips," he said.

Flicking her eyes up, she noted that his head was thrown back and a small tick had started in his jaw.

I'm doing this to him. He's in my control for a change. That idea thrilled her.

Then before she could ponder what to do next to him the tables were turned. Moving faster than she could have anticipated he had her back in the water, with her tail pressed up hard against his. His hands flanked hers as he positioned her arms on either side of her.

# Don't miss out!

Visit the website below and you can sign up to receive emails whenever Renee Field publishes a new book. There's no charge and no obligation.

https://books2read.com/r/B-A-HRN-SEAC

**BOOKS 2 READ**

Connecting independent readers to independent writers.

Did you love *Bliss*? Then you should read *Be My Vampire Tonight*[1] by Renee Field!

[2]

Bidding on a masked man at an auction is all for a good cause, but what happens when he turns out to be a vampire who has the power to unleash the wild woman lying dormant inside you?

As a Darklander vampire, Mitch has spent a century living in a bleak world, but all that changes when he sees Tina. The beast living within Mitch wants to stake his claim. Mitch knows taking Tina's virginity will change her forever, but try explaining that to a woman whose passion cannot be denied.

Tina holds the key to his freedom, but Mitch will be damned forever before he turns her over as a slave for his master.

*Book one in the Darklander Lovers series.*

---

1. https://books2read.com/u/3RoMDG

2. https://books2read.com/u/3RoMDG

Read more at www.reneefield.com.

# Also by Renee Field

**A Warriors of Maida Novella**
Love Me Wild
Love Me Tender
Love Me Strong
Love Me Wild

**Darklander Lovers**
Be My Warlock Tonight
Be My Vampire Tonight
Be My Werecat Tonight

**Elemental Love**
Heart of Mine

**Riverton Cove series**
Embrace

**Titan series**
Rapture
Bliss


**Standalone**
Claiming A Siren's Heart
Claiming Poseidon's Heart
A Siren's Wish
Fairy Cursed
Summer Heat
Queen of Dragons
Summer Heat
Electrify Me


Watch for more at www.reneefield.com.

# About the Author

Renee loves to write a variety of genres. She writes for HQN Spice Briefs and also writes sensual paranormal romance, and contemporary romance as an Indie author. Field also writes nitty gritty young adult and paranormal young adult romance novels under the pen name Renee Pace. Renee calls Halifax, Nova Scotia, Canada home and loves her view of the Atlantic Ocean. She is a member of Romance Writers' of America, and her local Romance Writers of Atlantic Canada. She juggles work, four children and is a firm believer in soul-mates and the power of the sea.

Renee loves to hear from fans. She can be reached by email at reneefieldauthor@gmail.com

Read more at www.reneefield.com.